Never Knew Love
Like This Before

Never Knew Love Like This Before

Maxine Thompson
Michelle McGriff
Denise Campbell

URBAN BOOKS
www.urbanbooks.net

URBAN SOUL is published by

Urban Books
10 Brennan Place
Deer Park, NY 11729

"The Value of a Man" copyright © 2007 by Denise Campbell
"Change of Life" copyright © 2007 by Michelle McGriff
"Katrina Blues" copyright © 2007 by Maxine Thompson

ISBN-13: 978-1-59983-024-7
ISBN-10: 1-59983-024-8

First Printing: June 2007

10 9 8 7 6 5 4 3 2

Printed in the United States of America

The Value of a Man

Denise Campbell

The Waking Hours

She licked her lips passionately as her body burned with passion within her. Desire had taken over and her body writhed uncontrollably as she struggled to breathe. Her knuckles turned white as she grabbed the red silk sheets for support. She gasped as his hot breath seared the skin on her neck as he whispered how badly he wanted to be inside of her.

The urgency was beyond what her mind could hold. She felt she would go mad as sweat seeped from her skin and she could feel his hard rippled body merge with hers, building in momentum as he found the valley of her desires, wetness drawing him to the point of no return, her moans and groans beckoning to him to fulfill within her the yearnings of her heart.

She released the sheets and reached for him, he hoisted her up from the base of her buttocks and positioned himself for the ultimate thrill, her eyes fluttered and her mouth fell open. Blood boiled like hot lava under her skin as she braced for impact. . . .

"Yes, please stop teasing me," she begged.

Just as the tip of him made contact her eyes squeezed to shut out the loud noise that violated the moment she yearned for. She fought against the rude sound that threatened to stop the orgasm that threatened to explode with just one thrust, but it wouldn't stop. She shook her head violently in protest.

"You want me to stop baby?" he whispered, his words kissing the already fragile heat that burned her.

"No, no pleasssse," she shouted and her body shot upright and erect in her bed, sweat drenched her sheets, her thighs leaked the love juice of unfulfilled desire and the loud piercing noise of her alarm clock mocked her. She reached for the clock by her nightstand and in one fit of rage she ripped it from the socket and flung it hard against her bedroom wall. Smashing it.

"Damn it!" she screamed in frustration. The closest I have come to having a good roll in the hay with a man and that damn clock ruined it. She lay back down, and her hands sought her heaving abdomen as it rose and fell under the moist sheets. Her hands caressed her inner thighs, trailed the hairy valley that dips into her love nest and picked up momentum, she twisted her body this way and then wiggling that, but to no avail. She tried to find that moment again, the point where she felt completely lost but it just wouldn't come back.

"Grrrr." Her hands flopped down in aggravation, annoyance rippling through her. She looked at the streaming sunlight coming through her window and sighed. It was at least 6:30 A.M. She had to get out of bed and get ready for work. She closed her eyes and licked her lips as she thought back to the delightful dream and smiled as she thought of Troy, then Bruce, but then the image of Isaiah came into her mind . . . she had to make a choice soon or she felt she would simply explode from sheer desire.

She took her time getting dressed since she was already awake and made herself a cup of coffee as she lounged, brooding over the loss of her unfulfilled dream. She sighed and draped her arms over the chair at her bar and stared out at the beautifully budding morning. It was Monday again and she was due in at the office with tons of appointments if she remembered right. She placed her coffee on the bar and began moving with a bit more urgency as the thought of her day propelled her.

"Good morning, Alex," Morgan answered on the second ring as she peered towards the clock on the wall and saw it was almost 8:30 A.M. "What happened to you? You are late?" she blurted out realizing in that moment she was also late.

"Don't start Morgan; I don't see you sitting at the door waiting with bated breath," Alexandra told her sarcastically as she turned off the ignition and waited in front of Morgan's penthouse high-rise building in the busy New York City streets where she double parked. "So how much time do you actually need?" Alexandra asked knowing that as the morning traffic built there would be blaring horns of impatient drivers driving her nuts. Morgan looked at her slipped top and stocking feet and sighed.

"Let me put something easy on and I will be down, ten minutes tops." She hung up the phone before her friend could make another sarcastic comment. She gingerly stepped into her unorganized walking closet and tried to find *something easy* to put on. She smiled at the comment knowing that with her, there was no such thing as something easy to put on.

As she dug through the pile of clothing both casual and formal she found a black pin-striped pant suit and grabbed it with glee.

"Yes!" she said exuberantly, "this will have to do." She struggled out of the closet and ran back into the bathroom. She threw on a pearl necklace and earrings and pinned her long auburn hair into a bun on top of her head, fastening it with pearl stick pins.

Walking towards her office desk, she changed handbags from the pink she had the day before, now to white, careful to put her wallet and keys inside along with her cell phone. Then hopping from one leg to the next, she pulled her pants on, a sheen white camisole top and her matching jacket. She looked out the window of her modest townhouse at an unimpressed Alexandra. "I am on my way down," she yelled.

As she stepped into the passenger side of the car and flopped down, Alex looked at her with a look of disdain.

"I had the hottest dream and it totally ruined my morning," Morgan blurted out to deflect Alex's lecture, and it worked. Alexandra knew Morgan and she understood that this was her way of changing the subject so she let it slide. Besides, Alexandra being a married woman loved the juicy dreams and tirades of Morgan, living vicariously through her as she liked to say now that her life with her husband had become comfortable.

"Okay, so tell me about this hot dream," Alexandra prodded, changing the mood from accusatory to a girl-friend tone. When Morgan was finished she let out a long breath and gingerly fanned her face with her right hand. "No wonder you are so grumpy. I should have shared my quarterly quickie with you." They both laughed heartily as she winked, resting her hand gingerly on Morgan's leg.

Courtship

Running to the office to beat time, Morgan and Alexandra got suspicious stares and furtive sidelong glances as the employees went about their way. Some were jealous of Alexandra for getting preferential treatment from the boss since they were close friends and others thought Morgan was being biased. But after years of trying to please people and worrying about how things looked, Morgan decided that she worked as hard as she did to be where she was so she could do as she pleased. And as chief executive of the upscale trendy magazine *Flowers Bed*, she was not in the mood to play petty games of jealously and favorites when she knew she worked hard and played fair. As she sat at her desk and looked out at the amazing New York skyline from the eighty-ninth floor of one of the most prestigious buildings in the city, she had to squeeze her legs together as she reminisced on how lucidly clear her dream was, abstinence becoming a more and more challenging ambition with each passing day. She chuckled privately to herself as she began sifting through her messages and files and began dialing, returning calls and focusing on the day's work ahead.

It didn't take long.

She noticed the messages but left those that were not as urgent as the copyediting meeting, press conference, and board of directors meeting on her agenda for early that afternoon that she still had to prep for.

"Ms. Quixotic, there is a Mr. Debauched on the line for you." There was a smirk in her secretary's voice that she didn't like and this was not the day to hear from Troy. He of all people was so full of himself, obnoxious and insolent. She took a deep breath as she answered the line.

"This is Morgan."

"So you foget 'bout me baby?" The deep sensual question that resonated from the depths of his throat caught her off guard and a smile snuck up on her.

"And what do you mean to say with such an accusation, Troy?" He liked games, and though she wasn't quite in the mood, his sweet disposition on the phone chided her to dance with him for the moment. This was one of the things that irked and pleased her about him, and he knew it. She could feel him slowly wet his lips on the other end of the line and run his fingers through his long dreadlocks with his right hand. She sighed, and she could see it as if she was there, his eyes closing to half-mast at the sound of her voice.

"Stop teasing me woman. You know I miss you. I cannot take this anymore. Let's stop these games. I want to see you, touch you, kiss you and . . ."

"Troy, we had a date two weekends in a row where you didn't show up, didn't call and left me hanging, and then you call me as if nothing happened and I am supposed to jump into bed with you as if everything is okay."

"You know I am sorry baby. Things came up."

"That's a problem, Troy, you don't understand what it means to have responsibilities; you make commitments and you don't follow through. How is that supposed to make me feel?"

"You are ova' reacting, baby love."

"Enough! I cannot bear this."

"You know what I want an' it's you. I don't want to go back to di man I was when we met; you have given me everything I need. I want that, I want to know there is one dime piece that's got my back."

Morgan quivered. Having never met a man like Troy, he was a bit of a thrill for her. Naughty, bad, everything she had been warned to stay away from. He took her completely by surprise. He wasn't what she thought a bad boy would be. She was from the right side of the tracks. She didn't have it all, but her parents worked hard to make sure she had what she needed. What they couldn't give her she made up for with brains, and a little beauty went a long way. It excited her the way he was gentle, affectionate, bared his soul to her even though at times he was lying through his teeth. Just the thought caused her to squeeze her legs together and feel the beginnings of desire creep up between them and nestled itself at her love spot. He knew what he was doing and he was good at it.

"You know I am a little confused. I need time to sort this all out."

"What time? Baby, I am your every t'ing. I will give you every t'ing. You know I can woman." And she sipped air slowly. The way he said that, dropping his voice an octave to a sultry offer, she knew what he meant and she knew he could do it. But that's not the life she wanted—well, not the way he wanted to give it to her. This was ridiculous. She didn't need to be taken care of by a man, she could do that ten times over on her own, but what he could do for her heart was quite tempting. She couldn't help feeling a tinge of fear. She wasn't sure if she was afraid of him or just his lifestyle but she knew fear was not a good component when choosing someone to love.

He felt her hesitation, and could taste her desire permeating the phone lines and smell her pheromones whiff past his nose. He sniffed. He wanted her bad. Yeah, he had his pick of the litter, but Morgan was different. She had class and wasn't just about what he had because she had her own. He knew she wouldn't betray him if she chose him, he knew she would have his back and maybe his babies. Granted he had a few babies already but he could deal.

"Darling, I cannot talk about this all right now. I have a few really important afternoon meetings to attend to. I will have to call you back later when I am home. Is that okay?" He was all rough around the edges but he was so sexy beyond her expectation. She thought about his long dreadlocks that would swoosh around her during their last lovemaking before she was thrust on this journey of celibacy; she remembered the way he walked around carrying her with her legs wrapped around his torso, rhythmically plunging away at her very soul as she hung on tight and screamed out his name. He did things to her she didn't know any normal man could do. He was strong and muscular, strapped to the bone with the most natural weapon of all. He was beautiful. The thoughts ignited the burning sensation that left her frustrated earlier that morning.

He heard her pant and he knew she remembered. The same way he remembered. No woman had dared say no to him. He was bad. Everyone knew of his reputation and when he had set his eyes on her all local competitors knew to back off, but he knew he wasn't the only one who wanted her, knew he had to compete with all the Goody Two-Shoe stuffed shirts she was used to. But he was used to competition and wasn't about to back down.

"Sho' baby. Anything you want. Holler at me later. I might be rolling but I will make time for my number-one lady. You know dat?" He hissed and then softly chuckled, almost hypnotically, sending shock waves of sensation down her spine.

"Okay baby. I have to go," she said and quickly hung up the phone. She sighed deeply and dropped her head back on her plush leather chair. She was going crazy and that man . . .

"Ohhhhhhhh that man!" she said more sensuously out loud, allowing her hands to slip between her thighs and squeezing her legs together on them. Pulling herself together she stood and took a few deep breaths; she ran her fingers through her curly auburn tresses that rested below her shoulder blades, a mass of gorgeous natural color courtesy of her half-Latina, half-black mother and her coolie Caribbean father. *What am I going to do?* she thought as she yanked at her collar and breathed out slowly.

"Shelly, please contact all departments involved in this afternoon meeting and tell everyone to meet me in the main conference room. Make sure we have fresh-brewed coffee and some pastries, please. It's going to be a long evening."

"Ms. Quixotic," Shelly paused and waited for her boss's response.

"Yes, Shelly."

"There is another . . ."

"I am not taking anymore phone calls outside of business today, Shelly," she snapped and she knew it. Shelly was new and a real sweetheart. She had been there only three months and had made her life so much easier. She felt bad that she allowed her sexual frustration mingled with her personal quagmire to surface.

"I am sorry Ms. Quixotic; I didn't mean to make you

angry. I only meant to tell you that you have a delivery. There was another phone call from an anonymous person who asked to be sure you received it before you left for lunch."

"I am sorry Shelly; I am a little tense today. You understand." Her voice threaded with an apology as she lightened her tone and mood. "Please bring in the delivery."

"Yes ma'am."

"And Shelly, could you please call me Morgan." She tried to lighten her voice, brushing Troy to the back of her mind and brightening up.

"Yes ma'am . . . I mean, Morgan."

She gathered her files and set her voice mail as she prepared to head to the main conference room, as she walked toward her door she was not prepared for what greeted her.

Shelly had requested the assistance of three other secretaries on their floor to help her take the delivery into Morgan's office.

"What are you doing?"

"You told me to bring your delivery in, Ms. Qui . . . Morgan."

"This is it?" Her voice cracked as she blushed and a smile replaced her surprise. "Is there a card? Who is it from? Did the delivery person say anything?" She was rambling and she knew it. But there was no way for her to know who would send her these flowers. It could be one of three men who desperately awaited her decision. She wasn't sure if she wanted to think about it. But after ten bouquets of three dozen long-stemmed roses of every color there were dropped at her feet, her curiosity got the better of her. Running out of room they placed some of the flowers on her office floor in every available corner.

"It looks like someone is really smitten," Shelly commented shyly.

"Or crazy," Morgan said as she reached for one of the cards discreetly snuggled between one of the bouquets and opened it. All color drained from her face as she shook her head flabbergasted.

"What is it, is everything okay?" Shelly rushed to her aid as she seemed she would fall. She brushed her hands away and turned her back to her as a tear slipped down her caramel rose-colored cheeks. She brushed it away quickly and smiled, slowly turning around as she quickly regained her composure. Isaiah was the closest to what she would want in a man. She wondered if she was overlooking a gem in him. Though he was quite a looker, she felt something was missing. She didn't feel that thing that Troy did to her with Isaiah. But he did offer her some whopping mental orgasms as powerful as physical ones. The man's brain was a wealth of power, information, and knowledge. She found it sexy and could sit with him for hours just talking and spending time; listening to him inspired her. But then, that was where it sort of ended. What was wrong with her?

"It's just the man who sent these. It took me by surprise is all." She smiled and shook her head slightly, causing her tresses to fall behind her shoulders and away from her face. Feeling suddenly hot she walked to her desk and retrieved a hair pin and swiftly wrapped her hair into a bun on top of her head. It is Mr. Isaiah Urbane who was causing the conflict in her. He is good, kind, thoughtful. He didn't harass her or press her for time. Having known him for almost four years at the brink of her now successful and budding career, he had proposed. But she wasn't ready for anything like that. Wasn't ready for marriage and children, all the things she knew Isaiah wanted. Sure he already had a son, but the circumstances are strange, and he hasn't had a chance to raise a child, be a father. Never married at forty-seven years old also held her reserve. He was almost perfect, and she didn't understand why she wasn't as attracted to him as she was someone she thought less worthy, less good for her, and in the future would probably be more problematic for her. Or maybe she was fed up with the fact that the few times they went away on getaway weekends, he only wanted to stay in bed and sleep when she wanted to go hiking and sightseeing. He was tired all the time after a few hours and she wanted to make love all night. His siblings were her parents' age and she wanted to join a family where she could have sister- and brothers-in-law to chat with and have fun with and share family events and holidays to help make them special. Maybe she just wanted too much.

"Okay Shelly, let's go. We have a deadline to meet and this upcoming issue of *Flowers Bed* is going to stun, shock and make lots of noise." She teased as she gently rested her hand on her assistant's shoulder as an act of repentance and walked out of her office door.

The day sped by and she was totally pooped. She had a productive day and was too tired to think about anything else but taking a long hot bath, climbing into bed, and sleeping the night away. Before she left she ordered everyone in the office to take home a bouquet of roses. She had to smile. They were indeed exquisite, just as the man who thought to send them. She didn't drive home with Alexandra this evening; her friend had a hot date and wanted to leave early, which she almost never did. She was happy for her so she agreed. She called a car service and reclined comfortably in the back in the plush leather seats as the air conditioner soothed her and closed her eyes. She felt the driver weave through traffic rushing her to her Upper East Side Manhattan penthouse condo as she planned out how she would end her evening.

She was soon forced from her state of respite as the livery service came to an abrupt halt, not three blocks from her home. There was a police blockade blocking traffic from entering the small one-way street on which she resided.

"Excuse me, driver, what's happening? Why have we stopped?"

"I am sorry, ma'am, but the police are blocking the street, seem to be searching vehicles," he told her uncertainly.

"Maybe they are looking for someone," Morgan said as she began digging in her purse to pay her fare. "I will get out and walk from here; I am not very far away from home." She stuck her fingers through the glass window and gave the cabbie sixty dollars.

"This is too much money," exclaimed the driver, flabbergasted.

"Its okay, I appreciate your speedy response in taking me home and you will be stuck in traffic for a while it seems." She smiled nicely at him, opened the door, and gently slid out the door, closing it behind her. She began to walk slowly and leisurely as she watched the roadblock unfold in front of her, and like her many neighbors and onlookers who had stopped to see the spectacle and inquire as to why there was a roadblock on a one-way residential Manhattan street in the middle of rush hour, she was very curious. The pileup was endless and as she got closer to her building she saw all the flashing lights and NYPD officers at her door checking ID of all females of a certain age group coming and going.

Increased curiosity prodded her onward. Walking briskly she arrived at her door and began searching through her pocketbook for her ID, her hands being filled with roses tumbling out of the vase as she fished around.

"Let me help you with that, ma'am," one officer said to her smiling shyly at her. Gratefully dropping her load into his hands she searched her purse frantically.

"Hey, that's her. We have found the woman we are looking for. Call off the block." She found her wallet with her driver's license and handed it to one of the three officers that approached her. They stared at her suspiciously as one officer looked over her license.

"Sorry, ma'am, my name is Officer Dudley and I have a warrent for your arrest."

"Excuse me?"

"Ms. Morgan Quixotic, you are under arrest for the suspicion of fraud and money laundering. If you don't resist we will take you in nice and quiet and we can avoid the embarrassing inquisition of your neighbors."

"What?" Her disbelief was evident and her anger rising. "I want my attorney, this is ridiculous."

"Ma'am, you can call your attorney from the precinct. It's best we get moving as soon as possible. The crowd is getting larger and we have caused enough of a traffic jam because of you. You really don't want a scene, I promise, and if you push the issue I will put you in handcuffs."

Thinking about her job, her status in society, her reputation, and the value of privacy, she agreed to go along and play along as if they were not trying to arrest her. She gingerly got in the back of a squad car and the sirens went blaring as they swerved through traffic to the 6th precinct.

"Excuse me officer but this precinct does not have jurisdiction in my neighborhood," she whimpered.

"No offense, Ms. Quixotic, but I am an officer of the

law and I should know what precinct has jurisdiction over what area."

"My apologies," Morgan stated, not wanting to cause the driver aggravation or show any form of disrespect. They pulled into the station and three other squad escorts pulled in too carrying cases of beer, balloons, and party paraphernalia. She was totally confused seeing these two gentlemen only hours before causing a roadblock barricade in her neighborhood and now partying like teenagers.

"Okay, I have been patient. I think I deserve to know what the hell is going on here." She got out of the car and looked to the officer who parked with a jovial smile on his face. She was livid.

"Why don't you just relax and follow me."

"Why? I have had enough of this game. Haven't you wasted enough of the people's tax dollars?" Her face turned beet red and steam seemed to be coming out of her ears.

"Fine then, why don't you ask him?" Feeling incredibly provoked and ridiculed she turned around and bumped into Bruce.

"Hello my *literary love*." He smiled proudly and brightly at her, causing her to hesitate. His voice dropped seductively as he sauntered closer, provoking her even more.

"What is it that you mean to ask me?" She was peeved, frustration rose to the extraordinary limits and the satisfied look on his face irked her so badly she wanted to slap it right off.

"Just come inside, honey. I want to show you something. Ignore the imbecile I call my colleague." He winked at the officer who gave him thumbs up and headed inside the station.

Morgan grew furious as it began to dawn on her that

he had arranged the entire thing. The immaturity of it all, the egotism, the insane fact that he actually believed she would like whatever it was he had up his sleeves. She was boiling beyond control, wanting to hear his explanation but afraid she already knew the answer.

"What is going on here? I had a long day and I am tired. Did you know there was a roadblock and a search on my block? That they carted me off here almost like a criminal threatening to cuff me in my neighborhood? You have any idea what such a thing would do to my reputation?" She fumed as she tried to catch her breath. Bruce pressed her against the car and looked deeply into her eyes as her eyes blazed back at him. Not yielding to her anger, he pressed his uniformed body into her, almost causing the police cruiser to rock. Then he urgently burned his lips into hers, stifling her complaints. Her moans invited him to pick up steam. They realized that they had an audience and the rest of the police officers in the precinct came out and began applauding. Horrified at the scene she looked to Bruce, searching his eyes for answers.

"Please tell me that you had nothing to do with this melodrama, Bruce." Rage riddled every bone in her body; embarrassment like she had never known threatened to stifle her words. The heat of his body paralyzed her; she hated that he had that kind of effect on her, that her knees buckled when he kissed her, that she warmed in the places his hands touched. Anger was not the word for what she felt; she was furious.

"I want to ask you to marry me." She moved so swiftly and slapped him so hard everyone fell silent at the unexpected turn of events. She was appalled; the gall of him for bringing her out in public to humiliate her, the nerve. What did he think, that she wouldn't say no? That she would allow him to corner her like that in a place where she was trapped to appease his ego. Never!

"You made a fool of me for this? Even after I asked for some space, to clear my mind?" Her questions flowed with contempt as her hands went defiantly to her hips, waiting for him to say another word that would fuel the anger she already felt.

"Morgan, please let me explain."

"You arrogant bastard, and you had to create an audience." Her statement was like a bullet to his heart as she stormed down the street, hailed a taxi and got in it.

"I thought women like this stuff?" He turned to his female captain and looked to the male officers who only shrugged their shoulders helplessly, while some snickered and laughed at him.

"Some women just like for a man to be simple, sincere, and honest, Bruce. If she asked for time that's what she needs, not a spectacle."

"I will never figure you women out." He held his face where she slapped him and touched his fingers to his lips to see if there was blood.

Letting Go

Morgan walked through the door of her home and slammed it. She was so angry she didn't know what to do with herself. This is what really pissed her off about Bruce, every time he saw her he had to grab and grope her body leaving her feeling like a piece of meat. It's always about sex or one big show. He had no idea how to just relax, settle down, and be romantic. She fumed, picked up the phone and dialed Alexandra.

"Hey, hot stuff. Enjoying being the envy of all women?" Alexandra answered the phone sarcastically.

"Oh, please don't start," annoyance canvassing her voice.

"I am only poking fun at you, I am one of the good guys, remember?"

"It's not that. I am sorry, but I am really not enjoying all this attention the way you guys seemed to be enjoying it. I cannot work like this," her exasperation becoming evident and finally gaining her friend's full attention. Alexandra could hear the defeat and sadness in Morgan's voice and she couldn't understand. She wished she had the kind of attention and courtship that was being thrown at Morgan; she couldn't even get anywhere near that from her husband, not before they married when they were courting and definitely not now after five years of marriage. She couldn't even remember if she was ever wooed so openly, so passionately and yet Morgan was shunning what she and most women would die for. Secretly she understood why men liked Morgan; her heart wouldn't let her lie.

"Why do you sound this way? You should be floating on cloud nine, now deciding who to pick." Alexandra giggled, trying to lighten the mood. When Morgan only sighed she put the book down that she was reading and sat up in bed. Envy ate at her as she looked beside her at the once sexy man she married who now snored heavily and in a short time had a growing beer belly, but she kept those thoughts to herself. She gave up a healthy dating life for him. "What exactly is the problem here, Morgan?" She pulled herself away from her own fantasies and returned to Morgan's predicament.

"I don't know. I just don't understand why they have to be so forceful, so demanding, and so arrogant," she blurted out.

"A little flowers and phone calls and you fold? I don't get it. It's not like you are being stalked, threatened or abused."

"Oh yeah, well then I was just practically arrested, thrown in the back of a siren police cruiser and taken to the police station."

"What?" The shock of it all bolted Alexandra from her bed and to the closet where she began throwing on her jeans and sneakers.

"I'm coming over."

"No, that's not necessary. I am okay."

"Then what happened? I am on my way," Alexandra insisted, hoping Morgan wouldn't say no to her again.

"Alex, I just said I am okay. The last thing I need right now is an audience. I had enough of that today already to last me a lifetime." Morgan was completely oblivious to the true motive behind Alexandra's dedication.

"What do you mean? Tell me what happened?" Alexandra sighed, realizing that she was not going to change her friend's mind. Morgan's words slowed her pace so she sat at her desk still dressed listening to Morgan tell her about the police barricade and the orchestrated proposal that was planned. Alexandra couldn't hold back any longer. She remained quiet on the phone line until Morgan was finished speaking and still she said nothing.

"Alex are you still there?"

"Yes."

"Then why aren't you saying anything?"

"Maybe a woman would be a better choice for you." Her words were said in jest and she laughed heartily waiting for Morgan to join her. When she didn't she stopped and got serious again.

"I am sorry, I didn't mean to joke. It's just because I am still trying to figure out your problem here."

"What do you mean you are trying to figure out my problem? My problem? I don't have a problem. These men with their controlling attitudes and selfish behaviors are the ones with the problem. Don't you see something wrong with that? Barricading the streets, sending so many flowers I have nowhere to put them and calling me so much at work that I am distracted from my responsibilities?"

"Actually Morgan, I don't see the problem. I think you have a problem and it's time you figure it out and face it. What is wrong with you? So many women including me would give our last breath for a moment of what you have and you are just so self-absorbed, so into you that you don't take time to be appreciative."

"Excuse me?"

"Yes, you are excused."

"Alex, don't try to put this off on me."

"Then who, Morgan? If you like these guys and don't want to make a choice then say you are dating and that's it. But you keep leading them on, telling them that you will make a choice. It's basic human nature, I would do the same thing too if I were in their shoes. I mean, what did you expect these men to do? Sit and wait for you to tell them no? Come on, for a smart woman you are really being dumb right now."

"Who the hell do you think you are talking to like that? Is this jealousy I hear?"

"Call it whatever you want, Morgan. Yes, I wish I could be in your shoes right now," stopping herself from really saying how she felt, "and that my husband did half of what he did before even though even that was not enough, but that's not the issue. The issue is that you need to check your behavior. I am your friend and so I will tell you the truth. If you don't want to hear it then that's fine but don't come crying to me because I will not lie to you and tell you what you want to hear to help you feel better."

The line was quiet and Alexandra wasn't sure if Morgan had hung up the phone or not, so she just waited for the dial tone. She was angry that Morgan was behaving the way she was. Sure she felt some jealousy toward her, but not in a malicious way. Sure her marriage wasn't what she envisioned it would be five years later. She wanted children and hubby didn't, but she loved the man despite it all. Morgan was her friend and she wanted to be honest with her, whether it hurt or not, but she didn't want to lose her friendship with Morgan either.

"So you finally told me off," Morgan stated somberly, her voice choked in an effort to speak. She was taken aback by Alexandra's abruptness, taking what was going on with her so personally, but she brushed it off as her friend really caring and looking out for her.

"Morgan, you know I love you. We are friends and I really want to see you happy."

"Please don't apologize."

"But I have to apologize; hurting you was not my intention. I just wanted to show you how lucky you were and that you should go a little bit easy on these guys. After all, you said you liked them equally for what they had to offer individually, right? So you play a part in how they behave toward you."

"I know you are right, Alex. I guess I just didn't see it that way and it's time I looked at me and not just them."

"Oh Morgan, sweetie, I am sorry." She heard Morgan sniffle and her heart sank. She wished she could put her arms around her. "Tell you what. How about I come pick you up, we go over to the Hudson Pier and grab some homemade ice cream. It's beautiful this time of night and I really could use a walk, you know how my butt is spreading like cream cheese these days." She chuckled at her own corny joke.

"Actually Alex, as tempting as that offer is, I think I am going to take a vacation."

"That's a fantastic idea. We will plan it for next month, by then all of our assignments will be covered and I will go with you." She thought this would be a perfect opportunity to spend some alone time with Morgan and maybe, just maybe she could share with her what she had been feeling.

"No, you don't understand." She paused and swallowed hard. "I am going to leave for a vacation tomorrow."

"Listen Morgan, you are not being rational. You can't just get up and fly off somewhere when you have responsibilities. You are one of the most responsible people I know," Alexandra urged, disappointment stinging at her.

"That's the problem, Alex, it's time for me to take some time for me. I am always doing everything even though the company is up and running efficiently. I can take a breather for a week and the world will not stop. I need to clear my head, Alex."

"Morgan, please. I want to go with you; I deserve a break from my Prince Charming here too. Just a few more weeks. Please." She smiled awkwardly, with her fingers crossed hoping her last ditch at a plea would go over well.

"As much as I would love that, girlfriend, right now it's an urgent necessity. I know I can count on you to cover the fort for me while I am gone." Morgan sighed. Her decision was made.

Relenting and not wanting to believe that Morgan would really leave she sighed and breathed hard into the phone.

"Then where are you going? Have you even thought about it?"

"Well, I have now. I am online as we speak with Expedia.com and they book flights, hotels, car rental, and everything-in-one packages. I think if I don't do this now I will loose my mind. These brothers are relentless and if I chose one or none I want it to be my choice and not because they twisted my arm."

"I understand how you feel, Morgan, but be honest, if you had to choose it would be Bruce wouldn't it?" She quizzed. "Tell me the truth."

"Bruce? Are you kidding me? No way!" She laughed, feeling the tension slipping away from her and walking towards her plush cream sofa love seat and curling into the softness of it.

"Why not? Bruce is hot."

"Yeah, of hot air. He is way too full of himself."

"But it's sexy, admit it. He's got spunk, he's gutsy and spontaneous. Not to mention he's got a body to die for." Alexandra drooled, that proposal thing he pulled was off the radar as far as cool goes, he definitely earned points with me.

"You think so? I don't think he's got a great body. Way too much hair on his chest, he's got these scrawny legs and is not as well packaged as say Troy for instance."

Getting up from her desk chair and falling to the ground Alexandra rolled on the floor, laughing out loud. "I just cannot find it in myself to trust Bruce. He's a player."

"What do you mean; you have never seen him with a woman."

"I don't have to, I know his history. Alex, his only child is the product of a booty call, how will he explain that to his daughter? That her mother is a woman he never dated, never cared for, and she was just someone willing to have sex with him at his whim. Not to mention his past ex-girlfriends were swingers and he is used to all that multiple sex partners. These are things I will never be into or condone."

"Wow, you didn't tell me that." Alexandra mused. She didn't come out and say it to Morgan, but she preferred that she was alone for a while until she was able to get her nerves together to really talk to her.

"Besides, three months ago he promised me for the third time to invite me to a family event, and never once have I met a family member." Morgan rambled on, laughing at the memory. "Once he invited me to a christening for his brother's child and hours before the event called and canceled. Honestly, I didn't really want to go because I wasn't sure how I would answer if people asked who I was, so he did me a favor, but the fact that he does this all the time. How serious am I supposed to take his behavior?"

"I see your point."

"So now you understand?" Morgan prodded, feeling vindicated.

"Yes, I guess so. Then who would you choose? It's not like any of the other guys have introduced you to family either."

Morgan thought about it and the thought really bothered her. Alexandra was right. As long as she'd known Isaiah, she had never even met a friend, nor had he ever invited her to meet his family. Worse yet, he had never referred to her as anything more than a friend to the people he knew or cared about. So what exactly was she stressing herself over? Agitation took mirth away as the thought pierced her pride.

"Troy," Morgan decided.

"Troy? Bad boy Troy? You only like the rush. You would be tired of him in no time."

"I don't think so. He's got dark creamy skin."

"They are all dark, Morgan," Alexandra chimed.

"Well, his skin is creamy and smooth. He is all up on the street lingo and stuff."

"Stuff like having a bunch of women, smoking weed and all the edgy stuff that you don't believe in. Imagine what your friends and family would think bringing him to a dinner party. He wouldn't know what fork to use."

"Okay fine, than what do you suggest? Isaiah?" Alexandra thought it wouldn't be fair for Morgan to date an older man. What if Morgan wanted to have children? Their dad would be almost at retirement age by the time they were ten years old. What child could truly enjoy their dad at that age? She just didn't think Isaiah was a good fit. Morgan needed a young, handsome charmer on her arm to wow the crowd and make her the envy of every woman within visional distance. "I don't think that would be wise. He's wonderful but he would bore you to death."

Morgan decided to get up from her seat and walk to the kitchen where she put on her teapot and turned the fire on to boil the water in order to make some tea.

"Isaiah is nice, charming and classy," Morgan chirped,

thinking of all the walks they'd shared, the long never-ending talks that had no limit or boundaries. She loved the way his eyes twinkled when he looked at her, the gentleness of his arms as they caressed hers and the hidden desires he fought to keep concealed below the surface of his gentlemanly disposition. She always wondered what it would be like to pry beyond the surface of his calm mannerisms. "At least I know he has prepared himself for a wife, and his choices in life tell me that choosing me is no light matter for him. That makes me feel very special. Besides he's great husband material, has a nice financial portfolio, and not bad looking either." Morgan thought about Isaiah's attributes and felt warm and safe with just the thought of him, but she thought his age might be a problem. She didn't want to be a widow at a young age, or limit her options of exploring all life had to offer because she had to be a stay-at-home caretaker to the man she wanted to share her everything with. Bruce, on the other hand, filled her with excitement and the promise of fun. He was young, strong, charming with the sense of humor that had women draping over his arms at his smile. Troy was passionate and sexy, he oozed dangerous sex appeal that was the ingredient of trouble and she knew it. Thinking of each man made her wish all their characteristics would be in one perfect parcel.

"I take it back." Alexandra rolled over on her back and stared up into her ceiling.

"What do you take back?"

"I take it back. I don't envy your dilemma at all. Yet again, I don't think I would be confused if I was in your shoes. I would definitely pick Bruce. You are more into the thug type like Troy."

"What are you trying to say? That I don't have any taste?"

"I didn't say it. You did." They giggled until their glee subsided.

"I cannot believe you are going."

"I have to, sweetie. But I know you've got everything covered and I will be back in a week. I just need to clear my mind and everything will be okay when I get back, I promise."

"Okay, well what time does your flight leave?"

"Six in the morning."

"Wow, I won't even be able to drop you at the airport," Alexandra mused.

"What are you pining about? Don't we see each other every day?" Morgan puzzled.

"I guess it doesn't matter. So where are you going anyway?"

"Germany."

"Why so far?" Alex asked, concerned.

"I don't know. It was the first thing that came to my mind when I clicked on the Internet. It's going to be fine, stop mothering. I will call you when I land."

"Well, you better go to bed now. It's eleven at night already. What do you want me to tell your fans when they try to contact you and you are not here?"

"Tell them I have gone on a business trip and you are not at liberty to discuss my location. That should throw a wrench in their inquisitions for a few days."

"I am going to miss you, Morgan," Alexandra stated quietly as she prepared to hang up the phone.

"I will miss you too, Alex, with your crazy self. But I will be back in no time."

"Okay, good night."

"Good night," Morgan said and gently replaced the receiver to its cradle.

Something New

Arriving in Düsseldorf, Germany, on a first-class direct flight, Morgan stretched her legs after her twelve hours and rubbed her eyes. She had traveled into time and it was very late as Germany is a whole six hours ahead of New York. A car service awaited her and she was whisked off to the Hilton.

"May I take these to your room, ma'am?" the bell service asked. She loved the sound of the people. Although to most the language was hard, rough on the ears and difficult to speak, she felt refreshed. A different country, a different language, a different feeling.

"Thank you. I would appreciate that." She looked at the man and smiled as his blond hair and dark eyes seemed to do a dance. "How do you say *thank you* in German?"

"*Danke schon,*" he explained and with a couple of tries she finally got it.

"That's not bad," he complimented. "And *you are welcome* is *bitteschon.*" She smiled at her own horrible attempt and joined the bellhop on the elevator to her room.

"Does everyone speak good English here or will I need a dictionary?"

"Oh no, in Deutsch, that's the German word for Germany. In Deutsch, the children begin to learn English in the fifth grade, so most people here speak good English. You will be very comfortable," he explained as he placed her things inside her suite and parted with a tip she generously placed in his hands. "*Danke schon.*" He smiled.

"*Bitteschon,*" she responded before closing the door.

She surveyed the room to her satisfaction and walked toward the large king-sized bed. *What do I do now,* she asked herself. When her stomach growled in response she knew the answer: dinner. But it was way too late for dinner. She took a quick shower and crawled into bed. It was almost morning. She could wait until then.

She awoke at almost twelve noon and she was starving. She hurriedly got dressed in a long cotton sundress, allowed her curly auburn tresses to drop to her shoulder, grabbed her purse and headed to the lobby.

"*Guten morgen!* ma'am." The same bellhop from the night before greeted her. "That means *good morning,*" he told her.

"Hello and good morning to you as well."

"Yes, it is a beautiful morning." The bellhop blushed and looked away. "If you need any help at all, please don't hesitate to ask. My name is Günter."

"Thank you, Günter, I will definitely do that." She turned to walk away and realized she didn't exactly know where to go. "Oh Günter," she called after him.

"*Ja?*"

"Where is the hotel restaurant or breakfast bar?"

"Oh, that's easy. Just take the elevator to the double lobby, take the long hallway past the gift shops and the recreation center and you will find the main dining area. They are serving a continental breakfast this morning."

"*Danke schon,* Günter." She smiled brightly showing him she remembered his lesson from the previous night.

"Wow, that's very good, madam. Very good." He smiled and walked away. She followed his direction and didn't have to look very hard as there were other tourists looking for the breakfast bar before twelve-thirty when they would stop serving breakfast and begin serving lunch. She only had to follow her nose as the aroma caused her belly to do flip-flops in anticipation of a good meal.

As she sat alone at a private area of the hotel restaurant, Morgan basked in the beauty of the ambiance around her. The brightly lit chandeliers, the deep plush comfort of the Asian and Middle Eastern fabrics of the chairs, and the Egyptian-type curtained drapes, swooshing throughout the restaurant giving it an air of intimacy. She stared at the picturesque walls filled with three-dimensional paintings and drawings that gave a great example of the German culture and history. It was beautiful. As she surveyed it she sighed deeply, lost in thought about all that faced her at home. She embraced the simplicity and serenity she felt in that moment and sighed again as she waited for the lines to die down by the omlette bar, where the cook was making them fresh to order according to each patron's desire.

Her thoughts trailed back to Bruce, Troy, and Isaiah. Maybe she should just be alone. Is it so bad that she is thirty years old and not married? Should she fall into the unnatural urges and pressure of her family and friends that her biological clock is ticking and therefore she should be married? That her twenty-five-year-old baby sister is married with kids is no consolation either. Confusion plagued her and she sighed again as the server brought water, clean utensils, and bread to her table.

"Entschuldigung! Darf ich mich Ihnen anschließen?" She heard the voice of a man and she looked up not certain of what she heard.

"I'm sorry, I don't speak German," she told him, blushing as she looked into his deep blue-green eyes and full curly blond hair. Her heart skipped a beat as he smiled at her showing even white teeth, sporting a white button-down linen shirt, denim jeans, and cowboy boots.

"*Es tut mir leid.* I mean, I am sorry," he smiled brightly at her, "an Amerikan woman," he stated as she smiled and nodded her positive response.

"What did you ask me before?"

"Oh, I said *Entschuldigung*! Which means *excuse me*, and *Darf ich mich Ihnen anschließen*, which means, *may I join you*," he told her.

"Oh I see," she said blushing again.

"Is it okay if I join you?" He stood, waiting for her to answer. She felt incredibly silly sitting there staring at him when he asked again.

"Yes, of course." She looked at this tall graceful creature that just happened to drop at her feet. She was completely taken by his height; he seemed to be no shorter than six foot six inches tall. His broad shoulders and confident disposition took her breath away. "I was just sitting here enjoying the view," she admitted, allowing her gaze to drift back to the window.

"I hope I have added to that," he teased, causing her to go from creamy olive to bright red. "I am sorry; I don't mean to embarrass you. My name is Seymen-Cansin."

"That's a mouthful."

"A mouthful?"

"Oh, that's just an American expression. It means that's a lot to say." She felt very silly and immediately felt awkward with the language barrier, but this man's presence made her feel very soft and gushy inside. "How do you pronounce your name? and could you please say it slowly?"

"Si-mon-Cansin."

"Oh, Simon Cansin, the *n* is silent in your last name."

"Yes, correct. You said it perfectly."

"That was very nice of you to say. I did horrible," she said shyly. The day just slipped away as they shared breakfast and sat through lunch laughing as he taught her all about his culture, education, and background. She laughed heartily at his quirky sense of humor and reverse sarcasm and tried desperately to understand his broken English, which only brought them more mirth. Before she knew it, the restaurant was just about empty with only two diners sitting on the opposite end of the dining room at just about midnight.

"Its getting close to dinnertime, Simon; I think they would like for us to leave so they can prepare the dining area for dinner."

"Yes, I think you are right to say this. I very much am enjoying your company." She laughed at the way he put together the English language.

"You laugh at me." He nudged her as they stood to get up.

"No, I laugh with you." She chuckled and felt the butterflies flutter her stomach as he took her fingers into his large hands and helped to guide her from where they sat for more than four hours deep in conversation.

"*Du bist ta Lügner.*" He laughed and she stopped to look at him quizzically. "Oh, I only say you lie to me that you don't laugh at me," he explained. "It is very difficult to be concentrated in English for so long. I never need here to use this language."

"It's okay, I understand. I am very impressed that everyone here speaks so well. In America, it is not encouraged that we learn different languages and cultures and histories of other countries. It's very limited and mostly geared toward America," she told him as they walked hand in hand out of the hotel.

They spent the next day together and emotions built quickly within them. She found that she liked his smile, his sense of humor, and the way he paid complete attention to her even when he could have his pick of all the women who walked by gawking at him.

"I like you a lot, Morgan," he told her, gently brushing her hair out of her face.

"I like you too." She smiled and they kept walking. As he pointed out different historical buildings, cathedrals, and tourist attractions, he would gradually caress her back, hold her hands, and brush his body against her. He loved the way she smelled, and her disposition of being a bit more open with how she felt. As they walked across the walkway heading back to the hotel, he turned and looked at her; he admired how the star's light bounced off of her reddish auburn hair and the twinkle in her eyes when she smiled; she felt her heart skip a beat as he placed his arms around her waist and pulled her into him. She could feel his excitement stir as he placed his lips to hers tentatively at first, then with passion he thrust his tongue into her mouth and kissed her freely for what felt like an eternity. She felt like she could stand there for an eternity. And when he pulled away from her, she couldn't breathe, she couldn't stand.

"Please don't let me go, I think I will fall." She smiled sheepishly.

"I will never let you fall," he whispered in her ear, causing his hot breath to sear her skin and palpitate her heartbeat. They seemed oblivious to the rest of the world, the stares of those looking at this black woman and this white man in the heart of Düsseldorf, Germany, kissing like longtime lovers.

He walked her back to her hotel suite and stood outside the door.

"Thank you for a very nice time, Simon, I didn't

expect to be enjoying myself so, and with my own personal tour guide." She licked her lips and hoped he would ask to come in. She didn't want to come off as being too aggressive, not knowing his culture and the ways of the women there, but she didn't want the night to be over, even though it was already so late.

"I had a wonderful time as well." He reached in and brushed his lips one last time gently against hers and then turned to leave.

"Bye," she said, moving to close the door.

"Morgan. I have a very important business meeting tomorrow early, and I am supposed to be heading back to Frankfurt on Thursday. *Aber*, I mean, but if you don't mind, I would like to hang around until the Monday when you leave for America. Maybe show you around some more. Go karaoke in Cologne and take the train over to Amsterdam maybe? What do think?" His boyish charm and exuberance for life titillated her.

"I would love that. If you are sure I am not interrupting anything," she agreed.

"No no, this is wonderful. The best time I have now in a long time, all because of you. You make me a happy man in this moment," he told her, kissing her once more before leaving. "I call you in the evening tomorrow when work is finished," he yelled back as she closed the door behind her, and with her back pressed firmly to the door she sank to the floor. *What have I gotten myself into now?* she thought, smiling broadly.

She looked at the time and calculated what time it was in New York. It was almost midnight in Germany, making it almost 6:00 A.M. in New York. She decided she would take a shower and order in a midnight snack. By the time she did all that it would be about eight in the morning and Alexandra would already be at her desk. Besides, she needed to check in the office anyway and see how things were going with her abrupt absence.

Alexandra shrieked when she heard Morgan's voice on the other end of the line.

"I was just thinking about you since you didn't call to let me know you arrived safely yesterday and that you were okay. I was starting to get worried," Alex told her, moving to her desk and sitting comfortably, kicking off her shoes and putting up her legs to rest on the edge of her deep mahogany desk.

"I am fine; you know you don't have to worry about me."

"Okay, spill the beans."

"What?"

"Girl you are as high as a kite and blushing like a Catholic schoolgirl who just got her first kiss; spill it now."

"You can tell all of that on the phone?" Morgan asked, surprised that Alexandra picked up on her happiness.

"Well, not exactly but you just sound so happy, nothing like the woman who left here almost two days ago."

"Really?" Morgan asked, blushing.

"Yes, now spill it!" her friend demanded, waiting anxiously to find out what had happened to change Morgan's disposition in such a short time.

"Okay, here goes. . . ." And Morgan told Alexandra what happened from beginning to end, moment by moment. Alexandra was on the edge of her seat drooling by the time she completed her tale telling.

"OH . . . MY . . . GOSH!" was all Alexandra could say. "What is it about you that you just keep reeling them in? Don't you ever stop? Girl, how do you do it? Please bottle whatever it is you have and sell some to me." She rambled.

"Oh stop, it's nothing like that. But Alex, he is so wonderful. He is nothing like the other guys. He is cultured, speaks multiple languages, well traveled, has everything he needs, his own business, his own job, his own home, and most importantly his own money." She bubbled.

"I know, and the thing about him that gets me is that he is younger."

"Younger? How much younger?"

Morgan pretended to cough and cleared her throat. "Seven years younger," she mumbled.

"Okay, a white guy, who's got it all together and seven years younger. Now that's something." She wrapped up nonjudgmentally, "I guess I would want a fine specimen like that too. You know they say that a man reaches his peak at twenty-one and a woman at thirty. Sounds like a perfect match," she teased.

"You know, you do have a point," Morgan admitted and they laughed heartily together.

"So what are you going to do about the guys here?" Alexandra questioned, thinking back to the original reason why she had to leave. "Are you over them, not going to pick any? What?"

"Well, I just met the guy, Alex; so much is not going to change in less than one day. I just wanted to tell you how good he makes me feel, how different he is."

"How do you think your family would take this? The guys?"

"My mother is white and my father is black. Both me and my baby sister are mixed, exactly how are they going to take it if I chose someone of a different culture? They did and things worked out just fine."

"I suppose you are right, but you know how things are on the racism tip. The brothers feeling like white men are taking all of our good women and the women feeling like all the good brothers are going to white women. Do you think you could handle an interracial relationship?"

"You know something, girlfriend. I just met Seymen,

and I feel wonderful. For once in a very long time my body is truly alive at just the thought of a man."

"You slept with him already?" Alexandra asked, incredulous.

"No, silly. I just said that my body feels alive. I am not stressing about picking a choice, I am just relaxing and enjoying myself. No drama and exaggerated courtship from men who won't even think twice to send flowers once they are married. Just pure simple hand holding, spontaneous kissing and enjoying a good time. Is that a crime?" Morgan asked, frustrated.

"I don't suppose it is, I just asked that's all." They paused for a minute while Alexandra absorbed Morgan's news.

"Well, if nothing else you are getting rest and something new is always good to uplift the spirit and shed new light on a situation." She smiled, hoping Morgan would get her drift. "Just do what you went there for, to relax and to think. By the time you are home you should be feeling bright-eyed and bushy tailed," she continued.

"You are right. Well, in other news, how is *Flowers Bed* doing?"

"Awesome, I told you I would be on top of things. That last advertiser we were waiting for came on, I signed on the dotted line and with that we have superseded our budget," Alexandra bragged.

"Awesome, I knew I could count on you."

"Thanks, Morgan."

"No, thank you, my dear. Now I have to get to bed and you have work to do." They said their good-byes shortly after and Morgan fell asleep and had a long peaceful, dreamless sleep.

She spent her time in Germany resting and not venturing too far away from the hotel for fear of getting lost and not exactly knowing what she wanted to do since her trip was impulsive. Thursday couldn't come fast enough and when it did, she waited for Simon to ring her. It was almost noon on Thursday before he arrived and knocked on her door and before that she felt as though he might have forgotten. She had a wonderful time in Germany as they rented a vehicle and traveled on the autobahn from Frankfurt, to Cologne, to Wiesbaden where he grew up, and to Berlin. They went dancing, sang at a few karaoke bars and listened some as Simon played his guitar and serenaded her. She met his friends, his sisters, visited his business and was able to see his home before he had to take her back to Düsseldorf to prepare for her long flight back to the United States.

Late that Sunday night as he kissed her passionately she began to cry and so did he.

"I will miss you, *schatzy*." He called her in the new name she had become accustomed to. A name commonly used in Germany to refer to your partner and life lover.

"I will miss you too," she told him curling into the comfort of his massive arms and broad chest, as they lay together in her hotel room, her things already packed for her early morning flight.

"What will I do now without you? I waited so long for a woman like you, I prayed so often for a woman to come into my life." He chuckled softly and she relished the deep huskiness of his voice. "I just never thought that she would be a beautiful black woman and from thousands of miles away in another country. No wonder you were so hard to find," he whispered playfully to her.

"It's not so bad. You can visit with me and when I have vacation I will also visit with you," she told him lightly.

At her words he gently eased her away from him to

look into her eyes. Tears silver streaking the beautiful sky blue of his irises.

"I don't want that we wait so long. I want you to be mine. Please Morgan, be mine?" he asked, his voice choked to an almost inaudible whisper. As she looked at him, felt the heat he created between her thighs, and ran her hands through his soft curly blond hair, she thought of a thousand reasons why she should say no. A thousand reasons why she could not just say yes to a man who had made her feel wholesome, complete, and loved in a genuine, sincere, and honest way. All things she wanted and hadn't had in any of the other men who sought to have her belong to him. But as she opened her mouth to say no, she too was surprised as she watched his frown turn to a smile.

"Yes."

"Yes? Oh *meine schatz, meine Machen, meine Prinzessin.*" He babbled on in German calling her his love, his woman, his girl and his princess. Swept away in his excitement, they made love for the first time and spent the night wrapped in each other's arms.

Saying good-bye to her on Monday morning was the most difficult thing he had ever done. He walked away the instant she went through the checkpoint. He just couldn't bear to see her leave him, for the first time he had fallen head over heels in love with a woman and he was letting her walk away. When she turned around he was gone and she felt completely sad and empty. Seymen sat in his car as tears cascaded down his cheeks and vowed that he would take the next flight to America the first chance he got to visit her.

Morgan's flight was long as she traveled back homeward bound. She had mixed feelings and felt even more confused going back home than when she left. Now she had another man to throw into the mix and the only problem she could see with him was that he was white.

When Life Hurts

Morgan dropped her bags and walked over to her phone pressing the voice mail button, which indicated that she had over thirty new messages. After playing them she found there was an almost even split between Troy, Bruce, and Isaiah all wanting to know where she was, why they couldn't reach her on her mobile, work or home number and when will she give them a call back. There were two very important messages registered on her phone that she had to respond to as the words caught her breath she began to dial.

"Momma, what's wrong? Is Sienna okay?"

"Hey baby, it's so good to hear from you. I was worried sick when you didn't call back after we left the message two days ago," her mother told her. She sounded as though she had been crying and panic overcame Morgan.

"What did they say Momma, is Sienna going to be all right? Is she still in the hospital?"

"Yes, baby. Normally when the sickle cells block the flow of blood, she would get the pain episodes and the last time she had lung tissue damage. But this time it's in her arms, legs, chest, and abdomen. She had a stroke baby. The doctors kept her in the hospital. She might also have spleen, kidneys, and liver damage." Her mother broke out into a fresh burst of tears.

"Morgan sweetie, we are heading out to the hospital now to see her. I will call you later, okay?" her mother said before abruptly hanging up. Morgan knew that her dad was having a pretty hard time. Her mom didn't handle stress or pressure very well. This is not what she wanted to come back to, her baby sister in the hospital.

She picked up the phone and began to dial when it rang.

"Hello Isaiah." Morgan was not happy to hear from him at this time. She just wanted to get a rental and drive up to Chicago. Driving would be better because it would give her a chance to think and not get there too fast. She hated seeing her baby sister in the hospital and it doesn't get easier with time.

"Hey sweetie, I have missed you."

"I am sorry I cannot talk right now Isaiah. I have to get to Chicago." There was a brief silence before he responded.

"Well okay, but can you give me a call when you get a chance, babe? I would like to talk to you." She snickered internally at his passive behavior. He never pushed the envelope, never asked that extra question even when she desperately needed him to. How was she supposed to know he cared? Well it didn't matter; she had to get to her parents.

"Sure, Isaiah, I don't know when that will be as I have an emergency in my family. But I will call you when I get a chance." She baited him, wondering if he cared enough about her and what she was going through to find out what was wrong. His answer disappointed her more, but she knew she couldn't be with someone who wasn't willing to go to bat for her, to put himself on the line.

"Okay baby, talk to you then." She hung up the phone feeling like screaming.

"Why do you have to be so damn predictable Isaiah, why?"

she screamed as she stormed through the house. She grabbed her purse and ran out without her overnight suitcase. She hailed a Yellow cab and was on her way to the nearest car rental spot. She didn't have to wait long before she was in a midsize vehicle and driving to Chicago like she had done many times before. When her cell phone rang she looked and saw it was Alexandra and answered.

"Hey, girlfriend. I cannot wait to hook up with you later and hear all about your German adventures," Alexandra chirped.

"That's not going to happen, Alex. I'm sorry."

"Morgan are you okay? You sound like you've been crying."

"I'm all right. It's just that Sienna is sick again. My mom says it's actually bad this time, the pain is so horrible they have admitted her now for a couple days."

"Oh sweetie, I am so sorry."

Morgan tried to wipe the tears away from her eyes, as her vision was getting blurry. She drove as fast as she could, taking the George Washington Bridge; she sped through New Jersey and was on 80 West to Illinois in no time.

"Just let everyone know you will be acting executive during this interim for me. I will be back as soon as possible."

"No problem, hon, just drive carefully, okay. Slow down and don't panic, your sister is going to be okay. This has happened before and she is always okay, right?" Alexandra tried to reason with her in order to calm her friend down. She knew Morgan was under a lot of stress even though she refused to allow her emotions to flow out into an obvious call for help, always afraid to rely on someone else, always insisting on being strong. Alexandra knew her friend's weakness and wanted to help her in whatever way she could without putting her vulnerabilities on the frontline.

Morgan kept wiping her tears. She knew she was only

feeling sorry for herself, beating herself up about not having a steady man in her life, wanting to have children, wishing Isaiah could be the man in her life, just a little more passionate; she would even deal with the age thing. The tears just kept coming. She reached to the glove compartment to retrieve a napkin and jumped when she heard someone blaring their horn at her. Swerving out of the way she realized that she had veered into oncoming traffic and quickly righted the car as the drivers cursed vulgarities at her.

"Whoa, what was that?" Alexandra asked concerned.

"Oh nothing, just some impatient drivers on the road, that's all," Morgan lied.

"Well, let me get off the phone so I don't distract you. Call me when you get to your parents and tell everyone hello for me." She smiled.

"No problem." Morgan sniffled.

"Please be careful, Morgan. I love you." Alexandra needed to let her know she was not alone and though Morgan appreciated it, she was not in the love mood and wanted to stay depressed for a while.

"Bye," she said and hung up the phone before Alexandra could say anything else.

She hung up the phone and paid close attention to the road. Though she didn't admit it, her veering off the road earlier scared her a bit, and left her nerves a little rattled.

She reached over and turned the radio on to some easy listening to calm her down. She drove in silent contemplation for a while until the phone rang again. She reached over to get her purse where she had dropped her cell earlier before. When she didn't see it immediately and it kept ringing, she released her right hand from the steering wheel and reached into her purse to fish it out. At the moment she grabbed it she knew something was wrong, it all seemed instantaneous. The blaring of the horns, the screaming of horror-struck onlookers in passing cars, she felt surreal and everything was in slow motion as she raised her eyes above the dashboard to see that she was completely in the lane of oncoming traffic; fear gripped her. Dread and distress sent off a distress of alarms in her but it was all too late. The shattering of the windshield sent splinters of glass into her face, head, and neck. She used her arms in an attempt to protect her face, releasing the steering wheel as it plunged into the oncoming vehicle. She saw herself in the most horrific way but there was nothing she could do. The air bag plopped out throwing her arms and neck back into the headrest of the driver's seat and she could hear the bones in her arms crack from the impact. She closed her eyes to stop the streaming of blood from entering her pupils. Her neck snapped to the side and she couldn't move, forced locked into position by her seat belt and the air bag, which felt like it was suffocating her. She could smell the scent of blood, smoke fumes, and gasoline as she struggled to move her legs and found that she couldn't. Pain tore at her body and her skin felt as though it was on fire. Her mind took her away from the blow, shock replaced her refrain and her screams were locked in her throat before she blacked out.

She came to vaguely, ambulance siren, fire trucks, and police cruisers swelled upon her and the surrounding area; she felt achy and groggy, and trying to move her head was difficult.

"Ouch!" she sluggishly whispered through the pained movements of her mouth. She tried to move and realized she couldn't. Tears of frustration and pain welled into her eyes causing her to flutter her eyelids. She couldn't move her arms as they were tied into restraints and the damage around her caused a new steady flow of anguish to stain her face.

"Whoa there little lady," one firefighter told her as

he held her head and steadied her. He motioned to one of the paramedics to assist him. The woman moved swiftly, putting a brace on Morgan's neck that extended to her spine.

"Oh this doesn't look too good," the firefighter said to the paramedic, "look." Alarms went off in Morgan's head as she tried to read their lips and to understand what they were saying. She couldn't completely comprehend their speech but she could see the panic in their faces as they tried to remain stone-faced and calm.

The paramedic woman walked over to another man and told him that she had to be airlifted back to New Jersey's closest hospital after noticing that she had broken her legs and was losing consciousness fast.

By the time they came back and prepared her for the arriving medical chopper, Morgan had passed out.

The hospital attendants answered Morgan's phone, deciphering next of kin and family who could be informed of Morgan's situation. Alexandra shrieked when the doctor told her where Morgan was. When Morgan didn't call her to let her know she had arrived safely in Chicago, she knew something was wrong. Alexandra asked the doctors not to call Morgan's parents because she was on her way there for her sister who was in the hospital and she didn't think they could handle both situations at the same time. So she got in her car and drove as fast and safely as she could to Barnett Hospital in Paterson, New Jersey.

Alexandra couldn't believe what she saw when she entered the hospital room. Her legs gave way and she began to cry. The smell of hospital disinfectants raided her nose and burnt her eyes. The sterility of the room and the sight of her friend centered amongst all the machines there to aid her back to health took her off guard. She was grateful that Morgan was still asleep so as to not see her react this way to the sight of her. As she moved closer to her friend she fought back tears as the reality of the tragedy bombarded her senses. The ticking of the machines felt like a time bomb about to go off, the scent of antiseptics nauseated her and tears flowed freely this time without restraints.

Her heart raced as if to jump from her chest as she gazed upon Morgan's once flawless features that were now riddled with broken glass wounds all across her forehead, cheeks, and neck. Both of her legs were in casts, hung from the ceiling and supported by strong ropes. Her hands were also broken and held in casts at her side. Her body was wrapped with body casts as if she was broken from the neck down and her head bandaged up revealing that her beautiful hair was cut away from her head leaving her almost bald. Alexandra couldn't help the well of tears that flowed like rain down her cheeks. She sat down as not to loose her footing as she began to feel faint. She sat down until her tears dried into a continuous stream of hiccups, and her heaving lulled her into a fitful sleep as she resolved not to leave her friend's bedside.

It was midnight the next day when Morgan moaned and let out a sigh of deep pain as she tried to move. She tried to open her eyes but couldn't, then she tried to adjust her footing and found them locked in place. Straining to open her eyes into the semi-lit room, her eyes began gradually scanning her environment. As she realized she couldn't move her head, a renewed fear grabbed her and horror riddled her. She began to cry.

The nurses, sensing movement through her monitors, rushed into Morgan's room to assess her lucidness, waking Alexandra in their hasty actions to attend to her.

"What's wrong, what's going on?" Alexandra asked, rubbing her eyes and quickly pulling herself to a state of alertness.

"Seems your friend is awake. Would you mind just stepping outside briefly and then we will call you back in once we have checked her out." The attending doctor looked at Alexandra understandingly, empathy filling his eyes and she knew he meant her well.

"Of course, but you will call me in as soon as you are done?" Alexandra pleaded, her voice brimming with excitement.

"Absolutely," the doctor told her as he returned to Morgan's side and Alexandra tentatively saw her way to the waiting area outside of her friend's hospital room. As she sat down she heard the strange ring tone in her purse and jumped at its abruptness. She had been on pins and needles and everything seemed to surprise her. The phone stopped ringing and she sat down, returning her focus once again to the closed hospital room wondering what was happening inside.

Suddenly the incessant ringing resumed, almost causing her heart to jump from her chest. Irritably she decided to answer; she was on pins and needles about what was going on inside of Morgan's room and felt rudely interrupted, but she knew she wasn't the only one who loved her friend and she had a responsibility to answer and inform others of the dilemma that Morgan now faced.

"Hello?" The person on the other end of the phone seemed hesitant to respond then it occurred to her that they wouldn't be expecting anyone other than Morgan to answer. "Hello, this is Morgan's phone, who is this?" she answered again.

"Hey, yeah. This is Troy an' I'm jus trying to reach Morgan," he told her tentatively.

"Troy, oh. How are you?" Alexandra asked, trying to decide if she should include him in on what was happening.

"Am doing fine baby love. But if yu don't mine mi askin', can I speak to Morgan please?"

"Actually Troy, she is a bit indisposed at the moment. She is going to have to call you back," Alexandra told him, still not sure of how to handle this scenario and waiting for the right opportunity that would help her to decide what was best and the right thing to do.

"Who's dis?"

"I'm a good friend of hers. My name is Alexandra."

"Oh Alex, how yu doing baby girl? I hear so much 'bout yu."

"Re: Alex, what do you mean?" Curiosity piqued Alexandra's interest and she wanted to know exactly what bad boy Troy knew about her, or if he knew as much of her as she knew about him.

"Naw man, nuttin' lik dat. Every ting I ever hear 'bout you was good sistrin." He chuckled and the lull of his voice and the deep sensuality that exuded over the phone told her why Morgan liked him so much. His ethnic vernacular added a sexy mix to the equation while his playful disposition heated things up and strung her along, made her want to hear him keep talking.

"Okay, I guess that's a good thing then." She smiled.

"Very good ting." He chuckled again slowly and then the phone got quiet. "So Alex. Yu don't mine if I call yu Alex do yu?" he asked before continuing.

"No not at all. What can I help you with?"

"I was jus' wondering why yu answering mi girl's phone. Usually if she not available it jus' go straight to voice mail," he pondered.

"Yeah you see, that's the problem. Morgan . . . ah. See, she is not well right now." She tried to gauge her words as not to cause any unnecessary panic, but the moment she opened her mouth she knew she was doing a horrible job of it.

"I see" was all Troy said, but before she could tell him she would pass his message on he continued. "So what's wrong with mi girl? She need me to bring har some ting to warm har up?"

"Oh no, that's quite okay. See Troy, I wasn't sure if I should say anything but Morgan was in a bad car accident and—"

"Yu was really goin' to keep a ting lik' dat from mi woman? Yu no see some ting lik dat important?" She could hear the angry annoyance in his voice right below his cool facade.

"Yes I guess I do, but I was informed to strictly disclose the details to family and very close friends, and well, I don't exactly know you." She held her ground firmly.

"Aaright, point taken. So tell me where mi girl at and I will be there as fast as di next plane, train or automobile can carry me." She could see why Morgan liked him. He was a man of action, he didn't sit on things and wait for something to propel it. It was absolutely sexy.

"She was airlifted to Paterson, New Jersey, Barnett Hospital," she told him, the words leaving her lips quickly as she saw the nurses begin to leave Morgan's room. She didn't hear what else Troy said as she quickly hung up the phone and was on her feet and at the hospital room door.

"Yes, its okay, you may go in," the doctor told her as she saw him exit and Alexandra made a beeline toward him. He didn't need to hear her question to know what she wanted. She just smiled and walked back into her friend's room, which was now well-lighted. In the light she looked worse. Her heart almost stopped as renewed tears welled in her eyes. She couldn't help herself as Morgan stared at her knowingly.

The Value of a MAN

The next day Troy barged into the hospital demanding Morgan's whereabouts and though he seemed rude, though calm, the attendant knew not to irritate him. He strutted into Morgan's room to find Bruce and half of his precinct comrades gathered around Morgan. He was taken aback by the group of five uniformed New York City police officers who had packed Morgan's room almost to capacity. He had to lower his defenses and asked politely to be allowed room to maneuver in closer to the patient's bed and take a look at her. Troy and Morgan worked the opposite side of the law, and Troy's appearance, though street and thug, was very *GQ* and stylish. Bruce, feeling a bit defensive and a little embarrassed that another man came to see *his woman*, stepped up, causing silence to deafen the room and all eyes on Troy.

"Excuse me, who are you?" Troy was not about to back down as he felt he had a right to be there, and the hardened look on his face brought Alexandra to her feet in an attempt to mollify the situation.

"Bruce, this is Troy, a friend of Morgan's. Troy, this is Bruce, another friend of Morgan's." Her voice was light and playful in the introductions but she wasn't prepared for them having already known of or heard of each other.

They both stopped and looked at Morgan who still struggled to talk or smile and the distress on her face, though bruised, was very obvious.

"Morgan, this is the thug you have issues with?" he asked, not wanting to let on to his buddies that she was actually juggling, choosing between the two men. Bruce did not feel that Troy was his equal or even of the same caliber. His ego was hurt as he looked him up and down causing his platoon members to draw back into a defensive stance in order to act on Bruce's word.

"Bruce, stop," was all Morgan could muster but the anger on the men's faces showed that they couldn't hear her. Troy set his face hard and stood cool and wasn't about to back down, so he held his ground and walked over to Morgan's side.

"Baby guirl, wha' you gone do to yu self baby?" he whispered close to her ears, forcing the audience in the room to strain in an attempt to eavesdrop on their conversation. "Yu don't look good yu no." He smiled sexily at her and used his fingers to brush a strand of loose hair from her face. He surveyed that they had cut most of it off and he fought to remain strong wrestling with his emotions in the face of his opponents. He kissed her eyelids, her forehead, her cheeks, and then her lips, gently lingering just long enough to annoy his adversary, and then backed away. Bruce bristled at his audaciousness, but there was nothing he could do.

Morgan held on to Troy's hand with her right fingers, which was the only part of her hands that were not cast. He slid his fingers to intertwine with hers and used his thumb to caress the palm of her hand. His need to hold her and kiss her and break down was very strong but he knew he had to face off in front of Bruce. He stared at her, dauntingly trying hard to use telepathy to express to her what he felt. Morgan didn't have to hear his words; she saw it in his eyes, he was scared. She didn't look like the woman he courted or pursued. She looked horribly banged up and probably no longer fit the mold of the type of woman he needed, or was used to having hanging from his arms. She squeezed the tears from the corners of her eyes and they rolled down her cheeks. She attempted and smiled and nodded to him, signaling that it was okay. He didn't have to hold on to her, she wasn't going to hold him to a promise. He was released. He bent over again this time tentatively, and he brushed his lips against hers; a tear discreetly left his eyes and landed on her face, blending with her own tears.

He stood, looked around the room and walked out. Alexandra couldn't help herself as tears created tracks on her face, boring through her makeup and running her mascara. Bruce swallowed hard as his comrades stared at him with the obvious question in their eyes. He choked up as he went and sat next to Morgan on the left side of her bed and smiled cheerfully at her.

"You know I am always going to be here for you, right pumkin?" He took her left hand and rested it on his lap. Leaning into her he winked and caused a smile to pull across her face. "Looks like it's just you and me now," he whispered privately. "Let me know what you need and don't hesitate to call me even if it means I have to camp out in front of your hospital room until you feel better." He waited until she acknowledged that she had heard him, and was grateful his precinct coworkers were otherwise engaged in conversation, hitting on Alexandra and having idle chitchat while he tried to schmooze Morgan.

"Thank you, Bruce," Morgan whispered in his ears. He turned and rested his cheek on her forehead and sighed heavily.

"Don't you know how badly I want to love you? I am ready, Morgan, but you haven't been. It's okay, though, I will wait for you," he told her near tears and she shook her head slightly up and down signaling that she heard him with his cheek still gently resting upon her head. He smiled and sat upright looking at her. "You are still the most beautiful woman I have ever laid eyes on." He blew her a kiss and stood to go.

"Okay boys; let's head back to the city. An officer's work is never done," he joked, sending his comrades into a fit of laughter. He decided to walk out ahead of the men to get a fresh breath of air before he had to deal with the onslaught of questions he knew was coming. And as he exited the door he heard them all one by one giving their last good-byes to Morgan and hugging Alexandra.

He walked down the hallway in search of a cup of hospital vending machine coffee when he ran right into Troy.

"What are you still doing here?" Bruce's hand went and rested on his nightstick and the other on his still holstered gun. His heart began racing and all the hatred he felt for this man in the moment that he had pressed his lips to Morgan's came rushing to the very surface of his skin, sending energy like wildfire across his body, making the hairs on his neck and hands stand up.

"Unless yu a one bline man, ar stupid, yu can see I bringing flowars to di pretty lady." Troy stood a foot below Bruce but was wider in the shoulders, and more muscularly built in his chest and arms. He had thick thighs from running and excessive working out. Bruce stood there looking from Troy to the large bouquet of wildflower assortment in his right hand and a huge two-foot white teddy bear with a heart that said *I LOVE YOU* in his left hand. Suddenly not only was he jealous, he felt stupid that he didn't think of it first. How could he visit Morgan in the hospital and not think to bring her flowers.

Bruce turned and looked behind him at the approaching officers engaged in laughter and conversation. They came upon the two men standing off and they knew it wasn't a good sign. They walked up to Bruce and pulled him to the side.

"Com'on man, this is not worth it," Officer Mike told him.

"Yeah, if he wants the chick so badly let him have her," Cabe whispered. "Besides, she ain't such a catch no more, those scars are gonna last for life, man." The guys pulled him away as he made one last posturing to save his pride and then allowed the men to pull him toward the elevator. Alexandra was walking up behind them in that moment and overheard what the men had said. Hurt stung at her heart as she made eye contact with Troy, who shook his head and walked up to her.

"Some tings are betta off keeping to yuself hear?" He looked her in the eyes till he was sure she understood his meaning. He didn't have to tell her. There was no way she would tell Morgan what Bruce's friends had said. And the worse part was not that they had said it, it was that he hadn't responded, defended or said anything back to deflect the statement.

Alexandra turned and followed Troy back to Morgan's room. Morgan, who was fatigued from the visitors and the emotional stress from the confrontation of two men she was choosing between, had begun falling asleep when Troy came back.

"Morgan." He knelt beside her. "I don't want to cause yu no stress, no worries, seen. So I man feel I should jus' step to di side and let di betta man win." Morgan wanted to laugh though she knew what he was saying was sincere. The only thing was that his motives weren't. He just didn't want to worry about taking care of a woman with scars and bruises. A woman who won't be such a looker to show off to his other boys and make bets on whose number-one dime piece looked better. There was a time he would have won that bet hands down. Troy was not the kind of man to take second place even on something so petty. But what else could she have expected from a man who lived every day for the moment and every moment on the line? She sighed heavily as despair took ahold of her. Things couldn't get any worse.

She somberly shook her head that she heard him but didn't bother to open her eyes. He saw that she was tired and stood up. He looked at Alexandra who glared at him with hatred. She couldn't believe that these men who had caused Morgan so much time and energy trying to decide who she should chose to spend her life with, had basically abandoned her in her time of need. Her resentment was insurmountable and she couldn't express in words the disappointment she felt as Troy stood there staring at her, knowing that he had just reached a level below the standards of a human being. But he couldn't help it. His life was about risk and people come and go all the time. Pain was a part of life for him and so was loss. He had become desensitized to the world that people like Morgan lived in. He cared for her but she was now a liability he couldn't afford.

Not having words to soften the blow of the pain in Alexandra's eyes, he stood straight, held his head high, and walked out the door. Morgan kept her eyes closed. She didn't want to face Alexandra, or even herself. She just wanted to sleep and pretend none of it ever happened. Alexandra wished she could kiss all her sadness away.

It had been almost a week since Morgan had her accident and Alexandra never left her side. When Morgan would sleep, Alexandra would caress her gently and kiss her face and fingers, encouraging her to stay strong.

Morgan's parents visited as often as they could from Chicago and brought love from Morgan's sister Sienna, who was now out of the hospital and also resting. They had removed most of her bandages but her legs and arms were still in casts so she couldn't move or feed herself or go to the bathroom by herself. She was completely incapacitated. Alexandra never let on to her friend what she heard and what had happened a week before with the men, but she remained optimistic, filling Morgan in on the happenings and goings-on at *Flowers Bed*. The doctor had told Morgan that she could be released if she was able to hire a home aide nurse to live with her and care for her until she was able to take care of herself. The road to recovery would be a long and difficult one.

Morgan was anxious to leave the sterility of the hospital. Being around all the sick people had her in and out of depression and the fact that she hadn't heard from either Troy or Bruce for a week had her in a deep state of sadness, misery, and anguish. She would brush the thoughts of them from her mind and wondered what Seymen-Cansin would do if he saw her right now. She lectured herself on her lack of good judgment and felt she deserved the punishment that had befallen her.

"I wish there was more I could do for you, Morgan," Alexandra almost whispered as her hands slid up and down the soft contours of Morgan's right arm. "I still think you are the most beautiful woman I have ever seen." She smiled charmingly at her.

"That's what a good friend is supposed to say." Alex blushed at Morgan's words but she knew this was the chance she had been waiting for. Years of watching Morgan strut her stuff around the office, throwing around provocative subliminal messages that would stir Alexandra like no man had. She had never thought of herself as gay, never before thought she could love a woman the way she felt for Morgan, but as their friend-ship grew, so did her love to an excruciating and painful blossom. She had taken little chances to flirt, touch and/or kiss Morgan in playful ways, but her friend had never responded in any way to make her feel that there was a chance.

"Hey Alex, anybody home?" Alexandra smiled and ad-justed Morgan's bedsheets when she interrupted her thought.

"Sorry, daydreaming I guess." She smiled coyly.

"Daydreaming about what?" Morgan prodded. "Com'on, you can tell me. This is the most embarrassing time in my life and there is nothing I can do but lie here. The least you can do is entertain me," Morgan said, her eyes drifting off to a vacant spot on the wall realizing how badly it hurt her to actually admit that.

"Naaw, I don't think this is something you want to hear," Alexandra said, hoping for a way to actually bring the subject up. She was in luck.

"Okay, now you have my attention. It must be juicy and you know being stuck in here, juicy is something I could use," Morgan joked. Alexandra looked at her and felt so magnetically drawn, so emotionally overpowered that she just couldn't help thinking just how wonderful it would be to just kiss Morgan. Kiss her a deep passion-ate longing lingering kiss that she had always dreamt about doing.

"Alex," Morgan said, tensing her neck by pressing her head into her pillow on the bed. Alex stopped and looked at her. She was face to face with Morgan, their lips almost touching. She was so close to Morgan's lips she could smell the Dentyne Ice breath mint that Morgan loved to pop into her mouth on the run, the ones that she had practically been living on since she found herself incapacitated.

"Oh" was all Alex could say as she gradually eased her body back into an upright position and bashfully turned her head away.

"Alex, would you like to tell me what's going on here?" Morgan asked, her fingers barely touching the tip of Alexandra's.

"I . . . am . . . so . . . sorry, Morgan," Alexandra stuttered. Blistering humiliation plundered her thoughts as her mind sped in various directions wondering what Morgan would do, wondering if she had just jeopardized their friendship.

"What were you doing just now, Alex?" Morgan asked again, confusion riddling her mind on top of everything else that had taken place with the men in her life.

"Morgan, I think I am in love with you," she slowly confessed. She turned away her face and placed her hands in her lap, twiddling her thumbs as a distraction to the obvious rejection she was about to be admonished with. The silence between them created a ten-inch concrete wall as Alexandra waited for Morgan to say something. Her heart felt like a thousand wild horses dragged it from Tibet to Egypt and then placed it in her body with the expectation that it would still function. Her mouth felt dry as her breathing became labored. "I have been in love with you for as long as I have known you. You are the light of my days." She spoke again, hoping to ward off some of the thickness in the room, hoping to get it all out before Morgan realized what she was saying and shunned her from her life for good. "I thought maybe you might feel the same way I did and—" She stopped when Morgan gasped.

"Feel the same, are you crazy?" Morgan looked at her, flabbergasted at what Alexandra had just said. "You see me running around here trying to figure out who my baby's daddy is going to be and failing miserably at it I might add," she chuckled, "and you think that I might decide to just throw it all away and be with a woman?" Morgan asked, incredulous.

"No, it's nothing like that," Alexandra started.

"Then what is it, Alexandra? Why would you wait until now of all times when my life is falling apart to pull some manipulating thing like this? Now, when I am vulnerable, helpless, and need your friendship more than ever?" Morgan looked at her as sternly as she could with her scarred features distorting the true intention of her expressions.

"That's not the way I was thinking about it," Alexandra whispered, her pride pierced and her dignity slowly slipping away from her.

"Morgan, I would never do anything to hurt you and I will always be your friend, please just don't be mad," Alexandra begged. "If you could just forgive me, just pretend this never happened I promise you I would never violate the boundaries of our friendship again."

Morgan looked away somberly. She couldn't believe what was happening to her. A bunch of catastrophes one after the other after the other, everyone she trusted and thought would be with her, people she thought she loved. What was going on here was the only question mark swimming around unanswered in her mind.

They stood there silently for what felt like hours before Morgan began to laugh. She laughed so hard she thought the stitches in her face would split open. She laughed until she began to cough.

"Water!" she gagged. Alexandra curiously looked at her and thought she was the final straw to push her friend's sanity to the brink.

"What is so funny, Morgan?" Alexandra asked, not amused as she poured some water in the disposable cup and helped raise Morgan's head to sip from it.

"Gay, Alex, are you telling me that you are gay?" Relieved that the mood had lifted the glum from the room, Alexandra began to smile.

"No," Alexandra playfully slapped her, "I am not gaaaaaay." She emphasized. "I love my husband," she admitted quietly, "I just happen to love you too." She looked at her from the corner of her eyes to see her reaction. Morgan raised her eyebrow and looked at Alexandra suspiciously.

"You're serious?" Morgan slumped into the bed; everything seemed so surreal, like an out-of-body experience.

"Morgan, I think you are amazing. I don't want to mess things up between us. I just love you." Alexandra poured her heart out, softening her voice and face in a silent request for understanding. "I don't know what to say, I don't know how this happened, I never would think that I could feel this way about a woman."

"Do you think you are bisexual?" Curiosity edged its way from Morgan's lips.

"I don't think so, it's not like I feel this way about other women. I think it could just be just you." Alexandra smiled sheepishly.

"Alex, I love you and you are my best friend. Nothing will ever change that. I understand how you feel but I cannot get involved with you that way." Morgan told her as tenderly as she could. "I hope you understand." Morgan smiled at her gently, hoping to soften the blow of her earlier reaction.

"Morgan, I am just so happy to finally get this off my chest. I have been walking around on pins and needles afraid of doing something stupid to destroy the trust between us. It won't happen again, I promise." Alexandra was so happy she turned to throw her arms around Morgan but hesitated, afraid of the connotation.

"Oh please, don't tell me we are going to be all

subconscious about every time we hug now?" Morgan teased. Hearing that threw Alexandra into her arms and squeezed her tight even though Morgan could not move her heavily casted hands; she knew she was hugging her in return. Then just as quickly she stood up and walked outside the door, excusing herself.

"Where you going?" Morgan asked, confused.

"Just for a quick breath of air that's all. I will be right back." Alexandra walked outside the hospital room and stood in the hallway until she could catch her breath. As she stood there she saw a delivery man looking as though he was lost. When he walked up to her she pointed out Morgan's room and then told him to bring what he had there. Walking back inside she grinned widely at Morgan.

"Morgan," Alexandra called her name, pulling her from her thoughts about what her friend had just disclosed to her.

"Please Alex," Morgan stated halfheartedly, dismissing whatever it was that her friend was trying to say. One more confession and she would ask the doctors to just pull the plug.

"Morgan, you have a delivery." She jumped up and down excitedly. This time Morgan decided to take a second look at her friend and try to decipher what the excitement was about. She didn't want to admit it, but the look of joy on Alexandra's face brought about the first stirrings of mirth in her since she returned from Germany. At least she wasn't trying to tell her another secret.

"Okay I will bite. What is it?" Morgan asked, struggling to adjust herself in her bed to get a better view, frustration tugging at her knowing that the little shuffling movements she made didn't bring her much leeway but she sucked it up and waited as Alex ran to her hospital bedroom door and swung it open wide so that the delivery man could walk in with twelve bouquets of three dozen roses of assorted colors. The nurses and hospital administrators all giggled as they followed the delivery men to Morgan's room, curious to find out who had sent all the flowers. One of the delivery men walked up to Morgan with a card the size of a greeting card and handed it to her. Realizing she couldn't take it he became flushed with embarrassment.

"No it's okay, don't be embarrassed; Alex, could you please open it for me?" Morgan asked, excitement now building in her. She felt vindicated after feeling abandoned by the men who swore to love her and chased her when she was whole. Now she was in need of true love and care they left her to face only herself and no longer hold the burden of a decision in her heart. It was a painful lesson to learn.

"It reads, *as beautiful as you are, as rare as precious diamonds, you deserve nothing less than to rest on flower's bed.*" Morgan smiled at the echo of oohs and aaaaahs that came from the awestruck women who now surrounded her speculating on who had sent the flowers.

"So who are these from?" asked one attendant as she moved from bouquet to bouquet smelling the roses.

"These are so beautiful," another exclaimed. "You are a very lucky woman, Ms. Quixotic."

"Well?" Morgan turned to Alexandra, her enthusiasm building with the anticipation of the women who now waited anxiously for the answer. Alexandra just stood there with a blank stare as she shrugged her shoulders to their urgent request. "What do you mean you don't know?" Flabbergasted, Morgan looked at the blank faces of the women waiting for her to offer some clue as to her secret admirer, but she too drew a blank. "Let me see that card, Alex." Looking over the card that was delicately embossed with typewritten words and no signer, she dejectedly sank deeply into her bed.

"But it's so romantic, Morgan," Alexandra chirped, trying to keep her on the brighter side of things.

"Ladies, please help yourselves to a vase and enjoy," she offered. "I really don't need so many flowers dying on me all at the same time in a place that is so reminiscent of death." Excitedly the women took a vase and proudly walked out of her hospital room until only she and Alexandra were left to speculate over the mysterious card.

"Well, I will go back to the city now and check on things. Are you okay?" Alexandra sat next to her and hugged her tightly. "Your color is coming back. I love you girlfriend." She giggled.

"You're just trying to make me feel better, but the fact is I am far from okay and far from looking the way I did before all this happened." Morgan brooded, trying to shake off the upbeat mood that Alexandra bore. She didn't feel like feeling better, being happy or cheered up. She wanted to just sit there alone by herself being miserable. Whoever sent the flowers obviously didn't want to see her ugly face, her now horrific scars, so instead they sent flowers to remind her of how she was once beautiful. Depression threatened to take hold of her once again.

"Now you know that's not true, Morgan. I will always be your biggest fan, and think you are the most beautiful woman in the world," Alexandra said, resting her head on Morgan's bosom. "I just don't like to see you like this." Changing the subject Alexandra sat up and smiled. "I am going now and I will be back to see you tomorrow, okay?" she told her, trying not to allow Morgan's somber mood to pull her down from the elation she felt about bringing all her thoughts to the forefront and dealing with her inner demon. Morgan had forgiven and accepted her, she couldn't be happier. Besides she had to stay positive in order to help Morgan through this time.

"I understand." Morgan looked away to the side not wanting to face Alexandra.

"Hey what's all this about now?" Alexandra quizzed. "You have so much to be happy for. You have your life, friends who love you. Your family who worries for you, and you are one of the most astute, accomplished, and successful people I know." She sighed, waiting for her friend to respond.

"Thanks for saying those things, Alex, but the fact is that no amount of money can buy love, and now for the first time, I understand that. I haven't heard from either Bruce or Troy, and what's going on with Isaiah? He's just totally just dropped me. I cannot imagine that he doesn't know that I am ill or even tried to contact me. Someone would have told him, don't you think so?" Shame burned in her words as she sought Alexandra's eyes for answers.

"I don't know what to tell you, hun." She lied, refusing to divulge what she knew about Bruce and Troy, but she honestly hadn't heard from Isaiah. "Maybe something's happened to them. Maybe they are busy." Her words sent Morgan into a fit of sarcastic laughter.

"Now that's the funniest thing I have ever heard," she said between giggles, then getting a bit more serious she looked at her friend. "In all the time I have known these men, neither of them has *ever* been so busy that they couldn't pick up the phone and call. They certainly knew how to harass me when I had something they wanted. It's amazing how easy it is to change people's minds."

"Normally that would be true, sweetie, but I have never stopped loving you then and definitely not now." Both women were totally taken by surprise by the man's voice that had completely snuck up on them and turned to look in the direction of where the voice had come from.

"Isaiah?" Morgan gasped. Alexandra looked from one to the other as the statuesque man sauntered toward Morgan's bed.

"*That's* Isaiah?" Alexandra's shocked expression tickled Morgan pink and all she could do was shake her head to answer as words evaded her at the moment. She looked at the man who had just walked in and brought with him joy beyond compare.

"I guess you are Alexandra," Isaiah said, stretching out his arms to greet her. His smile was soft and warm, his eyes twinkled brightly.

"Yes, how did you know?" She knew she sounded really stupid, and she admonished herself for her awkwardness.

"I will take that as a rhetorical question." He chuckled deep down from his abdomen, sending a wave of sensuality across the room. Morgan couldn't remember him looking that great. He had lost weight, must have been working out because he looked like a Greek muscular Adonis. His black skin glowed healthily and the casual linen outfit he wore clung to all the right parts of his body.

As he approached Morgan's side, Alexandra excused herself and a twinge of jealousy stabbed at her.

"So I guess I will see you tomorrow, Morgan." When Morgan didn't respond she let herself out and was gone, leaving the two to talk privately.

"Hun, you look scrumptious," he joked, "especially lying there looking so vulnerable." His smile was genuine and sincerely ebbed his words.

"Liar."

"Now you know I would never lie to you." Breathy words escaped his lips as they pressed against her mouth.

"I don't feel that great right now." Morgan shied away and tried to hide her scars from him.

"Morgan, it's not the end of the world. With a little love and care you will be back on your feet in no time, and if it really bothers you, there are great cosmetic surgeons who are available just for circumstances like this." His words were tender and careful. He didn't want to offend her but he wanted her to know that she was every bit the woman he loved and if she so chose, could be every bit the woman she needed to feel she was.

"I just don't know how I got into this mess." She choked on her words, stifling her tears.

"Mistakes happen, that's just like honey." He smiled, resting his right arm across her while sitting in the spot on the left side of the bed that Alexandra abandoned. He took his left hand and lifted her chin to him, forcing her to look him in the eyes.

"Now, if you would let me, I would love to show you how beautiful I think you are, how rare as precious diamonds, and I want to take care of you allowing you to rest on a bed of flowers that I will prepare for you." His eyes glistened with moisture as he brushed his lips lightly against hers.

"It was you? How could I have not figured that out?" She tried to speak but he cut off her words with a deep kiss, sending shudders down her body that had been numb since she returned from her short one-week vacation in Europe. For the first time in what felt like forever, Morgan felt happy, hopeful, at peace. She was ready to begin her healing with Isaiah by her side.

Healing

Morgan was happy to be back in her home. It seemed like so much time had passed, but the home she returned to was definitely not the home that she left almost two month before. She returned to her bedroom scattered with flowers, and so many petals on her bed that she wasn't sure if it was a bed or a flowers bed. Isaiah had kept his promise. He stopped work and completely dedicated his time to her. He was there with her every waking moment and kissed her passionately each time she closed her eyes at night. He served her hand and foot, washing her in her most embarrassing and private of places. He never made her feel helpless or vulnerable and they grew together laughing, talking, sharing, and getting to know each other in ways that only love grows and through the day-to-day grind of a tragedy.

Morgan felt loved like she never had; in his eyes her scars disappeared, under his loving touch she healed; in his arms she found safety and security. She was never more sure that this was the man for her. This is what she had always wanted, and needed. A man who would give to her selflessly, love her no matter what, guide her without condescension, seduce her without her feeling used. She felt like screaming his name from the top of a mountain.

Only two weeks of him taking care of her and she felt like love had grown a garden in her heart.

"Could you get the phone, honey?" Morgan yelled from her wheelchair as she ate the egg-and-grits breakfast Isaiah had made her. She could feel her face glow with joy as she watched Isaiah strut from the kitchen in his boxers and a cotton shirt to grab the cordless telephone. When he came back looking somewhat puzzled she placed her fork on the table and swallowed. "What's wrong? Who was on the phone?"

"I don't know," he told her, heading back to the kitchen but she could see he was bothered.

"You look a little disturbed Isaiah, what is it?" She wheeled her chair over to the kitchen and stared at his broad shoulders. His back was turned to her and she could feel the energy of his pain radiating from him.

"It's just that since I have been here, I have been receiving the same call from the same international number. At first the gentleman asked for you and I told him you weren't here, now the same number just calls with a string of hang ups." He turned around to face her as the last words left his lips. He braced his hands against the kitchen counter and looked softly at her. "Is there something going on here that I should know, sweetie?" His words of anguish pierced her heart. She had completely forgotten about Seymen-Cansin and the last thing she wanted to do was to hurt Isaiah, but telling him the truth was the only thing she could do. She also knew that telling him the truth could cause him to walk away from her. What she did was reckless and irresponsible. She went to a different country to choose between three men and added another to the mix. Not only did she add another man to the equation, she had slept with him and now she had regrets though her time with him was wonderful, he took her breath away and had the circumstances been different, he might have been her choice. But it was a slap in the face to know that Isaiah had been right under her nose and she didn't see it. Shame riddled her in the light of her clarity; hindsight is 20/20 and she could not take it back, nor could she take away the pain she now saw in the eyes of the man she loved.

She raised her chin so her eyes could look upon him, but she couldn't get the words out to answer right away. Isaiah turned his back to face her for a few moments, then took the dishcloth to wipe his hands; he replaced it on the counter and walked away.

Morgan followed him, rolling her wheelchair.

"Isaiah, please stop." But he kept moving. He walked away from her to the bathroom and closed the door. "Isaiah, please come out so I can talk to you."

"I just need a few minutes. I will be out in a second." She knew he was only saying that so as not to face her. She felt stupid . . . why couldn't she just tell him what the situation was? Why was she stalling? She knew why, she was afraid to loose Isaiah. She sat outside the commode for what seemed like forever until Isaiah felt like coming out.

"Are you okay?" she asked, trying to find a way to break the ice.

"I am fine; you wanted to talk to me?" He closed the door and sat on the marble-tiled floor in front of her waiting for her to speak. Her eyes became watery as she tried to hold back tears of confusion and regret knowing she better say something very fast before she lost his attention.

"Isaiah, Seymen is someone I met recently. Remember a few months back when you couldn't reach me, I had taken some time and took a trip to Europe to clear my head. I met Seymen-Cansin there. It was nothing." She hoped that Isaiah's laid-back personality would let this one slide, but the fact that he wasn't saying anything bothered her. "He was just someone I met that helped me around the city, that's all." Her voice became shrill and urgent, but Isaiah only looked at her.

"Okay," he said, standing. He reached over and brushed his lips against her forehead.

"Okay?" Morgan rolled behind him once more as he

stalked back to the kitchen. "Isaiah, what do you mean okay?" she asked, guilt biting at her soul.

"You said it was nothing and I say it's fine, darling." He turned to her and offered her a tight smile, then placed his now cold breakfast in the microwave to reheat it and place it on the table, then following suit with hers.

"You don't have to do that. I am no longer hungry," she told him, wheeling herself to the living room to look outside of the large bay windows of her penthouse suite. Isaiah decided to leave her to mull over whatever was on her mind and finish eating his breakfast before it was cold again. If and when she was ready to talk to him he knew she would, so he let it go.

When the phone rang again Morgan made it her business to answer; she was very relieved that it was Alexandra.

"Hey Morgan, are you excited? Today is the big day." Her friend's jovial disposition irked her in the moment but it triggered her attention as she was completely at a loss as to what her friend was talking about.

"Alex, could you please just cut it out and tell me what you are referring to." When Alexandra got really quiet on the phone she knew she sounded a bit bitchy. "I'm sorry, I am just in a foul mood."

"What? Trouble in paradise after only two weeks?" she teased but realized it was in bad taste and bad time, though she had discussed her feelings with Morgan, she couldn't help feeling resentful that she now had to share what little attention she got from Morgan with a man. She shook it off and went back to the matter at hand.

"Morgan, today is your surgery to remove the scars from the accident, remember? I thought you were anxious about this day to take the first step towards getting your drop-dead gorgeous good looks back without blemishes." Alexandra remained upbeat. She knew Morgan had looked forward to this day since she first awoke in the hospital more than two months ago now.

"Oh my goodness, thanks for calling, Alex, it had completely slipped my mind."

"Do you want me and David to come over and accompany you to the hospital? We don't mind and I have been on pins and needles waiting for this day myself. I really would like to be there, Morgan." Morgan thought about it. Yes, her arms were out of the cast but her legs were still healing. She could roll around but she really needed help. She felt bad about asking Isaiah to help her knowing he was mad but she needed to get dressed.

"How soon can you be here?" Morgan asked quietly into the phone not wanting to disturb Isaiah.

"We were already on the way. David will drop me off and I will drive with you and Isaiah if you don't mind the company," she chirped.

"That sounds good. Hurry, I am still not dressed. I don't know what to wear and I could use a woman's perspective." Morgan lied; Isaiah was as good at dressing her as he was at dressing himself. He had a refined taste and had been able to coordinate her essentials as though he had been doing it for years.

"Who was that on the phone, hun?" Morgan turned to find Isaiah sitting on the floor not far from her, pain in his eyes as if she had literally slapped him.

"Alex, I had forgotten that I had my first cosmetic appointment today to remove the glass scars from my face." She looked down at her socked toes and tried to look anywhere but at Isaiah.

"I didn't forget sweetheart, your appointment is not for another couple hours. That's why I had this great breakfast, your attire is already prepared and waiting for you to slip into them and the house is clean just the way you like it." He shrugged bashfully as he realized how he sounded. He hoped she realized how much she meant to him even though he knew he hadn't been as forthcoming with telling her he loved her. He had bought her a white four-karat solitaire engagement ring that he had kept for almost six months now hoping he would be her choice. He knew it was probably a foolish move, but he had to have faith that she would see the treasure in him that he had found in her.

"Oh thanks darling. You are always anticipating my needs. How can I thank you for being here?" She rolled the chair closer to where he sat so his head could rest on her inner thigh. "I am sorry to have hurt you Isaiah; I never want to hurt you. That was a different time for me, and now it seems like a lifetime ago." She smiled down at him and hoped he heard what she was trying to say with mere words that didn't do it justice. He didn't say anything for a few minutes, but then he slowly raised his head from her lap and looked up at her.

"Let's get you dressed, lady. You have an appointment with destiny." He winked lovingly at her causing butterflies to form in her stomach. She really wished at that moment she could make love to him, but she knew that she would make it up to him once she was fully healed. Only another month and she could remove the leg casts and begin rehabilitation for walking. By then she should have finished the three stages of cosmetic face surgery that it would require to bring her facial looks back to almost normal. Her doctors were optimistic, which filled her with excitement of what the end results would look like.

"I think that's Alexandra at the door," Morgan yelled from the bathroom as she finished applying a little foundation to somewhat camouflage the scars that caused her self-esteem to plunge below confidence.

"Is everyone ready?" Alexandra asked as she rushed into the bedroom to see if Morgan needed any assistance. Isaiah just smiled having now become accustomed to her friend's outgoing personality. "Okay children, let's go!" she commanded as they left the suite.

Confronting the Past

It had only been three days since her facial cosmetic surgery attempt and it was very successful, though depending on the healing she would have to do at least two more. Alexandra stayed with Morgan despite the complaints of her husband David while Isaiah went on an important business trip and was not expected back for a few hours. Morgan was excited about his return because tomorrow she would be able to remove the Band-Aids to see the first healing results. She couldn't wait.

"Morgan, I have to tell you that I really underestimated Isaiah," Alexandra said, putting down the magazine she was reading and looked over to Morgan who was stretched out on the sofa with the Bose speaker headphones on her ears jamming to one of her favorite songs by Daniel Bedingfield. She had always liked the song but loving Isaiah had brought new meaning to it. She never thought she would really say those words and mean it, or have a song like that have personal meaning in her life. She was at peace.

Alexandra looked over and realized that Morgan couldn't hear her. She walked the short distance to where she lay and removed the headphones.

"What did you do that for?" Morgan protested playfully.

"Because I want to talk to you." Alexandra laughed, falling to sit next to her on the floor.

"What's wrong, Alex?" Morgan turned slightly to her side as she was able to maneuver a bit more as she healed, even with the casts still on her legs.

"I was just thinking about Isaiah. I wanted to apologize for the way I talked about him in the beginning." She smiled up at her friend. Morgan just allowed her hands to gently caress the thick Afro puffs of Alexandra's natural do. She loved the ethnicity about her, the way she loved her people and her culture, the way she was knowledgeable about Africa and all the things that they usually don't teach you in history books. Morgan appreciated her friendship with Alexandra and felt so blessed to have her there in her time of need. No amount of money could buy the love she had bestowed upon her in the past three months.

"You don't have to say that Alex, I know he has charmed his way into your heart too." Morgan smiled proudly though it hurt for her to put any kind of excessive expressions on her face. It felt tight, almost numb.

"He is really wonderful, Morgan. I cannot believe all that he's done for you, waited on you hand and foot as though you are the last breath he would ever take." A touch of melancholy hitched her voice. "It's what I have always wanted for you and what I thought I had found in David." She looked at Morgan who now strained to keep focus through the bandages on her face. "You really are a lucky woman, and it was Bruce's and Troy's loss the way they behaved so stupidly at the hospital. Them not wanting you was a blessing in disguise," she finished, allowing her gaze to drop to the marble floors and shuffling to adjust her bum on the large throw pillow on the floor next to the sofa.

"What do you mean their behavior at the hospital? They were surprisingly very civil to each other," Morgan reminisced.

"Yeah, in your presence, but those two are ridiculously childish." She shook her head as she thought back to the conversation she overheard.

"Wait a minute. You mean to tell me that something happened so long ago and you haven't told me?" Morgan turned to her side and looked at her friend.

"It was a very fragile time for you. I didn't want to make it worse," Alexandra reflected. Trying to compose herself, Morgan knew she couldn't be angry at Alexandra. She was doing what she thought was best for her and if she were to be honest with herself she had to accept that.

"Well, are you going to tell me or what?" Morgan asked nicely. Alexandra looked at her, contemplating whether this would be the right time and somewhat kicking herself for saying as much as she did. Looking at Morgan she realized that she was not going to get away with not spilling the beans so she did.

When she was finished, all Morgan could do was lie where she was, numbed by the information. She couldn't believe all that had transpired. She couldn't believe they disrespected her like that in front of her friend, behind her back, after all the aggravation they put her through. But she was a grown woman and she didn't have to allow herself to go through that. She snickered when she thought of Bruce's proposal.

"Good thing I didn't marry him," she uttered.

"What?"

"Nothing, I just cannot believe them. I knew that my spirit was in a strange place and I couldn't understand why it was so hard for me to make up my mind."

"Well, that's all in the past now. Look at your consolation

prize. He turned out to be better than the prize and the surprises." Alexandra smiled broadly at her. "I totally approve of this choice though it was by default," Alexandra taunted her.

"Yes, Isaiah is a special man. Sometimes I wonder how he truly feels, though."

"What do you mean?" Alexandra turned almost 180 degrees to face Morgan. "Well, I know he cares for me a great deal, but I don't know if he loves me. What if he is just feeling sorry for me and doing all this until I am well and then leaves? What if he feels like Troy and Bruce does, that I am now damaged goods?" She sighed, not wanting to get too emotional about it. She had thought about it quite often but she didn't expect to be baring her soul about the situation in that moment.

"I see what you are saying, Morgan, but it's obvious that man loves you deep down to his bones. I cannot imagine anybody doing this just to do it, and there is no way you will get that man to walk away from you unless you do something really dishonorable to him," Alexandra reassured her, but when tears began running down Morgan's face, she stopped.

"I guess you are right. I am just so happy. I hope he wants me, Alex. I hope he still finds me beautiful. Here I was worried that he would be too old to have children with, worried that he couldn't give what I needed when he was *all* I needed all along." She smiled. Alexandra looked up when she heard the doorbell.

"Isaiah is back already?" Alexandra smiled as she braced herself and prepared to stand.

"Why would Isaiah ring the bell, silly? He's got a key. Let's see who it is," Morgan told her, reaching for some pillows to put behind her so she could sit up.

"Okay," Alexandra chirped as she walked to the intercom phone and picked it up.

"Hello, Ms. Q. There is a visitor here for you," the doorman exclaimed. "Should I send him up?" Alexandra turned to Morgan quizzically and then returned her attention to the doorman on the other end of the line.

"Well, we weren't expecting anyone. Who is it?" Alexandra asked as Morgan sat up in an alert state completely at a loss as to who it might be. Alexandra heard the doorman ask the stranger in the background a question and then returned to her.

"He said his name is Semen," the doorman quipped, trying to hide his mirth.

"Semen, are you sure?" Alexandra asked amused.

"That's what the gentleman said," the doorman insisted.

"One moment please." Alexandra muted the phone and turned toward Morgan. "The doorman said the visitor's name is Semen." She looked at Morgan for any kind of recognition. "He sounds like he had an accent."

"Oh wait, Seymen-Cansin? But that's not possible; he is thousands of miles away from here." Morgan's heart began to race and she felt frightened as her heart began palpitating. It couldn't be, not now when she was all broken up and bandaged up. Not now when she had decided; what would she do?

"Whoa, hold up. You mean to tell me that you think that's that Semen German guy you met on your trip?" Alexandra was flabbergasted and her hand went to cover her mouth that flew open. "Say it ain't so?" she hoped, genuinely concerned seeing the horror on Morgan's face.

"Well, that's the only Seymen I know," Morgan barked, not finding the situation in the least bit amusing.

"What should I do?" Alexandra asked, wondering how to handle the situation. "You can't exactly not see him; he flew all the way here to see you. But why didn't he just call?" Alexandra asked.

"Actually, I think he has been trying to call. Isaiah got really upset a couple days back because he kept getting hang up calls from an out-of-the-country number. I mentioned Seymen to him but not in detail. Oh my gosh!" The full spectrum of the situation dawned on her.

"What?" Alexandra mouthed.

"I don't have time to explain now. Invite him up," she ordered.

"With you looking like that?" Alexandra surveyed Morgan's haphazard attire and sickly appearance.

"All the better, Bruce and Troy ditched me so he would too, since he is much younger and I am sure twice as vain as Bruce."

"Send him up please," Alexandra told the doorman in her most polite voice knowing that she had kept him waiting a while. She knew they would have to slip him something extra on the way out next time. Money always made people feel better. When Alexandra hung up the phone she turned to Morgan for more information, but before the first words were to leave her mouth, the doorbell chimed.

"Well, at least I get to see this fine specimen of a creature that rocked your word for a few days while you were incognito." She winked as she went to the door. Opening it left her in awe. He was majestically tall, at least six foot six inches from the ground, and though he looked a little rugged as though he had a long flight and a really hard time, he was beautiful. Gorgeous big blue eyes, curly blond hair, pink rosy cheeks and lips and very muscular and hard-bodied. She looked like he spent time in the gym, and though he had on a loose T-shirt his pectorals and six pack begged to be noticed. She almost drooled as she must have stood at the door for at least a minute without greeting him.

"Hello Seymen-Cansin," Morgan said, helping out her

awestruck friend who just simply stepped aside so that he could enter.

"Morgan, oh baby, what's wrong? What has happened with you?" Alexandra listened to the way he rearranged his words and sighed, while behind him she looked at Morgan wide-eyed with admiration.

"Oh I had an accident," she told him casually, "the day I returned I was driving and ran head-on into oncoming traffic. That's why I look like this." She tried to explain, embarrassment pierced her but something familiar stirred in her loins as she looked at him.

"Oh baby, *ich vermisse dich mein schatz.* I missed you so much darling." He told her in German and then translating it to English as he reached over to embrace her. Morgan put her hands against his chest to stop his progression but he gently pushed his body against her futile resistance and allowed his lips to rest passionately upon hers. Alexandra was stupefied. She didn't know what to do so she just stood there watching.

"Seymen-Cansin, we cannot do this," she told him, forcing him to pull his face away from her. "Please stop."

"Baby, so many bad things happen now to me. I fly here with a special surprise for you. When I don't hear from you so long, I was afraid you forget me." He searched her eyes for a response and tears turned his eyes red as he looked at her bandaged face and her bruised skin.

"What are you saying?" Concern laced her voice and finally brought Alexandra back to earth propelling her feet to sit next to him by Morgan's side.

"Oh, I am here in Amerika now at two o'clock maybe last day in the evening maybe." He began his story struggling for the words to explain how he felt. "I think someone might see that I am not from Amerika . . . oh *schatzy* you were right. It's not safe to be here alone in this

county." He looked at her with huge blue puppy-dog
eyes. Alexandra was so drawn into his accent she was
almost right upon him. The sincerity in his voice and the
tears in his eyes brought forth empathy as he swallowed
hard and continued. "Someone I think was following me
from the Manhattan island. Oh darling I changed three
trains and I looked the large plans in the subway to find
where you told me you were living."

"You mean the subway maps?" Alexandra asked, wondering what plans he referred to.

"*Ja ja* . . . maps. Then I was to get off the train in Manhattan and it starts to get dark when I am out because I
go always wrong." Frustration strained his words. "And
this man was also with me when I am off the train."
Drawn into his words both Morgan and Alexandra
waited for what he would say next.

"Oh I am so sorry your first experience in America is
this way, but it's not safe to travel alone when you don't
know where you are going." Alexandra tried to soothe
his pain. Morgan felt numb and she still didn't know
what to say, how to feel or react. She knew Seymen-
Cansin was charming and wasn't surprised that not one
logical thought went through Alexandra's usually analyt-
ical head.

"I was beat up pretty bad, *mein frau.* He knocked me over
the head with a large piece of wood and I was feeling me
falling to the floor. They stole all my money, video camera,
digital camera, and baby; I was having for you an engagement ring. I wanted to make a nice *vorschlag* for *meine
madchen* . . . ah what is it you say in English." He held his
head as he tried to make the translation. "Propose! I want
to make nice propose to my girl." He stopped and gazed
up sadly at Morgan trying to gauge if his words had im-
pacted her, but she didn't understand.

"I don't understand why you would come here like

this Seymen-Cansin. It was dangerous and reckless and irresponsible." She admonished him trying to stand her ground. What was she going to do?

"*Ich liebe dich schatzy.* I love you. I must come," he maintained. "You don't want me?"

"We spent a few days together. We are strangers. It's not right to just show up at my door by flying halfway around the country. How can you love me?" She told him, hurt that she had to say those words. Isaiah! What was she going to do?

"You don't care that I was attacked?" Incredulously he stared at her. "That the man he steal now from me everything? I have it no money. He tried to take my backpack but I punched him with my fists. Look!" he showed her his scarred and injured knuckles. "Here, feel my head." He took Morgan's hand and began probing around for where he was hit with what he believed to be a stick.

"Wow, all of that really happened? I never would think that people are knocking people over the head with sticks these days, more like guns and gangs." Alexandra tried to see Morgan's line of reasoning, but the tears just came when Seymen-Cansin looked into their eyes and saw disbelief.

"The police came, the ambulance came. It was so funny; they turn the lights on that makes the noise. I only see that on television." He smiled behind his pain. Morgan and Alexandra couldn't help smiling at his childlike glee experiencing what is an everyday annoyance in New York like a new toy. "They take me to the emergency room where I was in the night with a doctor and a police officer. Then in the morning they were with me at the German embassy in Manhattan and they take me to a hostel. I told them I know I don't have to stay long when I again with my beautiful woman." He smiled sexily, flashing his even white teeth.

"Oh Seymen, you cannot stay with me." Her words timidly left her mouth as she tried to make it not sound as bad as it did. "I had an accident; I have to have multiple surgeries on my face before I will be anywhere near normal. I cannot be a host to you. This is just a very bad time," she reasoned, but it didn't take the shock away from his face.

"I don't care. I can take care of you. *Ich leibe dich* . . . I mean it that I love you. I think you are beautiful. I will never leave you," he told her, wrapping his arms around her thigh as she lay across the sofa helpless to resist him.

"You don't know me well enough and I don't know you well enough to allow you to stay here in my home," Morgan told him almost inaudibly.

"What is it you mean to say to me?"

"Morgan, why don't you just tell him?" Alexandra interrupted, startling the two. They had almost forgotten that she was there. Morgan couldn't help feeling horrible. She really liked Seymen and he was so good to her, he made her feel welcome in his country and showed her a nice time; she felt like an ungrateful American, after all, that's how the Europeans refer to us. Her thoughts crumbled in her mind as she fought to find the words to express how she felt.

"Tell it what to me?" Seymen asked incredulous, wondering what was going on, anxiety building in his chest and restricting his breathing. Alexandra took Morgan's hands as she stood there stone face, shame, embarrassment, shock, and anger; emotion piled on top of emotion fighting for dominance.

"Morgan, he came all this way, he has to leave, tell him about Isaiah." Seymen-Cansin became frozen; words failed him as his mind swam with question after question.

"Isaiah? Who is it this Isaiah?" Seymen asked, now standing upright, his statuesque frame towering over her as she sat vulnerable to her indiscretions, face to face with her past.

"Yes, Morgan, tell him who is this Isaiah." All eyes shot towards the door. No one had heard it open, no one had heard his heavy footfalls, no one had witnessed the crowd that Isaiah had brought with him, coworkers, his son, and his parents who he had decided he would use as leverage to show Morgan his true intention. To show her his love. He held his face hard, his jaw set firm against his usually soft gentle features.

"Isaiah," Morgan exclaimed, not able to say anything to ward off the disgrace and humiliation that glowed in his eyes.

"So this was the big secret Morgan? This is what you couldn't tell me? That you had someone else, while I toiled and cared for you, all along I was a joke."

"It was nothing like that, darling."

"Isaiah, calm down, this was all unexpected and . . ." Alexandra was not able to finish her thought.

"And you knew, didn't you Alex, you knew all along and I was the laughing stock of your jokes." He hadn't moved from the spot where he stood when they first looked up and saw him.

"She is *meine schatz, ich immerr noch hier*, it is to say I am here now." Seymen-Cansin stood towering about Isaiah and looking down at him. Though he was well built, Isaiah outweighed him pound for pound, but his gracious matured demeanor exuded strength, calm, and wisdom. Morgan heard Isaiah laugh like she had never heard him laugh. The laugh was condescending, cynical, sarcastic, and downright rude, she didn't know he had it in him, another underestimation of the man she had truly grown to love. She was impressed by the deep baritone timbre that reverberated across the room and down her skin causing the hair on her body to prickle.

"What you laugh at me? I am now here in Amerika one day and now I get to be a joke." Seymen-Cansin was obviously intimidated and Isaiah's body hadn't budged, but his chest heaved beneath his shirt. Overwhelmed by the sight before him he was terrified of what this day would cost him but he was cool under his dress slacks and tailored blazer.

"Seymen-Cansin, sit please. You don't understand." Morgan looked up at them both, her face half covered by the healing scars that strained to come undone under the pressure of the fear that spoke volumes on her face.

"It's not what you think, Isaiah." Alexandra tried to calm the situation.

"For once Alex, let the woman speak. It is time I hear her. Hear her heart." He set his face hard and refused to shed a tear. Not now. Not in front of these people whom he had never taken to introduce to a woman; not in front of a white man who had shown superiority and for centuries whose kind have had the best and prime pick of black women; not while his entire existence and his life was on the line; not while he was praying to God that right now in this moment of truth all that he had gambled on wouldn't fall around him. Not now while he waited for her to finally love him. He searched her eyes for clarity, some way to hold on to the hope that her apprehensiveness was not because all along he just wasn't young enough or white enough for her.

Alexandra drew close to Morgan and sat next to her on the sofa where she had not moved for hours as Seymen told his story, she felt the tremor in Morgan's touch and knew she feared losing Isaiah more than she feared having to take her last breath.

"I love you," Morgan uttered so quietly everyone was jerked at attention and almost missed it. She ached to go to him and touch him but her legs were cast and she could not walk. Isaiah's heart was about to jump out of his chest as he tried to figure out if she had just told the man she had a tryst with that she loved him. He did not hear her correct. Didn't she realize that he understood confusion, that he too had made mistakes, that a roll in the hay while uncommitted was no crime as long as there is no heavy consequence to bring a lifetime of burden? Didn't this woman know he would do *anything for her*?

He tried not to allow his legs to fall from under him as he looked at her tortured with the agony of defeat, trying to tell her with his very existence that he loved her.

"I love you, Isaiah," Morgan said as she slowly raised her frightful eyes to look at him. "I am sorry. I made a mistake and I almost didn't see the treasure you were until I almost lost me. I found my life again in your love, purpose in a way I never dared to dream." Tears found her cheeks as they poured freely from her river of grief. Hurt stung at her as she watched the weight of this grown man overpower him as he could no longer stand and he finally fell to his knees.

"I don't want to live without you, don't want to wonder again if I am loved, don't want to search in the arms of frogs if I have yet to kiss my prince, I only want you." Isaiah's relief brought on the tears that his ego wouldn't allow before and he strained against the gravity of sorrow that was now being ebbed away by his overwhelming joy to reach her. He went to his pocket and pulled the small velvety box from it.

"Morgan, honey. I have been waiting for so long to hear you say you want me. I had almost given up on whether you might finally remove that naive veil of life from your eyes." He smiled as he reached her, engulfing her into his massive arms and lifting her from the sofa, bringing her to rest on his legs as he stretched out on the floor. "Marry me, sweetie. Marry me and honor me. Marry me so the rest of my life may finally find purpose in you. Marry me so I can love you in all the ways you want to and ways you never dreamed. Be my wife?" His words came out so hard and fast that he couldn't breathe when he was finished. He only slipped the ring on her outstretched finger and watched as it slid on in a perfect fit.

"Yes," she cooed in his ear and nuzzled her face in his neck. "Yes, I will marry you."

"Aren't you guys supposed to kiss or something?" Isaiah's fourteen-year-old son quipped shyly. On that note, Morgan looked at her man and gently took his face into her hands and purposely tantalized him with the promise of a kiss, slowly wiping away the tears from his eyes, kissing each eyelid, the tip of his nose, the creases of his forehead before raising his lips to meet hers.

Alexandra walked over to Seymen, empathy working her over.

"Are you going to be okay?" She gently rested her hand upon his as a sign of understanding and support. "I know this must be really hard for you."

"Oh yes, it is. I only come here now to see her beautiful face. I have it no money, I wait for the police report and I stay in a hostel in a strange country with nobody." He said the words jerkily but held back his emotions. "I think I go now." He turned to walk away and was almost out the door through the parted gathering of Isaiah's entourage.

"Seymen-Cansin, wait," Morgan said and looked to her fiancé for support. "I am sorry." He looked at her and shook his head, then continued walking away.

"Hey man, one second," Isaiah said as he gently replaced Morgan to the sofa and walked over to Seymen.

"I am not angry. Thank you for being respectful of her wishes." Isaiah removed his hand from his pocket and came back with a few hundred dollars that he discreetly placed in Seymen-Cansin's hands. "My car service is still downstairs, I was supposed to go and take the rest of the surprise out. How about I walk you down and the service can take you back to wherever you need to go," he offered kindly.

"*Danke*," Seymen-Cansin told him sincerely. "Thank you very much for being so kind."

"You are welcome," Isaiah told him and watched him exit the penthouse suite. Turning around he couldn't hold back the joyful exuberance that built in his chest and poured out into a scream of relief. . . .

"Yes, yes, yes . . . she said YES!"

Change of Life

Michelle McGriff

Prologue

The hotel was expensive. But there was no way he was going to take her to a cheaper one. Besides, he would just write it off on his expense account. It wasn't as if he'd ever used his entire stipend. His boss would never question this one time.

They were always telling him to have fun on these conference trips and so, *Dammit, I'm gonna have some fun . . . right now,* he thought, grinning wide and goofy at the young blonde as she looked around the room. It was as if she'd never seen anything like it before. She was impressed, he could tell.

"So you like it?" he asked.

"Sure I do. It's really cool," she answered, tossing her blond mane over her slender shoulder. He couldn't resist. He kissed her. She responded with a fire that shot quickly to his loins.

"I'm glad, baby . . ." he purred, trying to sound hip—youthful. He knew at times his flirtations sounded lecherous—or maybe it was just that he felt that way, being twice this girl's age and all.

Her name was Candy. He wasn't sure if that was her real name but nowadays, kids had funny names like that so maybe it was. He thought about his high school days and how all the hippie white kids were changing their names to things like Summer, Autumn, and Freedom, so *Candy* wasn't so bad. Perhaps she was a product of one of those "types."

They'd been seeing each other for about three months, ever since she was hired on as his assistant. It was an automatic attraction.

She had mistaken him for the vice president of the company. He was pretty close to being that, but, "No, I'm his assistant," he confessed, stretching his actual position as far as he could. Sure, he was indispensable, but not for the reasons he wanted her to believe.

It only took two dates to get her to bed. And funny thing was, he wasn't even trying to get her there. She brought it up.

Even now thinking about the young girl's firm body and loud passion-filled outcries, he weakened, nearly overcome with lust for her.

Running to the bed, she jumped on it, bouncing high and giggling.

"Come on, join me," she invited. "We have two hours before the seminar."

Two hours?

It took longer than that just to get his wife to agree to come to bed. She was a workaholic and now with the department she headed up under review, she was a downright drag. She was always overworked and stressed out and far too serious.

Candy began to strip while standing on the bed. She loved to tease and play.

Naked, she began to bump and grind, moan and

other obscene things that he had only seen done once at a stag party—many, many years ago.

Before he stopped himself he had joined her on the bed, pulling her down to him and covering her body with kisses, closing his full lips around her firm pink nipples, seething with the fever she had caused to come up in him as she quickly reached into his trousers, stroking his manhood.

"Take your suit off so we don't have to get it pressed," she whispered, while working on the buttons of his shirt.

The contrast of her fair skin against his darkness would always make him pause for a second. It was a reality bite that would cause him to think . . . but only for a moment.

Back when he was a young man, a white woman was all but taboo—available to only the most radical black man. Radical was not him. He was shy and reserved, so needless to say Candy was his first.

In the beginning, it bothered him—maybe even scared him a little. But soon, he figured that all he had to do was turn out the light and that would take care of all his fears. Once in the darkness, he could only feel her—tight, taut, and smooth to the touch. She smelled of peaches or some other fruit most of the time. The combination of that scent, his cologne and their love would nearly take him to madness. And the way she would wrap her legs around him, pulling him in all the way . . . well, it wasn't uncommon for him to go on for nearly a half hour. At first, he worried if she was satisfied. She wasn't as easy to please as his wife. He knew his wife was always satisfied with what she got, because, what did she know about anything? She was a virgin when they got married and he hadn't been with many girls prior to that. Together they had managed to fumble their way into a rhythm that, up until now, had worked for them.

Maybe it still worked for them.

He didn't know. Maybe he was just fooling himself with Candy. But as he closed his eyes and took in the sounds of he and Candy, working together, creating a new cadence, all he knew was this was the beat he wanted to drum to from now on.

He entered her forcefully. She liked it like that. He figured it was part of the myth she had envisioned when seducing him to bed. She told him that she had never been with a black man before, so he figured it was what she expected—rough sex. Therefore, he tried to oblige. He had to admit he liked it too—pulling her hair, biting her. Sometimes she would want him to call her dirty names and he liked doing that too.

When he would release into the sheath that she insisted he wear, she groaned as if receiving his seed with pleasure and full acceptance and then would scratch his back like a cat, purring, moaning, and writhing beneath him, sliding her silky long legs up and down his thighs before going into orgasmic jerks, settling finally into a comfort zone. He had never worn a condom with his wife, but Candy insisted upon it, and it was okay. He was getting used to it. As tight as she was, he almost felt the same sensation as the real thing.

Her pushing against his chest would give the sign that he could pull out—which he would then quickly and carefully do. She was so tiny, and he knew his weight was probably more than she was used to. Having been a football jock—a lifetime ago—he still carried a few extra pounds, of course now it wasn't all muscle like it used to be. But he tried to take care of his health. His wife was a fanatic about it, but then she went overboard on stuff like that.

"I love you," he told Candy after wrapping a towel

around his waist and climbing back in the bed on top of her, kissing her excitedly and rubbing up against her.

She grabbed his face, kissing him full on the lips, "And I love you too," she said. "But we better get in the shower and get going."

The shower.

He knew what that meant. It was usually where Candy treated him to oral sex.

Another intimacy no longer performed on him by his wife.

Maybe he would make a move when he got back home. Maybe he would just tell his wife *what was what* and get in with Candy for real, in the open. Yes, he needed to make this thing with Candy permanent before anything happened—before anything changed between them. Before Candy woke up and moved on to someone her own age.

Life had a way of changing that way, just when things got good. And things were sure good with Candy.

At this point in his life he deserved something good.

Chapter 1

Glenda was dragging. Two morning cups of coffee and even an afternoon trip to Starbucks wasn't helping put the spring back in her step.

She read the same sentence three times before finally giving up and closing the file.

Corporate work wasn't always the most exciting occupation in the world, at least not at her age. At forty-five, staring at the picture pinned to her corkboard, the one of that house nestled in the plush greenery on that hillside, the house with the white picket fence with the colorful pansies creeping along it. . . . "Now that was exciting," she said aloud, taking the picture from the stickpin and getting a closer look at it. She sighed heavily and put it back on her corkboard.

"We're going for drinks after work today," Dave said, peeking into her office, smoothing down his combover. Dave was a wannabe overachiever. Glenda felt he was more of a brownnoser than anything, but his department was always winning service awards—thank goodness. Being his boss, she would hate to ever have to fire him for poor performance after all these years. Who knows what he would do. He didn't seem to have much of a life outside of this job.

Dave didn't linger at her door; he had simply announced their plans and then disappeared without waiting for an answer from her. It was as if he knew she would decline. Lately she had been nothing short of a wet blanket—always so tired. But then, how could she expect a man to understand what was happening to her? She was forty-five now and the dreaded change was upon her. Glenda could tell by the signs. She was coming into menopause.

She was willing to accept it. It wasn't as if she hadn't expected it. Actually as soon as she turned forty, she began reading up on the subject.

"I'm an intelligent woman," she reasoned. "Why live in denial over the inevitable? It's a fact of life, can't run from it," she had told herself.

Her husband, Simi, was a handsome man, barely showing gray around the temple. And a good man, although she'd not reminded him of that much lately and she knew Simi loved her, it wasn't as if she had to be told all the time either.

"So are you going for drinks?" Gerri asked, stepping into her office, breaking her reverie. Gerri was her assistant.

"Oh . . . oh no, I'm gonna head on home. Simi is supposed to get in this evening and I want to be there when he gets in," she answered, before realizing she still had the picture in her hand. Gerri looked around nervously and then closed the door behind her.

"Glenda, can I talk to you?" Gerri asked.

Glenda sighed, knowing before she spoke what the young woman wanted to talk about . . . that man.

These young girls these days, Glenda mentally fussed. *They just don't know how to keep their relationships afloat, they are just so fickle;* she went on thinking. She had been married to Simi her whole life. He had been her first and only lover, so she didn't have anything to compare him to, but even with that, she had to figure he was one of the good ones, lord only knew her brothers were no angels. Just remembering them as young bucks sowing their wild oats gave her a chill.

All the girls . . . the babies . . . the babies' mamas' dramas . . .

Despite how much she liked Gerri, Glenda felt she was about the worst—always whining and crying over her relationship. Why Gerri went rounds and rounds with that man was beside her.

"It's about Harold," Gerri began, sitting down quickly.

"I told you, just make up your mind about him—all this back and forth," Glenda fussed after hearing again about the planned breakup. Gerri shook her head, allowing the tears to flow now. "Gerri, either get out or you need to try to work it out, but settle on something, all this bickering is distracting to you and your work."

"But Glenda, you don't understand. How can you. You have a good husband and . . . besides, life isn't all about my job."

"Gerri, please, your job needs to be given a much higher priority, my dear. With your work you measure your worth," Glenda lectured. "You have to think about what's important and fighting with Harold isn't it."

"Glenda, I can't believe you can just say that to me, as if love isn't important," Gerri whined.

"Love? Is that what you call this?" Glenda laughed. "Please, I would never let my personal life get so distracting and convoluted as you have done with yours . . . honey, love just isn't crazy like this. Love doesn't have you acting a fool and—"

"God . . . you are impossible to talk to, Ms. Never Had To Work Out A Thing In My Entire Life Dixon," Gerri growled.

"And what does that mean? You know Gerri; you come in *here* to complain," Glenda fanned her hand. "I don't come to you, but then again, I don't have complaints."

"Ms. Perfection, here we go again with the lecture on how to have the perfect man, the perfect life . . . well, Glenda, life is just not that simple."

"Gerri, it's not about simplicity really. It's about having yourself together and organized, prepared for the unexpected and you don't know about that. You think that each day is supposed to be an adventure but it's not. You are supposed to live by the rules and in doing that life won't rule you."

The conversations with Gerri always led to heated debates between the two of them and Glenda never understood why they even would *go there*. Yet, Gerri would always start it by coming into her office, not the other way around.

"It doesn't matter who he is or where he is," Glenda began, trying to keep the sanctimonious tone out of her voice. "If you have love and trust in your marriage . . . the key word being *trust*, then it's all good, and especially if you have children with him. You need to give your children a balanced home and two parents that love and respect one another. And . . ."

"So you're saying that once we set the rules we just live by them as if nothing is going to ever change between us. People change, though, Glenda, life is full of new things and . . ."

Glenda knew from experience at this point in the conversation that no matter what she said, Gerri was going to try to prove why putting Harold out . . . again, was going to be the wise thing to do.

Young folks, Glenda began to believe they just didn't have a clue what real love meant. It was all a game to them. Thank God she and Simi never had to play this game. Simi would never pull the infidelity card—why would he? She was a good wife. No, she was a perfect wife.

"I suppose if you really love Harold you work it out. Nothing should matter."

"It does matter," Gerri cried, tossing her thick mane of red hair over her shoulder. Her face was flush and she was mess. Her eyes were bloodshot and strained. She pulled out a few tissues from the box that Glenda held out to her just in time, as if habit.

"Well thanks to you I guess I'm gonna go home too . . . my night is shot to hell." Gerri stood, blowing her nose and pouting. "Now I'm feeling all guilty for something I didn't even do."

"I didn't do anything, either," Glenda defended. ". . . except state the facts on how to make a relationship work. It's all very logical. You get what you give. You give your all and you get it in return, it's simple really. Remember Gerri, life is tough, but it's tougher if you're stu—"

"I know, I know. Don't even . . ." Gerri held up her hand to stop the words from coming. "I don't know why I try to talk to you. I . . . you're . . ." Gerri stammered and then quickly stormed out, slamming the door behind her.

Glenda wasn't stupid and so life was easy. Actually going along with things had made life very easy. She would never understand why these woman had made life so hard on themselves by complicating the simplest of things, like their relationships.

The expensive mahogany wood desk clock that she had received as a gift from her best friend Minx said five P.M.

Glenda felt that familiar weight lift off her shoulder and the smile part her lips. Standing quickly she took her coat from the back of her leather chair and swung it over her shoulders. She reached under her desk and pulled out her purse from the small compartment.

Rising, her head lightened. She saw a flash and then felt the pressure against her shoulder as it hit the floor.

Chapter 2

Gerri bit her nails while waiting with Glenda in the ER. Glenda wanted to tell her to stop doing that but her head ached and frankly, at that moment, she didn't care enough about Gerri's annoying little habit to say anything. Glenda wanted to know what was wrong too; she wondered if it was her blood pressure, her cholesterol or one of those other little things that go suddenly out of whack with the onset of menopause. She was ready to hear the worst.

The doctor walked in. His expression was unreadable and Glenda felt a little uneasy. She glanced over at Gerri whose eyes were wide with concern. Her gold contacts made her already large eyes look even bigger and wilder than normal.

"Well Mrs. Dixon, I'd say you're looking great for a woman your age," he said.

"Thanks," both she and Gerri answered at the same time. Glenda smirked. She knew Gerri was nervous but still she was starting to work her nerves a little.

"Gerri, why don't wait out in the lobby. I think if it was bad the doctor would have told me already," Glenda explained. "So what he needs to say to me from here on out is probably a little personal."

Gerri's expression fell but she stood slowly from the little stool beside the bed, still clutching her bag. Glenda felt instant regret. She felt what she had never felt before toward the young woman. Glenda felt friendship. She realized suddenly how many personal things Gerri had shared with her, yet she didn't even want to share the slightest of things in return. She wanted to change her mind and ask her to stay. But she'd already told her to leave and changing her mind was never one of Glenda's habits. Gerri hesitated slightly but upon seeing that neither Glenda nor the doctor was going to budge, she left.

"Well, Mrs. Dixon," the doctor began speaking, sliding the stool up to the bedside. "Like you said, it's nothing bad . . . I guess. But it's definitely personal."

"What does that mean? You guess. It's menopause and it's not bad . . . perhaps personal but . . ." Glenda chuckled smugly. "It's something a woman must face in life. It's part of what we do. It's—"

"It's not menopause, Mrs. Dixon," the young man chortled. "I see you were more than ready for that one."

"Then what is it?" Glenda barked, slapping the sheet, growing instantly irritated, without even knowing why.

"You're pregnant."

The room grew silent enough to hear the sirens outside the hospital—to hear the traffic in the street, to hear the babies crying on the fourth-floor maternity ward.

"What did you say?" Glenda asked, her voice squeaky and pinched-sounding.

Gerri asked more than once or twice regarding Glenda's hard to read expression but Glenda said nothing. Gerri just drove in silence to where Glenda's car was parked at the office with the curiosity killing her.

When Glenda's cell phone rang and she glanced at the number but didn't answer it, Gerri knew then what the doctor had told her privately was serious. Glenda was probably dying or something. It was going to be hard not to answer inquiring minds Monday with her own deductions on Glenda's medical condition.

"Glenda . . . will you call me?" Gerri asked her, leaning over the passenger seat.

"Probably not Gerri," Glenda said. "But thank you ever so much for getting me to the hospital. You are just the sweetest girl and truly, I thank you."

Gerri was shocked but tried to hide it. Glenda had never said such a thing to her. Yes, she must be dying.

Chapter 3

Glenda sat on the sofa, waiting. Simi had promised to be in by Friday evening and now it meant everything to her for him to keep his word. Even if he never did again, tonight he would have to come home. Minx had called her earlier but she couldn't bring herself to even speak to her. She wasn't in the mood to hear her rambling on and on about this, that, and the other thing. Minx could catch Glenda up in a conversation better than anyone could and so surely she would blurt out the truth to her before Simi and that just wouldn't be right. Glenda was a nervous wreck, thinking, rehearsing, and planning how she would tell him he was going to be a father for the first time.

Finally sighing heavily, breathing in deeply after what seemed to be hours she slapped her forehead and collapsed against the back of the sofa. Just then she heard the keys in the lock and sprung to attention.

"Hey, you waited up." Simi smiled weakly, closing the door behind him.

"Of course Simi, you know I missed you," Glenda said, while holding her hands folded in her lap, unconsciously covering her flat belly as if it was protruding and showing her condition. His face showed concern . . . maybe the hospital had called him. Simi, as was common, held out his arms for her to come embrace him, but Glenda hesitated. "Simi, we need to talk," she began.

Had Candy called? Simi thought. *Had someone from the hotel gotten their signals crossed and maybe let the cat out of the bag?*

Guilt covered his face.

"About what?" he asked, dropping his arms to his side and shifting uncomfortably before shoving his keys into his pocket.

"Us, Simi," Glenda said, standing now to fix him a drink. He was gonna need it.

She handed him his regular, he gulped it down, surprising her just a little, but then again, maybe he felt the tension in the air. Glenda knew she needed to spit it out.

"I got some news today . . . unexpected. And frankly, I'm not sure how to take it, but I do know that our marriage is forever changed," she began.

"Well, it needed to change . . . something needed to change," Simi blurted.

"What?"

"Okay, so now you know," he said.

Glenda stared at him, looking deep in his eyes for clarification of his statement. "Yes and it wasn't what I expected. I was shocked and—"

"I figured you would be, but then . . . as you always say . . . life happens or some kinda thing like that you always say."

"Well that's not what I say but . . . go on," she said, allowing him to speak his mind first. Maybe the hospital had called him. That was all she could figure.

"Life with you is dull, Glenda," Simi said, leaning towards her face tauntingly. She could feel her eyes widening but said nothing. "And well, a man gets tired of so much predictability. I needed a change. I needed something more than what you were offering me."

"Okay," she said, leaning back from his face. "I guess I didn't realize you felt this way about us."

"I've felt this way for a really long time and well, Candy makes me feel alive."

"Candy . . . ?" Glenda asked, even more confused than before. "What are you talking about?"

"My feelings Glenda . . . my feelings for once, I do have them, ya know. I'm not some robot. My life is not all planned out and—" Suddenly he threw the tumbler. It hit the plush carpet without breaking as was intended. They both stared at it for a second before Glenda picked it up and sat it on the coffee table.

"That's exactly what I mean Glenda, why can't the damn glass stay on the floor, why can't I just—"

"Because it doesn't go there," she interrupted.

"Glenda, I'm leaving you. I'm leaving you for another woman and you are too busy picking up a glass to even listen to me! That's what I'm talking about! That's what I'm saying!" he screamed. Glenda spun on her heels facing him now. Her heart was beating so hard she could swear it was in stereo. Her brain soared and her stomach tightened, yet her brain could not release the appropriate emotion.

"Oh really?" was all she could ask. "So are you planning on getting another woman or have you already picked her out or . . ."

"I'm having an affair, Glenda, with Caaaandyyyy," he yelled some more, leaning forward again to make sure she heard him this time.

The heat from his words scorched her face and she could swear her hair moved backwards, as the sound of his voice resonated through the large foyer where they stood. She was stunned and could not speak. Everything she knew to be real, honest, and true died without so much as a serious illness to explain it. All she felt was coolness growing inside her tempered only by the burning in the pit of her belly, a heat that suddenly got her attention—her baby . . . her baby, no longer their baby . . . that she decided immediately.

"What do you have to say, Glenda . . . nothing, that's what I thought. You see, you need time to plan it out; you can't even be a woman and just speak from the heart. Everything is always so planned with you," he taunted, sounding as if he'd already had a few drinks before getting home and was empowered by them.

Feeling her eye twitching she stepped backwards instead of giving in to what she wanted to do. Slapping his face would be juvenile, right? Screaming and crying would be something Gerri would do. Cussing him out would be Minx. But Glenda would . . .

She had no idea what Glenda would do and that was what was scaring her. "Simi, I think you should leave. Sleep on all this and get back to me tomorrow with your final say." She sounded professional and knew that was a good start. *Yes, keep it professional, Glenda,* she told herself. *No one can fault you if you keep it classy.*

"You want my final say Glenda . . . divorce. That's my final say." Simi stormed out but then suddenly burst back in. "I'll come get my things tomorrow . . . that's what I'll do . . . so put that in your little planner."

The door slammed behind him.

Chapter 4

Simi had only been gone an hour but Glenda felt as though it had been weeks. She'd already emptied the closet of his clothing and the walls of his picture. It was all methodical and precise. Before this day, she'd done some thinking on what she would do if Simi died and since this incident felt pretty close to it she put those plans into action.

She had told herself she wouldn't grieve him when he died, that she would be strong, stoic, and brave. No tears or any of that whining and sniveling stuff. She would wear black for six weeks and hold her head high when people offered their condolences. "Yes, he was the love of my life," she would say—when he died. But then, he would be dead—not like now. Now he was just gone—gone to be with another woman. A woman named . . . Candy at that. Was it the same thing?

"Hell no!" she exploded, glancing at the clothes she'd so neatly spread out on the bed. His suits and shirts that she'd painstakingly picked out so that he would look stylish and tailored all the time. She had laid out her favorite of his suits, on the top—the burnt sienna–colored one. It always made him look so sharp and handsome, with the copper shirt and matching tie that went with it.

She felt the tie—rubbing it against the skin of her face. On the bedside table she then noticed her shears. She had them there to cut out articles of interest, but suddenly, she had a new use for them.

The slivers of the tie fell to the floor, the shirts came next. Excitedly she then went through the dressers cutting up all his ties and underwear and T-shirts. She cut all the little alligators off each polo shirt, carefully staking the little gators in a pile, while sitting Indian style on the floor amidst all he owned—clothing-wise.

No, Simi wasn't dead, just gone, and she was disappointed at how much the whole situation was going to require some rethinking on how she was going to handle it.

About that time the doorbell rang. She stopped what she was doing and went to answer it.

"Girl, where have you been? Why aren't you answering the phone?" Minx asked, poking her head in, looking around suspiciously. "Simi must be here."

Suddenly just hearing his name became all too much. Glenda burst into tears.

"What is the matter? Tell me. Talk," Minx said after fixing herself a stiff drink and sitting on the sofa next to Glenda, who with her feet pulled under had covered herself in the colorful afghan. She'd had a wonderful cry and now her eyes were puffy and nose stuffy. She blew it one more good time. "So, are you ready to speak English?" Minx requested, moving a strand of hair out of her eyes and draining her tumbler.

"Simi left."

"Simi leaves all the time, what suddenly is the problem?"

"No," Glenda sniffed, shaking her head. "He's having

an affair and he left to be with her. Candy," Glenda said with a sneer that caused bitter secretions to come into her mouth and her face to twist up.

"Girl, shut up!" Minx exploded, finally getting the full understanding of Glenda's words. Minx realized that apparently Glenda had been trying to say this a few times but between the sobs she was just too hard to understand. But now . . . now Minx got it. Weaving in the shock she turned up her empty tumbler hoping for one more drop.

Glenda nodded. "I was going to tell him about the baby but before I could even tell him, he told me that . . . that." Glenda frowned and growled, unable to formulate any civil thoughts. "Cannndeee," she growled again. "He just got all in my face and . . ." Glenda's face twisted with the memory.

"What baby?" Minx then asked, finally hearing that too. She was stunned and looked at the glass and then at the bar, willing the two to come together without her having to move.

The silence between them got thick so Minx took advantage of it to slide finally off the sofa and pour herself another stiff one, gulping while still at the bar. She then turned to Glenda on the sofa. "You were going to tell Simi what?" she gasped, half from the burn of the liquor, half out of shock. Glenda just stared at her. "You want one?" Minx finally asked her, sounding odd and the question, out of time with the situation. Glenda just shook her head.

"I can't," Glenda said.

"Of course not, you're preg . . . Glenda, what in the hell are you talking about . . . a baby?"

Glenda threw back the covers and ran toward the bedroom where she had her purse. Inside was the confirmation of her pregnancy. Minx followed but stopped abruptly at the sight of Simi's clothes in shreds all over the floor. "Oh girl, you have lost your devilish mind up in here. What the hell?" she asked, picking up the slivers of his ties and other pieces of silks and fine fabrics. "New craft project?" she asked.

Suddenly Glenda broke into laughter.

Chapter 5

Morning found the two women sprawled out over Glenda's California King.

By the time Glenda finished telling Minx all she knew to tell about Simi's affair, which wasn't much, Minx was tipsy, so by the time they got to the real issue at hand . . . the baby, Minx was almost sloshed to the wide. Giggling and laughing about the whole thing like a high schooler, she spoke with confidence on how they together were going to raise this baby.

"Now, never having been a parent myself, I'm not too sure about all this but I think if we put our heads together," Minx began, slurring slightly.

"Once you get sober," Glenda assured her, while shoving the last of Simi's clothes in the large garbage bag.

"Exactly!" Minx agreed. "But see, I was drinking for two," she giggled.

"You are one crazy heffa."

"Glenda, how in the world did this happen . . . when?"

"I don't know?"

"Girl you getting it like that? Damnnnn gwon wit cho bad self," Minx teased. Glenda for a second realized what she had implied about her and Simi's sex life. Yes, it was good . . . before. Now it was over.

"Please, I can't even think about that. I've got so much else to think about," Glenda voiced her thoughts.

"Tell me about it," Minx said, pulling the comforter over her when she rolled on her side. "We're gonna be way past busy," she went on as if thinking clearly.

"I've never been alone before. I've always had Simi. I'm sure I'll be just fine but still. I've never been . . ." Glenda looked over at Minx who was drifting into some ugly sleep. Her mouth dropped open and a snore cried out. "Alone," Glenda said, with a sigh following her words.

Was Minx her support group?

"What am I going to do?" she asked herself.

Glenda felt hungover herself when the doorbell woke her up. One eye glanced at the clock—six A.M.

"Why is someone at my door at six A.M. on a Saturday," she asked out loud, knowing the answer. She jogged with her nephew Glen on Saturday mornings. It was something they did, rain or shine.

"Somebody is at your door," Minx groaned, rolling over, pulling the comforter over her head when Glenda dragged out of the bed to go answer the door.

"What is wrong with you? You sick?" Glen asked with concern showing on his face. He had rung the doorbell several times and was knocking by the time she reached the door and now he was eyeing her tussled clothing.

Glen was her namesake, her nephew, who truly held her heartstrings, having been abandoned by his teenage mother and left for his father to raise. Glenda's brother—Glen's father—in turn, married one irresponsible woman after another, leaving Glen with the need of

a mother figure in his life, to which she and Minx—
Minx, ever so reluctantly—filled the bill, as best they
could, considering neither of them had children.

He ducked his head in and looked around, "Simi here?"

Normally she was decked out in a bright jogging en-
semble and matching running shoes. "Glen, I'm so
sorry, but I had such a rough night," she said with a sigh
this morning, realizing how she must look, having slept
in her work clothes.

"Where is Simi, what's wrong?" he asked again. Suddenly he noticed Minx coming from Glenda's bedroom
instead of the guest room, where she usually stayed when
visiting over the weekend. Minx headed to the kitchen
and filled a wineglass with a red liquid that looked like
Sauvignon maybe. Glen grew immediately irritated. He
had mixed feelings about Minx, although she'd been in
his life most of his life. Where she exactly fit, he was
never sure. Sometimes he felt like he hated her and yet
other times he felt . . .

"You drinking already today?" he asked rudely. Minx
just flashed him a tight sarcastic smile.

"Yeah, holy woman that I am, I've managed to turn
this cranberry juice into wine."

"Nothing is wrong," Glenda answered his question,
trying to keep his focus. Glen too was easily distracted.
Between him and Minx she often felt as if speaking to
herself when talking to them. She was about to explain
but suddenly a handsome young man joined Glen on
the porch. Glen didn't bother to introduce him.

"Holy, I think not," he called out to Minx, who was on
her way back in the bedroom but stopped when hearing
his comment. "Why do you look a mess?" he then asked
Glenda, giving her another side glance on his way into the
house to start an argument or continue one with Minx, who
stood ready for whatever, with her hand on her hip.

"She doesn't look a mess. She's positively glowing," Glen's friend said, pulling Glenda's attention to him. His eyes were rich with all the colors of the earth, browns, gold, and shades of sage, dancing and alive, filled with the passion of youth.

"Glowing?" Glen asked, overhearing him yet continuing to where Minx was, taking her glass from her and giving it a sniff.

"Boy, get your face out my . . ." Minx fussed.

"How many months are you?" the young man asked Glenda, who nearly gasped. "Oh, my name is Tim, how rude of me."

"Somebody needs to police your actions," Glen fussed on from inside the house, taking a sip from Minx's glass.

"How did you know?" Glenda asked Tim, her voice just about a whisper.

"Your eyes drew me in but while there I saw something. . . ." he reached up and touched the side of her face by her eyes. It was almost a stroke of his hand down her cheek but not quite. ". . . right here. I'm studying the eyes. Have you ever heard of iridology?"

"Iridology?" Glenda asked, now coming under the spell of his gaze, no longer hearing Glen and Minx going at it.

"It's the alternative study of one's health through reading the eyes," he said. His voice was low and deep . . . affecting. Glenda had to nearly shake her head to break the trance he was putting her under.

"You said it, not me, Minx the cat!" Glen sounded off, catching everyone's attention finally.

"You two stop it," Glenda said, smiling all the while. Glen and Minx always went at it like this. She had to wonder why there was always so much tension between them.

"Are we running or not?" Glen asked as if his attention had never been diverted from what he originally came to ask.

"Sure," Glenda said, sounding a little perkier now. Tim had changed her mood although she would be the first to deny it.

"Are you sure you should?" Tim asked.

"Why not?" Glenda asked.

"Well, with the circumstances," he said. Glenda's mood instantly changed to irritated. *How dare this kid try to be my daddy,* she thought.

"Why not?" Glen asked at the same time. Tim's hands went up in surrender.

"It was just a suggestion . . . a word of caution maybe."

"My aunt doesn't need any caution, dude! Look here, go get changed and let's go, Auntie. And Tim, just because you're studying to be a *woman doctor* doesn't mean you know everything about every woman you meet." Glen went on, while heading to the kitchen. "Where is Simi?" he asked again while sticking his head deep into the refrigerator.

Chapter 6

After the run, Tim parted company with them. He had to get back to his practice. Glenda found it fascinating that he was a practicing doula. Glen was wrong; Tim was a male nurse and newly certified doula. He had plans on going to medical school in the future maybe, but for now, he was enjoying where he was, career wise. She didn't know much about the profession of doula, but she was impressed just hearing him speak about it. He was so passionate about his role in helping women give birth and his voice was enchanting . . . deep and soulful. She wondered if he sang, and if so, did he sound like Barry White.

"So how many babies have you assisted with?" Glenda asked, slowing her jog to a quick walking pace. It seemed psychosomatic almost that she had tired so quickly. Glen left the two of them to drag behind.

"So far none, I just got started. But I'm more than ready." He laughed, causing Glenda to take note of her heart and its beating. Everything about Tim was attractive. She felt a little embarrassed, surely he was no older than Glen and if so, not by much and that put him around fifteen years her junior.

"Ready for what?" Glen asked, passing them on his second round of the track. He too had slowed to a power walk, yet his pace was still faster than theirs.

"Childbirth," Tim yelled towards his back. Glen stopped abruptly.

"What the hell are you two talking about?"

Glen and Glenda entered their regular eating spot. It was such a habit for them to go there after a run they didn't think twice about it.

"Are you going to be all right? I mean, what does Simi have to say about it?"

"Glen, you have not been listening," Glenda finally sighed.

"I've been hearing you. You're pregnant. I got that loud and clear . . . thank you very much. And how crazy is that, Aunt Glenda?"

"Well, I'll find out Monday just how crazy it all is. I go see my regular doctor and—"

"What about Simi."

"Dammit Glen, Simi is not here. He's gone. He's very, very gone. He's having an affair and last night he left me."

The silence covered the table. The waitress sat their plates in front of them and smiled but they did not see her, they were too busy staring into each other's eyes.

"Simi left you . . . with a baby. He left you?"

"No, he doesn't know I'm pregnant and I'd rather not tell him until I'm sure what I'm going to do about this."

"What you're going to do?" Glen asked.

Just then, Simi walked into the café and stood stiff and tall as if suddenly realizing a habit of his own. When in town, he met her and Glen there on Saturday, after their run. It was pathetic in Glenda's opinion his being there. But then she was no better—a creature of habit. She and

Glen had even sat in the same booth. "This is so ridiculous," she sighed at that fact as well as the other one—the fact that he was here. Glen's large hand covered her as if he felt her growing tension.

"What do you want?" Glenda asked, her words coming through gritted teeth. She felt so out of control. It was so unlike her to grow angry in public this way. She hated this moment in time and wanted it over.

"Don't let this clown upset you, Aunt Glenda."

"Glenda, I want to talk today, I told you that," Simi said, and then quickly looked at Glen with his face twisted up. "And what did you call me, boy?"

"There is nothing to talk about," Glenda said, standing and gathering her purse.

"Don't do this, girl, there needs to be some closure," Simi added.

"Closure?" Glenda laughed out loud and then with a sudden charge of emotion she slapped his face. "When you closed that door last night you got all the closure you're gonna get," Glenda said, hurrying out.

"And shame on you, caaaalown," Glen threw in. Simi noticed, cutting him a reprimanding eye. Glen paid it no mind as he rushed out to catch up with Glenda. Just then the waitress came up slapping the bill in Simi's hand, as was usual for her to do. She'd missed the angry exchange.

"You always get here in time to pick up the tab, Mr. Dixon. You're such a great husband," she said with a grin.

"Damn," Simi groaned, reaching in his pocket for his wallet.

"Want a doggie bag?"

"No, apparently I'm the only dog here and I'm not hungry," he mumbled.

* * *

By the time Glenda and Glen reached the car, Glenda was shaking, livid, and nauseous. They drove off. Realizing that she hadn't paid the tab she slapped her forehead.

"What?"

"I didn't pay, now I'm going to have to send Simi a check."

"You're kidding, right?"

"No, I don't want him in my life at all. He has no rights to pay my bills or anything. I'm done with him!" she yelled, digging in her purse for her wallet. Suddenly, throwing her head against the seat, she hollered out. "I'm sick!"

Glen, shocked at her outburst, pulled over. "Glenda, stop it! You have to stop this. You are acting crazy. You and Simi have been married too long for you to just act like it's as simple as writing a check, like you can just go on your way and have this baby like Simi is no part of your life. I know what you're thinking and this flight to Egypt isn't leaving tonight. Besides, you're not in condition to fly anyway."

Glen knew her too well. She was not ready to face all this.

"I'm not in denial, nowhere near it, and I'm doing just fine," she lied, tossing a peppermint she took out of the bowl on the restaurant's counter into her mouth.

"Please, last night your marriage ended and today your man showed up and you slapped the taste out of his mouth, and now you're popping hard candy like you've been riding in a car through a windy mountain range . . . you're not doing well."

"Well? I'm not well?" Glenda screamed. Just then nausea got the best of her. She threw open the door and vomited in the gutter. After a moment of regrouping she sat back in her seat, totally humiliated. "I'll tell you what is not well," she began, with tears steaming down her face. "This . . . this is not well," she said fanning her face. "This crying, and screaming and . . ." she closed her eyes. ". . . throwing up and otherwise acting a fool in public. No, this isn't going to work. I've got to see my doctor and then my lawyer. I've got to get all this mess behind me. I can't do this. I can't have this baby and I can't forgive Simi for any of this. I have things to do at work. I have a simple life."

"What the hell are you talking about? Abortion?"

"It's too big of a change Glen, I can't do it," she sobbed into her hands. Glen began to rub her back in a circular motion the way he remembered her comforting him when he was a little boy . . . crying, lonely, and scared. Glen was always scared of something, bugs, bullies—the new mother that came every year, it seemed. But Glenda was constant and maybe Minx too, as much as he hated to admit it. He wouldn't know what to do without them, and now one of them was hurting. No, things were not at all well and it was all Simi's fault.

Chapter 7

The evil alarm bellowed out its hellish call at four-thirty A.M. as was its usual task. But this morning, it was a wicked assignment. Hung over, bloated and swollen from her night of binging on Big Macs and whipped cream–topped coffee drinks, Glenda was regretting life. After she got home from the attempted jog and run-in with Simi she cried a little longer before realizing her hunger. Rubbing her belly she felt the rumble. "Yeah, yeah, you're hungry . . . always hungry . . . like Simi," she sniffled. She then chuckled at the one-sided conversation. "No, Glenda, you will not be one of those women talking to their bellies," she reprimanded.

Noticing the soft jazz coming from the stereo she decided on something a bit more upbeat before venturing into the kitchen.

"Break it down," she called out, dipping low and swinging her hips to the rhythm of the dance beat. Tossing the salad she began to feel the effects of a lightening heart. Before she stopped herself she even fantasized about Tim, his strong youthful physique, and how it would feel to have him spinning her on the dance floor under a disco ball.

"Hell, if Simi can cheat I can too . . . even if it is in my mind." She giggled at her mischievous thoughts.

Soon her craving got the best of her. Opening the cabinet, she pulled out a can of kippers, eating them right from the can with her fingers before opening a package of crackers to lay them on. After she finished them, she looked for something to wash them down. Not finding it, she grabbed her keys and headed out the door. "What I want has to be out there somewhere."

At the time, it all felt so good. But now, with a full day of work ahead of her, she felt worse than she ever thought possible. Stepping into the shower, she was regretting life. Her breasts were full and tender to the touch. They had been overly sensitive for a while now, only before today she had tried to pay them no mind, as Simi had noticed their fuller look and was giving them a little extra attention . . . much to her pleasure. But today they were in her way and painful and for the first time she noticed the slight pudginess under her navel. "This can't be, this is all too soon," she said to the mirror, shaking her head. She didn't want to think of her last true menstrual cycle or the possibilities of being too far into this pregnancy to get out.

Beating most of the East Bay traffic, she'd made it into the city and to her doctor's office by eight sharp. This was crazy, living, driving, and commuting for the most part, but until now she just did it without a thought, but now suddenly she wondered about all of it—the stress. How would she manage all this stress?

The nurse called in back within five minutes. "What's up, Glenda," Dr. Margau asked, pushing his glasses up on his nose.

"You're not going to believe this but . . ." Glenda chuckled, trying to sound nonchalant. His face was serious. She'd sounded nearly panicked when making the appointment, and now she was trying to laugh it off. "I went into the ER Friday . . . silly really, I was light-headed and well, they said I was pregnant."

"Really?" His brow raised and his mouth dropped open.

"Yeah, isn't that crazy. Me?" She placed her hands on her chest dramatically; again her tender breasts caught her attention. "Crazy hormones of mine must have had that little test strip reading incorrectly." She laughed loudly . . . a little too loudly.

"Well, it's not really all that crazy Glenda," he answered, opening the door and calling in his nurse. Glenda could hear herself swallowing. The nurse came into the room.

"We want to get a pap, pelvic, and blood draw on Mrs. Dixon and a transvaginal ultrasound."

"Now, what are you about to do? No . . . I don't want to do this." Glenda began to panic again, the same way she did in the ER after Gerri left the room, while the young man was trying to convince her that she was pregnant. "I can't be pregnant. I . . . I can't have a baby," she told that young doctor and now Dr. Margau.

"And that means?" Dr. Margau asked, prepping the room for the exam.

"I can't do this. I want an abortion."

"Just relax, Glenda, and let's take one step at a time. Let's first establish viability, okay?"

"I don't see the point, I don't want it," Glenda fussed, stepping behind the curtain and sliding from her tight skirt and wrapping the paper around her.

"Why not, you're as strong as a horse."

"What did you say?" she asked, showing irritation in her tone.

"Get up here and slide to the edge," he said, patting the table, prepping her for the exam.

After removing the speculum, he reached inside her with one hand and began to push on her belly with the other. She flinched at the discomfort, feeling as though she had a hard tennis ball in her abdomen. "That hurt?" he asked. She refused to answer, fighting to keep the grimace from coming to her face. "Ummhmm," he mumbled.

Moving the monitor where she could see the baby if she wanted to, he readied her for the ultrasound. "Now relax, this won't feel any different than a pelvic okay?" Dr. Margau said, placing the ultrasound scope inside her. Glenda turned her head away so she wouldn't see the picture that started coming into view.

"I want to come in as soon as possible for the procedure," she said, trying to make conversation.

"Right," he said, sounding as if only half listening and concentrating on his job.

"I'm not going to go through all this," she went on.

"Wow, looking real good," he and the nurse said, conferring on the picture they saw coming into clear view.

"What do you see?"

"You should look," he told her.

Glenda gulped air, fighting with all her might not to turn her head facing the monitor. "You see something?"

Dr. Margau clicked a button on the ultrasound machine. Glenda then heard the sound of the fast-paced metronome.

"What's that? What's that?" she asked.

"It's your baby," he said, a smile parting his lips. He'd been her doctor for nearly twenty years, but Glenda had to admit, this was the first time she'd seen him smile. "And if next time you come this child is flash dancing like this we'll be able to clearly see if it's your son or your daughter."

* * *

Glenda finished crying and blowing her nose finally, as Dr. Margau patted her shoulder. "I'm going to send a referral to a perinatologist I know. I believe you should see him instead of me. Just your age alone makes you a high risk and if you are sure you want to go through with this I want you to only have the best of care."

"You think I'm at risk?"

"I would say no, but Glenda, this is your first baby and well . . . a few tests wouldn't hurt."

Glenda raised her hand to stop the rest of his thought from coming out. "And I'm old," she said, finishing what she thought to be his next words.

"Not old . . . mature," he chuckled, looking younger than he'd ever looked. Glenda laughed.

"Fifteen weeks? How can I be so far along? I'm so into my body, how could I have not known?" she asked.

He shrugged. "Maybe you missed something besides a period, Glenda. Sometimes when you think one thing so adamantly, you can ignore the reality of something else."

"Like that flu I had at the start of the year? The one you said was probably just stress because you couldn't find anything wrong with me."

"Exactly," he agreed, patting her shoulder again.

Chapter 8

Glenda was in a daze by the time she reached the office. She didn't even remember the heavy traffic and congestion. She sat in her car, listening to her jazz CD, for the first time thinking of her baby. Had she felt it moving thinking it was gas or just a hunger pain?

"A baby," she said in an undertone, stepping from the elevator.

"Hey there Glenda," Dave said, nearly bumping into her. It was as if he had been waiting like a puppy by the door, for her.

"Oh Dave, hello," she greeted, a little surprised at his *in her face* presence. Had the grapevine gossip already started? She looked for Gerri, who sat working hard, no doubt filling the void that a morning at the doctor's office had caused. Gerri was a hard worker, despite her domestic issues. Glenda hadn't given her much credit for that lately, nor had she delegated much to her, but things around this office were about to change. As much as she hated to admit it, Gerri did a darn good job considering all the craziness she lived under. Glenda realized that here she was simply pregnant and about to fall to pieces and yet Gerri had had four children since she started working there and had only taken six weeks off per child. She and her husband had been through hell . . . money problems, infidelity, in-laws . . . sickness, the works and yet Gerri never had taken any unauthorized time off because of any of it.

When she went into her office, Gerri followed with a notepad in her hand. They had worked together for five years and Gerri knew her well, she was ready to get to the business at hand. Glenda smiled.

"What?" Gerri asked, looking around.

"Nothing."

"Glenda, this morning, we had calls from just about everyone and—"

"Aren't you going to ask how I'm doing?"

Gerri looked at her closely. "No. It's not like you're going to tell me. You all but said get my nose out of your business and soo . . ." Gerri huffed. Glenda fanned her hand at the door, noticing Dave hovering.

"Close the door."

Gerri's eyes bugged out of her head and she ran to obey. Tossing the pad onto the desk she put her hands on her hip and took in a ragged breath as if she'd been holding it all morning.

"Tell me, I can take it," Gerri began, sounding altogether serious. "Just lay it on me." She sliced the air as if having braced herself. Glenda laughed, pulling the picture of her dream house off the small corkboard and holding it. "Oh my God, the picture . . . you're holding the picture . . . you're dyin'," Gerri gasped, covering her mouth.

"No, crazy. You are so crazy," Glenda giggled. Gerri, noticing the girl-like giggle, took a closer look at her.

"I may be crazy but if I didn't know better, I'd say you were positively glowing."

Glenda felt the heat come to her face. She pinned the

picture back on the board and picked up the pad off the desk, shaking her head. No, she wouldn't tell Gerri yet. She'd wait until the ultrasound, the tests . . . the confirmation that yes, she was indeed going to have a healthy baby, and a life without Simi—pity was something she would never be able to live with.

"I'm so hungry . . . want to take an early lunch. I need to talk to you about some changes I want to implement here in this office."

"Changes?"

"Yes, Gerri, you are my administrative assistant, but how about a promotion to executive secretary, and more responsibilities . . . if you want them, if you want it."

"Heck yeah, I mean, sure . . . I mean . . ." Gerri grabbed Glenda's arm. "What about Dave?" she whispered.

"What about him? He has a department. You are my assistant; you are in line for this promotion, not him."

"Lunch sounds real good then," Gerri purred excitedly.

The position had been on boards as open for the longest time, but never filled before now. Glenda had never felt anyone was qualified to fill in for her this way. Executive secretary was basically a clone of herself, with a nearly matching salary. The powers that be had told Glenda she needed one yet she only worked harder to prove that she didn't. But now . . . all that was about to change.

"Glenda," Gerri said then, serious now and in a low voice. "Are you dying?"

Glenda laughed. "No."

When they reached the restaurant, Glenda quickly ordered. She was starving. Just knowing about the baby now justified her appetite and she had no intention of fighting the feeling any longer.

"Wow, you were serious about lunch," Gerri said, ordering only a salad after hearing Glenda ordering so much food.

"You got that right," she giggled.

"What's gotten into you?" Gerri asked. Her question was probing and curious. Glenda caught the inquiry and just smiled.

Just then laughter came from another table, familiar laughter. Glenda turned to see if she could find the owner of it. It was a sound that tickled her ear and only one person had that effect on her.

"Tim," she uttered.

"Who?" Gerri asked.

"Oh, a friend of my nephew," Glenda said, still looking around trying to follow the voice.

"He must be someone interesting, you're breaking your neck to find him," Gerri noticed, glancing in the dessert menu. It was only around one o'clock now but something sweet was good anytime as far as Gerri was concerned and since Glenda was in such a good mood she was gonna order a big piece of pie to have after her salad. Glenda cut her eyes back to her.

"No, no, I was wondering if my nephew is with him."

"Ah, but I doubt it. Glen's schedule never allows for him to have this time of day free," Gerri said.

"How do you know that?"

"I know his schedule as well as I know yours, missy. See, I know more about you than you think." Gerri winked.

"You didn't know I wasn't dying," Glenda smarted back.

Just then, Tim's voice closed in around her. She glanced over her shoulder to see him standing there. He waved good-bye to two other young men who looked clean-cut and professional. Gently he laid his hand on the back of her neck, sending chills through her body and a shiver down her spine. He pulled his hand away as if he too felt it and rubbed his palms together.

"Hey, Mommy," he said, flashing a beautiful smile. Glenda blinked slowly and then her eyes darted to Gerri who didn't seem to catch the comment. Glenda cleared her throat.

"Hi Tim, I'm in a business meeting right now if you don't mind," she quickly said. Tim stepped backwards, realizing his mistake and carelessness.

"I am so sorry, gosh, I wish my boss took me to lunch sometime," he said toward Gerri.

"Please, she's my boss but don't get excited. This is truly the first time," Gerri rambled before catching her professionalism or lack of.

"Oh Gerri, you sound like I'm a tyrant," Glenda said, fanning her hand. Gerri just gave a tight smile, which made Tim laugh aloud and again pat Glenda's shoulder. It was almost as if he wanted to test the heat again to make sure the fire had only been his imagination.

"Well, I won't interrupt your meeting. Oh, by the way, I would really like it if you would come by my clinic. I would love to give you a massage and show you what we do there at—"

"Okay," Glenda said, cutting off the rest of his statement just in case his clinic had some name that had carried the word *baby* or *mother* or *birth* in it.

"Wow, can I come," Gerri asked. He glanced at her, his eyes staring into hers.

"Well, I don't think our service is for you," he simply said, bending over, sliding a card from his pocket under Glenda's water glass. She stared at it, afraid to pick it up and then feeling the heat on her face. She glanced at him out of the corner of her eye. His face was close, his skin smooth. He smelled good. His hands were large and strong looking. The thought of them on her aroused her. Hardly ever had she thought of another man touching her and never with the excitement the thought of Tim massaging her brought.

"I'll call," she managed to say.

Just then, the waitress came to the table with the black book that contained her credit card. Her face was tight and concern was showing. She stood until Tim moved away from Glenda and then whispered in her ear while laying the black book on the table. "Ma' am, I'm sorry but this card didn't clear."

"Excuse me?" Glenda said, her voice reaching a high pitch.

"Do you have another one?" she asked. Her voice rose a little louder now and Gerri immediately saw what was happening and heard her. She reached for her purse. Tim too reached for his wallet. Glenda held up her hand.

"Guys no, please . . . hold on, there must be a mistake," she said to the waitress, who shook her head, buckling her lip in embarrassment.

"Wow," was all Glenda could say, rubbing her forehead. She didn't even want to verbalize her instant thoughts.

Simi.

She opened her purse and pulled out cash and paid the tab along with a large tip for the girl's trouble. Her stomach was turning and churning the whole time. "Please bring me a doggie bag. Gerri, I saw you looking at the sweets. Do you want something? I'm not in a hurry, just not hungry any more."

Gerri shook her head and quickly folded the menu closed. Glenda shook her head and handed the girl another ten-dollar bill. "Bring us a couple of slices of cheesecake too please," she said, hoping to show Gerri she truly had no financial worries. The waitress nodded and smiled, walking away from the table happily.

"Well, that was scary," she said to both Gerri and Tim. "I guess my husband has been doing a little shopping," she said sipping her ice water. Again, Tim slid his large hands over her shoulders, easing the immediate tension he saw come up in her face.

"Call me, Glenda . . . tonight," he said, in her ear.

Glenda hated that Tim no doubt knew about her separation. She could tell by the compassion in his voice. Glen had told him. When he walked away Glenda watched him a long time.

"Okay, spill it," Gerri said, bringing her back. Glenda assessed her emotions. No, she would not cry. She was actually a little ticked off at Simi's audacity. To max out the cards without telling her was downright rude.

"Gerri, Simi and I had a little misunderstanding about finances, apparently," she added, rolling her eyes. Her mind was soaring.

"And so big hand handsome dude just happened to be available to . . ."

"What are you talking about? Tim is my nephew's friend. Come on now, he's a kid and I'm a grown woman. Actually, I've been thinking of having a masseuse come in once a month to give massages to all my leads."

"And so you were just gonna try him out first?" Gerri asked. Glenda nodded and pointed at her.

"Exactly," she said. Gerri and Glenda burst into girlish laughter. The waitress brought the doggie bag and pie, only to find Glenda eating now and she and Gerri engaged in lively business conversation about Gerri's new work duties.

Chapter 9

Glenda went back to work without concern over much. She felt good about her conversation with Gerri and both had a full understanding of what was going to be expected as the months continued. It was easy to talk to Gerri, easier than Glenda thought possible. Even when Gerri's curiosity over who Tim was came into the conversation, Glenda wasn't even rattled. She had an answer for that one. He was Glen's best friend, nothing more, right? Sure, he always seemed to be there when she needed him but still . . . he was Glen's friend, not hers.

Thinking about Glen, she called him to tell him what had occurred during the lunch break.

"What? Your card didn't go through. Is Simi nuts? How can he use up all the credit when you're gonna have a baby. How can he do that to you and the baby?"

"Glen, he doesn't . . ."

"I realize that he doesn't know, but even still, how could he just take money like that? How could he leave you and then take money? I mean, I'm sure he was embarrassed when you popped his chops in the restaurant the other day but still . . ." Glen was fuming. Glenda had never seen him have so much anger towards Simi before. She wasn't sure how to feel about it.

"Well, I called the bank and closed the joint checking accounts that we have. They were my accounts anyway and therefore I just had to close them and move my money to a different primary account. I want you to be on it with me," she said. Glen was so busy fussing he didn't hear her right away. "As well as my IRA and well, I've got to meet with my attorney but . . ."

"You want me to what?" Glen snapped to attention, shaking his head at the same time on his end of the phone. "No, I don't want to, Aunt Glenda. It's too much pressure."

"Pressure?"

"What if Simi finds out, I mean . . ."

"He won't find out and what if he does?"

"I don't want to end up fighting him. He's so jealous."

"Jealous?"

"Oh yeah, didn't you know that. He's always been jealous of me and you and our relationship. I'm so surprised you didn't know that."

Glenda laughed aloud. "What is there to be jealous of, Glen?"

"Well, like when we start going to your appointments together he's gonna flip!"

"You're going with me?"

"Of course I am. I would never let you go through this alone. I already told Tim we'd be there next week."

"You told him what?"

"He was saying that he wanted to be your doula or whatever the hell he is, maybe you should let him deliver your baby . . . or whatever."

"No way," Glenda giggled. "He's not a doctor . . . anyway, no. I'm not going to let him touch me." Glenda felt the heat on her face, whispering loudly into the phone as if someone might be overhearing. Once again,

Tim had come up in conversation. He was becoming a *somebody* in her life . . . who, in particular, she had no idea.

Just then, Dave peeked his head in the door. Glenda held the receiver to her chest. "How can I help you, Dave?"

"Need to speak with you for a minute," he said. He had a bit more of an edge in his voice than Glenda was used to. She held up her finger for him to hold on a moment but instead of his usual compliance, he rolled his eyes. "Some people need to get to work around here," he mumbled. She heard him.

"Let me let you go," she told Glen before hanging up quickly. "You have a problem, David?"

"So, Gerri's role in his office has changed?" he asked, sounding a bit off the wall. Glenda leaned back and folded her arms.

"She's my assistant, Dave . . . same position she's always had."

"Well, she's acting like you and her just had some friggin' power lunch or something because she's out of control. Whatever you broke, you need to fix."

"Pardon me?" Her body language said it all. How dare he question any decision she made.

"She just asked me to bring my department stats for the week to her. I'm thinking to myself, what does she want them for? She can barely read, let alone . . ."

Glenda's hand flew up. "End it right now, Dave. Don't say another word. Gerri is my assistant. Reviewing stats is in her job description. She's good at her job and does it well. It's called delegation. Good-bye," she added, looking over the stack of papers on her desk. He stood there for a moment longer before pushing up his glasses; he realized he'd been dismissed and left in a huff.

"You must have bumped your head when you fell,"

he mumbled again under his breath. Glenda pretended not to hear.

Dave wanted Gerri's position. Glenda wasn't sure of that fact until now but suddenly she was very aware. Over the last few days Glenda had teetered on softness but she needed to keep her wits about her in the workplace. Yes, there were changes at home but here, whatever different was going to be happening she wanted her hand on the trigger—making it go. There was no room for pliability and tenderness in the corporate world. She knew that and wanted to believe that she hadn't given Gerri the added duties in error, or out of some kind of tender emotion. If Gerri made a mess of things it might cost Glenda more than she was ready to give up. Just then she felt a pull in her belly. It felt like a hunger pang but maybe . . .

"It's too early, Glenda," she told herself. Thinking about Tim suddenly, she reached for his card. "A doula . . ." she thought out loud and then chuckled. "Are you easily distracted or what?"

Just then, she heard a ruckus coming from the front office. Stepping from her haven, she found Dave and Gerri going at it in a verbal altercation. His files were scattered about on the floor.

"What is going on here?" Glenda exploded, looking around the office realizing that clients were sitting, staring, shocked at the unprofessional behavior they were witnessing.

"You bitch!" Dave yelled. "I'm not giving you a flippin' thing. I'll quit before I allow you to double-check me! If you want my files pick them up yourself!"

"Let's not get personal here, David," Gerri said calmly.

"Personal . . . Ha! That's a laugh. You're personal life is all over this office . . . and the bathroom walls."

The air cracked from the stiff silence that suddenly froze the room. All Glenda could do was stand there and wait to see what Gerri would do next. This was her test, her first one. How would she handle this situation?

"Well, if that's true, David, then I suppose we should call maintenance or better yet, my lawyer for copyright infringements, because I don't remember giving anyone the right to put my life in print that way," Gerri remarked coolly. Keeping her cool, Glenda realized then Gerri had been indeed listening to her lectures. Dave's face went beet red as he stormed off.

Before Glenda could apologize for her employee's actions, Gerri was already handing out gift cards to the waiting clients. They always kept complimentary coffee-house cards for clients who had waited too long to be seen or were otherwise not totally thrilled by their visit there. On her way back to her desk, Glenda nodded approval and headed out to look for Dave, but his jacket was off his seat and his cubical was empty. His cube neighbors were all busy with clients and had apparently either missed the loud exchange or wanted to pretend they had so as not to jeopardize their jobs as Dave had.

Later when Gerri wrote up her incident report, it showed Dave in a very bad light. Apparently he was bringing his personal life to the office. "His wife left him. I know he's upset about that. It was so unexpected, but still . . ." Gerri divulged. It was gossip and maybe a little bit of a rumor but still, it would explain Dave's change of demeanor. "You don't go off in front of the clients. Even I know that. I came in here and cried in your office . . . sheesh," Gerri said, handing Glenda the report.

Too much stress, Glenda thought now, pulling out Dave's personnel file, giving it a look over. He was up for review and this go-round wasn't going to be as pleasant as the last one was. His resentment over Gerri's increased responsibilities coupled with dropping department scores this quarter were, unfortunately, damaging.

Glenda could relate, though. This separation from Simi was turning out to be a bear and all she could hope was she could handle the pressure.

When Glenda got home that night, she was met at her door by a small gift. A peace offering from Simi was her first thought. Picking the single rose up, she gave it a sniff. The flower immediately affected her. "Can I forgive him?" she asked herself. "Can I take him back after all he's done?" She shook her head. No. Simi had showed his ass for the last time as far as she was concerned. Now he was trying to hurt the baby. Sure, he didn't know there was a baby, but still. How dare he try to take money from her when she needed everything she'd saved over the years to support this child—to give him or her everything he or she needed.

Glenda huffed and shook her head again. Yes, it was a sweet gesture but just not enough to change things.

Walking in the house she glanced at the phone, the message light was blinking. Laying her purse and the rose on the coffee table she pressed the play button.

"Glenda, call me." Minx.

"Aunt Glenda, call me." Glen.

"Girl, have you lost your damn mind, Simi was here all tow up. What's going on? Call me," Glenda's brother yelled into the phone.

Glancing at the card hanging from the rose she read it. "I hope life gets better real soon. Tim."

Tim?

Glenda gave way to coquettish giggling and then stopped herself and looked around.

Tim?

What in the world did getting this rose today . . . of all days, mean? Timing was everything in Glenda's mind and Tim had been *right on time* more than once since this all began. He was becoming as mystic as the contents of a fortune cookie . . . and maybe as sweet.

Chapter 10

It had been a month since the separation and Simi was doing just fine, well . . . considering all the weirdness at the job. Looking in the mirror, he smoothed back his hair and straightened his new tie. It had cost him a mint replacing all his clothes. He'd not had to buy so many things in over twenty years. Glenda was gonna flip when she got that bill. But then, "Glenda and her crazy ass, cutting up my clothes like that. What got into her? Minx, no doubt! I hate her," he lied. He actually always liked Minx. She was an exciting woman, much like he wished Glenda was. He had always hoped being friends, that Minx would have rubbed off on Glenda. "Maybe it has . . . but it's like, really bad timing."

He had a date with Candy tonight. She'd been hard to catch up with since her little promotion. She had been given half his territory to work. It was strange, but according to the grapevine the presentation she used to show the big dogs why they needed another salesperson in his region sounded a lot like one of his, one he was planning to use for his next step up the corporate ladder. It wasn't time for an assistant or partner. He needed to be the big dog running the show alone a little longer—proving his worth for a minute or two more before then showing his ability to delegate. It was all in the plan. But now Candy had rushed it.

"No big deal," he first thought.

"Man, Candy took your idea, though. You just gonna take that layin' on your back?" his colleague, who had seen Candy's presentation, asked after the e-mail had gone out announcing Candy's promotion.

"What idea?" he asked, trying not to get overly excited at just the mere sound of her name. Still no one knew about their affair. It had gotten around about his separation but not his affair with Candy. She was still very insistent on keeping that private. And considering she'd not given him any in over two weeks, it hadn't been hard to do.

"I think she's after your job, man . . . not just part of it—the whole thing."

"Please, nobody is after my job and especially not a sweet girl like Candy."

"Sweet? Don't let those blue eyes fool you; she's a snake in a miniskirt."

"Not Candy. And besides, from what I hear it's just a lateral move, nothing to get all excited about. I've still got my position secured and retirement set. I'm still going to be her superior."

"Well, I'd watch my back if I were you . . . might find yourself sitting in the unemployment line—superiorly."

"No biggie, I'll just work on another proposal," he told the reflection. Candy deserved this little advance and besides, it wasn't as if she wouldn't ask him to come along with her on her out-of-town trips, turnabout was fair play, right? It wasn't as if she knew the ropes. She was green and needed supervision . . . and that would be him, right? Also, Simi had to figure that he was next in line for a promotion, "Yeah, maybe now I'm not going to be just the West Coast sales division head but, instead, head of the whole West Coast region."

Gathering up his keys and jacket, he noticed his mail on the bed. Simi had not opened his check stub yet. He knew what it would say but out of curiosity he opened it now. The shock wave cut through him. With the cut in his division also came a cut in commission pay and a short letter of explanation.

"They can't do this!" he yelled, grabbing his phone. "Friday night. Nobody is there, Simi," he gasped.

What had gone into his account was barely enough to cover his expenses incurred while staying in the fancy executive hotel suite he had rented. "My money!!" he groaned, grabbing his head.

He called the bank to verify that yes, the automatic deposit had gone in and no, it wasn't enough to cover the checks he'd written.

"Overdrawn? No way, I've got plenty of money," he said, laughing nearly hysterically now. The IRAs, the savings he and Glenda had stashed away over the years. . . .

"Talk about a rainy day," he said aloud, smoothing his hair back. Sure Glenda had stopped the little credit card he was using, but that was a small drop in the bucket. "And she was just being evil when she did that."

Come Monday, he would simply need to go to the bank and pull out a few thousand to hold him over until he got his mess straightened out with his boss. Sure, Candy could have half his region but no way was she having half his money. "We're not married yet." Even then, he'd been very careful with money matters over the years with Glenda, just in case. There was no way he was just going to hand over his life's savings to this kid— Candy. It wasn't as if he'd asked for Glenda's forgiveness but still, it wouldn't be right to allow Candy to have what he and Glenda had worked so hard for. He and Glenda had money stashed everywhere. Yeah, he would just go to the bank on Monday and get some.

"Maybe I should let Glenda know what's happened," he asked the reflection and then frowned up his face.

There was no way he was going to tell Glenda anything. She was so selfish and into herself. He'd seen her over the last couple of weekends at the track with Glen, Minx and that other kid. ". . . must be some friend of Glen's."

Simi thought about last weekend seeing her there. He remembered thinking about how fat she was getting. He figured it was because he was gone she was letting herself go. He always knew he was the motivator in her life. Without him she didn't have a life worth living. "No imagination." He smirked. I need to call her tomorrow, he thought. Maybe even stop in and see how she's doing. "Give the girl a thrill," he said out loud, grinning at the thought of Glenda's face and how it used to light up when he came home late at night and crept into bed. How willing she would be to give herself to him freely no matter the time. She loved him unconditionally, unlike Candy who now all but required an appointment.

Sucking in a chest full of air he gave his expensive executive suite a once-over to make sure nothing was forgotten and headed out to meet Candy.

Reaching the restaurant, Simi found Candy waiting at the table. She was looking at her watch as if short on time.

"Hey baby," he said, leaning to kiss her cheek. She reared back, causing him to miss the mark.

"Please don't do that in public, Simi," she whispered.

"Excuse me?"

"We are colleagues and I would hate someone to get the wrong idea."

"Excuse me? We are a little more than colleagues, deary," he corrected.

"And I wanted to talk to you about that too, I think we should cool the umm . . ." she gulped her ice water. "Sleeping together thing," she said quickly, again looking at her watch.

"Are you breaking up with me?" he asked, sounding naive.

"There is nothing to break up, actually. I'm just saying that the more I thought about how you've been taking advantage of me over the last few months . . ."

"Taking advantage of you?"

"Well yes . . . I mean, you've all but made me feel like without sex I would lose my job."

Simi rubbed his forehead. "You are insane," he finally managed to say. She had ordered wine before he arrived and when the waiter opened it, he had him fill his glass without the customary approval sip.

"I constantly think of all the money I could have been making if I hadn't felt so held back by you and your non-verbal threats."

"Threats?" he said, nearly choking on the wine.

"My attorney said . . ."

"Candy . . . come on; if you want to end this thing just end it."

"No, ending it isn't the issue." Her voice turned cool and austere. "I want the whole region," she said.

"Then what will I do?"

"How about retire?" she asked coolly, sitting back in her seat, folding her arms over her chest. Simi burst into sardonic laughter. He couldn't help but think of his friend's words—snake in a miniskirt.

Just then a young black man joined the table kissing her lightly on the lips. He then looked over at Simi and outstretched his hand.

"Hello, you must be Mr. Dixon. Candy has told me so much about you. It's really nice to meet you. I'm Stan Givins, Candy's fiancé."

"What did she tell you about me?" Simi asked, trying to quickly gather the facts of the situation unfolding in front of him.

"How wonderful you've been training her to replace you. Must be nice taking an early retirement . . . where are you and the missus gonna go to celebrate?"

"By the way, is she joining us tonight?" Candy asked, still holding onto the man's arm, urging him to settle into the seat next to her. Simi felt sick . . . fat, old, ugly, and sick.

He'd been played. It was crystal clear.

Just then, the waitress came over to the table with the black book to collect payment for the wine. Simi looked at the total. "A hundred dollars for one bottle of wine?" he gasped. Candy and her young man just stared at him, letting him know that they had no intention of paying the hefty bill.

Reaching in his pocket, he pulled out his wallet, emptied it into the black book, and stood. "Actually, what I was going to tell you, Candy, was that my wife can't make it tonight. She's under the weather and so I just wanted to meet your friend here, and then I was going to have to take off."

"Oh, I'm sorry about that," the young man said, standing to be polite. "Well, perhaps at your retirement party, we'll get to meet her." Out of the corner of his eye, Simi caught Candy's wink. He was more than confused now.

Chapter 11

From the first time Glenda walked into that clinic, she knew she was going to like Stephanie.

At first, she had to admit, she was a little nervous about the whole doula thing. Especially since her doctor had immediately referred her to a perinatologist as a high-risk pregnancy. Just the term *high risk* scared her to death so needless to say anything that didn't involve standard by-the-book activities made her nervous. When Glenda first found the address, she was a little put off. Thinking Tim worked in a true clinic, finding the old Victorian in the middle of the Haight-Ashbury district made her hesitate.

Walking in, the bell on the door jingled when she entered. Joni Mitchell was playing on the stereo. The smell of sea salts filled the air and pillows lay all around.

"Hello." Stephanie grinned broadly. She had on wide-rimmed glasses and a polka-dot dress. She was an earthy white girl who dressed as if she was from 1969 instead of being a member of the Generation Xers.

"I'm looking for Tim Hannon."

"Oh he's in the back with a mother meditating. It'll be a minute," she said, grinning again. "So is this your first?"

she asked, no doubt seeing her pregnancy in her eyes as Tim had the day they met.

"Yes."

"You waited?" Stephanie asked and nodded all at once.

"No. I slipped up," Glenda answered flatly, not meaning to sound so unfriendly. Stephanie's frown covered her face as she stepped from in back of the counter. She touched Glenda's belly.

"No little guy, she's not speaking to you. It's all good in your hood," she said, directing her words to Glenda's belly.

"Why are you doing that? I'm the only one who's hearing you."

"No, you're not. Your baby hears all you hear and feels all you feel, Mama. That's the first thing you have to realize, okay. If you decide to walk out of here and never come back, just remember the learning has already begun."

"But the book says . . ."

Stephanie shook her head, "No Mama, despite what you've read, life started the minute you and Daddy planted that seed." She smiled broadly.

"There is no daddy. I'm in this alone," Glenda confessed. Stephanie smiled again.

"No worries. No judgment. This time is for you and the life inside . . . no time for stress, hate . . . or even bitterness. Just you and baby," she said, touching Glenda's stomach lightly.

"You guys touch a lot here."

"Our hands are our tools. Look around. Check us out. Tim will be out in a minute. He's awesome."

Glenda could tell Stephanie admired Tim and had probably learned a lot from him. She had his demeanor and groovy air about her. Glenda liked that about him and now she realized she liked Stephanie too.

About that time, a very pregnant woman came from the back room with Tim on her heels. Both their faces were calm and filled with peace . . . it was a calm and a peace that Glenda immediately saw and wanted.

When she had thought about going, she told Minx but then again, Minx wasn't one who really thought things all the way out when it came to men.

"Hell, I'd let that little Negro massage me in a heartbeat. He is too fine!" Minx admitted. Glenda giggled.

"It's not that kind of massage," Glenda told her between chuckles.

"Look at you blushing," Minx noticed.

"Stop it. I'm not," she lied.

"You should go. I'll go with you if you want."

"There is no way I want you there embarrassing me. It's bad enough you and Glen are all up in the doctor's office with me."

"Please, girl, ain't nothing I haven't seen before," Minx guffawed. "Beside, I need to see my little dude as much as I can now, because once you have him and that fool Simi starts coming around . . ."

"I told you. Simi is having no parts of my baby."

"Glenda, don't say that. It's not good to exclude him this way. I can't believe you still haven't told him. This is gonna tear him apart."

"Please. He'll live," Glenda said.

"This is too not like you. You've changed."

Glenda didn't want to answer the phone, seeing that it was Simi. He was probably calling about money. He was so on the late freight with that mess. It took a while but finally she had locked all the joint funds and cut off all of Simi's access to her money. She'd transferred more funds and she felt like a money launderer. All the money he insisted she hid so that his pride would not be touched by the fact that for most of their marriage she made more money than he did. He insisted that she put the money *away* so that by the time her check actually came home it was little to nothing compared to his. And now, he was trying to blow it. "What was he thinking, taking an expensive suite in a hotel when he could have very simply just gotten a studio apartment for a quarter of the cost?" All Glenda could figure was he had moved in with that woman, and there was no way she was going to pay for that mess.

The thought made her laugh aloud. She'd been doing that a lot more lately and it felt good to give into the joy she was feeling in her heart instead of the bitterness, which Simi was trying to force in there each day with his actions. She never realized how oppressed she felt all these years trying to make Simi feel better about himself. And for what? For him to just walk out without so much as even an attempt at reconciliation. And this call tonight, it wasn't to make up . . . it was for money. She was sure of it. But she wasn't about to give in to what Simi was trying to make her feel. She was learning a lot from her sessions with Tim at his clinic. She was learning to take control of her emotions in a whole new way and it felt wonderful.

In just the last few weeks, watching Gerri run that office, Glenda was more than happy about her decision in that area too. Dave, on the other hand, was becoming a problem.

"He's like a ticking bomb," Glenda told Stephanie.

"Ticking doesn't sound cool at all," Stephanie said, working her shoulders in a deep massage. Tim wasn't there this evening. He was at the hospital.

"It's not cool and I'm worried that he's gonna go off."

"Fire his ass then. I mean, seriously. Send him

walkin' . . . poison air is what he's got," Stephanie said bluntly. Glenda changed positions so that Stephanie would work her belly a little bit so as to stimulate the baby into movement. As if waiting for this, the baby began to move.

"I'm shocked you said that. I thought you would suggest I take him some tea or something."

"Please, I'm into babies, not jerks with 'tudes," she explained, measuring Glenda's tummy. She was good at what she did. For a young woman she knew a lot about babies. "Like Tim, no matter how much I love this job. If he was a jerk, I'd be soooo far south of here he'd need a map to find me."

"So you and Tim seeing each other?" Glenda asked, finally getting out the question that had been burning a hole in her brain for weeks. She just wanted to know. There was nothing behind the question . . . okay, so that was a lie; she was fighting jealousy every time she saw them together. The way they laughed and hugged. The comfort level between them was enviable. Surely, they'd slept together. Glenda just wanted to satisfy her curiosity.

"Seeing each other? Oh, you mean sleeping together?" Stephanie asked bluntly. "Oh no, I have a partner and he and I are like sooo faithful and rich in our relationship. He's like, my soul mate . . . of course I hate him today. He's being like . . ." Stephanie fanned her hands wildly. ". . . such a boy." She went on, sounding more and more like Gerri every minute. That's when Glenda realized that most relationships truly did have ups and downs. Maybe that was her and Simi's problem, it was no longer up and down, it had flatlined years ago.

"Besides, Tim has a crush on someone. He's keeping it a big fat secret but I know him and he's in love with someone, and he's got it bad too," Stephanie said, grinning slyly.

"Really?" Glenda asked.

"Oh yeah, he's always writing love letters and then tearing them up all fast . . . he's so cute. He needs to just come out and tell her."

"Yes, he does," Glenda said.

Her curiosity was beyond piqued now.

Chapter 12

Glenda had left the perinatal clinic. It was part of the main hospital where she had planned to deliver her baby. Stepping from the elevator onto the seventh floor, she had again decided against a tour of labor and delivery and veered in the opposite direction. She could almost hear the women screaming bloody murder.

"I can't imagine going through all that," she mumbled, shaking her head trying to clear her mind of where her imagination was going. "Legs tied up like I'm some kind of wild animal . . . what a visual." And the longer she could put off that reality the better.

As a young woman, she had never had discomfort during her time of the month, never even a simple bladder or yeast infection . . . nothing. And now, for the last few months, she'd been nothing less than miserable. She'd already had a bladder infection and some other foreign issue that caused her to require a suppository to relieve the itching and burning. She was puffy, swollen for the most part, and her skin was horrible—worse case of acne than puberty could have ever caused. Looking at her brittle fingernails, she figured a manicure was sorely needed as well.

She'd never had such issues with her appearance as she had now. "Glowing. What a big fat lie." She giggled thinking about the day she met Tim. Those were the first words out of his mouth when he saw her, however, he'd not said it recently and she had to figure *glowing* was no longer the term that best described her.

Looking at her growing belly, she could not believe how big it was getting. She was sure she was waddling a little and her thighs rubbed too, causing her gait to widen just a little to avoid that friction.

Tim had offered to massage her thighs on her last visit to his clinic. Glen was with her and so she refused. There was something in the way Glen looked at Tim when he asked her that told her perhaps a nearly intimate massage like that wasn't a good idea. Glen, if she recognized the look, was jealous of Tim. "Crazy boy," she mumbled, climbing into her car—besides, Tim had a girlfriend, at least he was working on one.

Glancing at her watch, she saw that she had time to grab a sandwich and still make it to Tim's on time. "Maybe Stephanie will be there to work my legs," she reasoned, feeling the start of leg cramps. "Because this is like no joke," she groaned, reaching down and rubbing on her calves.

Stephanie smiled at Tim who was busy folding blankets and straightening pillows. Finally, noticing her goofy grin, he looked at her. "What?"

"Nothing," she answered, placing new bottles of lotion on the shelves.

"Her who?" he asked, sounding innocent.

Just then, the doorbells jingled. Tim quickly turned to the door with almost a look of guilt showing. Stephanie burst into laughter.

"What?" Glen asked, looking serious.

"Oh nothing, Tim thought you were somebody else," she answered, not realizing the somebody else was just who Glen came to talk about.

"Hey, um Tim, can we talk?"

"Sure." Tim folded up the last blanket and glanced at his watch. Glenda would be here soon. His heart raced. How foolish he felt. This all caught him so off guard, these feelings for Glenda. He'd yet to sort them however, and maybe it was just as well. She was married and he was younger . . . a lot younger. Just those two factors made anything on his mind nearly impossible—not even adding her baby into the picture.

"I want you to stop seeing my aunt," Glen said, as soon as the door to the meditation curtain shut behind them.

Glen . . . a factor he hadn't even thought about adding into the equation.

"Excuse me?"

"I . . . I don't like it, man, it's kinda freakin' me out, you touchin' on her like you do. And now she's thinking about you being there when she has the baby, no, I don't like it."

"She is?" Tim grinned, smoothing back his freshly tended too twists. He was leaning towards dreads but right now he wanted to be able to change his mind, so he'd only had his hard twisted.

"Tim! I said I don't want you seeing her anymore. I'm sure all this that you do here is legit and like with Stephanie, I'm sure you two are on the up-and-up and all but this is just not cool with me anymore."

"But Glen, you are not having a baby and you are not the father of this baby so your stake in this baby is . . . what?"

"Glenda is my aunt and you are my best friend . . . why can't you just respect my discomfort with all this."

"Because it's unfounded. Glenda enjoys her sessions

here. She's got a high-stress job and coming here relaxes her. This is her first baby and she's well over the normal age of having children, Glen. She's dealing with scary possibilities and the least I can do . . . we can do," Tim corrected quickly, but not quickly enough, Glen caught the slip. "Is make her feel better about this whole thing."

"I've stated my peace and well, frankly, I think you're using her and this baby for your own motives and it's wrong. It's unprofessional and . . . wrong."

"Would you feel better if I didn't touch her anymore?"

"Hell yeah!"

"Would she?"

"I happen to know for a fact that Glenda is uncomfortable with you touching her like you do."

Tim's heart sank. Perhaps Glenda had told Glen something she had not told him. Perhaps he had been out of line and he didn't even realize. Maybe where he thought they were bonding he was, in fact, crossing that forbidden line between client and doula.

"Then fine, Glen, I won't touch her anymore, but I'm going to continue our meditation sessions because she needs them. She's too far from focused and . . ."

"Whatever dude, just stop touching her."

"Hello, Glenda," Stephanie said loudly, as if she knew the men were behind the curtain discussing her, besides the fact that she had overheard a little bit of what they were saying.

Glen quickly exited the room and joined her in the main part of the clinic. Glenda's eyes widened in her surprise to see him.

"What are you doing here?"

"I just stopped by to see Tim for a minute. We are pawdnas ya know. I mean, before he got all wrapped up in all this baby stuff," Glen said, working hard to keep the jest in his tone. Glenda caught his effort and looked at Tim for an explanation of why he was really there. Tim said nothing but instead pulled his jacket off the rack.

"Trudat and I forgot that I had another appointment . . . a date. Actually she just called and well . . . new relationship and all that," Tim lied. Glenda grew instantly flustered. "Stephanie can handle the session today right?" His words were curt as if he hadn't thought them completely through before they flew from his lips.

"Well . . . sure," Stephanie stammered, caught off guard slightly. Tim rushed out, leaving Stephanie, Glen, and Glenda standing there.

"Wow, she must really be something." Glenda sighed heavily. Glen caught it and felt instantly remorseful.

"Yeah, she is," he said. "He cares a lot about her."

There was a long silence between all present until Stephanie finally clicked the stereo system, filling the air with natural sounds.

"Okay Glenda let's get started. You've grown since I've seen you last."

"Tell me about it, and my legs hurt like heck," she said, easing down to the floor with Stephanie's assistance.

"Well, let me check out," Glen said, backing out of the front door. Glenda gave him a halfhearted wave as she was concentrating too much on getting to the floor carefully.

Chapter 13

He and Glen had had words over the sessions and Tim was going to make a point of staying on his side of the tracks where Glenda was concerned. It was not worth it to lose his friendship with Glen and the respect of an admirable woman like Glenda Dixon.

Apparently, Glenda had told Glen about the sessions and spoke with an air of sensuality attached and that was not good. It was clear that Glen was okay with Stephanie touching Glenda, but Glen was not cool at all with all the personal attention Tim was giving her. Tim had to wonder if Glen had seen the truth. Maybe it showed in his eyes or the way he and Glenda would walk around the track on Saturdays talking about life, her dreams and goals . . . maybe Glen was jealous.

And that's stupid, Tim fussed internally. She is my client and since when can't I handle a client . . . since when can't I work with a patient. I'm a nurse for crying out loud. I've seen women naked many times and . . . and more!

Turning his car around Tim headed back to the clinic where he found Glenda and Stephanie finishing a massage on Glenda's thighs. Stephanie looked up at him and smiled, glad to see that he had come back, proving he was the man she had figured he was.

"Do you want to take over from here?" Stephanie asked. "I really do have a date," she whispered in his ear as she passed by him closely. Tim smiled at her, feeling the heat coming up in his face.

"Sure, I'll do it," he told her.

Working her feet, Tim noticed the tension. "What's on your mind?" he asked her finally. They'd both been silent for about five minutes.

"What did I miss here today? I mean, I'm not dense but I have been a bit distracted lately, however, I could swear something weird happened here today."

"Nothing to concern yourself with," Tim told her. He didn't want Glenda to feel one way or the other about what Glen had told him. If indeed he had been improper with her, it would never happen again, as he planned to be the utmost professional with her, but on the other hand, he was not going to stop servicing her if it wasn't what she wanted.

"Good, because for a minute there I thought you were changing the guard on me. Like I told Glen, I've been thinking of you assisting me in my labor, Tim," Glenda told him. Tim stared at her, while still holding her foot. His heart was pounding.

"Really? Why . . . I mean . . . yeah, why?"

"Because, I trust you and . . . well, I can't imagine having to go through this without you. I know we just met not too long ago, but you are a very special young man and well . . ." Glenda stopped herself, feeling as though she was saying too much, getting too personal. "And whoever the women is that you are involved with . . . she's very lucky and I just hope she understands our relationship . . . I mean . . . the relationships you have with all your clients," Glenda corrected.

Tim was speechless. "Of course I'll be there for you, Glenda. I'll be whatever you need me to be . . ." he said before stopping his words. He didn't even attempt to straighten out his last comment.

Chapter 14

Glenda carried the picture with her everywhere she went these days just in case she ran across the home of her dreams. She was going to put in a bid on the spot. And today she found it.

It was Sunday and she and Minx were out shopping for the baby—as usual, when they ventured to Half Moon Bay. There were some trendy shops there and she was hoping to find just the right bassinet, but instead she found the house.

"It's perfect," she told Tim during their session later that afternoon. Stephanie was out with her partner and so Tim was planning to both massage and meditate with her. Glenda had to admit it was way past wonderful when Tim touched her. Intimacy was never one of Simi's strong suits. Sure, he remembered her birthday and their anniversary, but just spontaneous lovemaking . . . especially the nonsexual kind, was not his forte. It was hard to keep it professional when Tim's strong hands touched her feet, calves, and back but she promised herself she would work harder at it. Maybe that was what Tim was trying to say to her . . . that he was too young for her to have any of those ideas about and maybe she was embarrassing him with her feelings . . . that were way too hard to hide, especially when then they would meditate. It was so easy for Tim to take her and her unborn child to a heavenly place. His voice alone could transcend time and space. Sometimes she would shed a few tears from the inner peace he helped her find. By the time she left his clinic, she always felt beyond satisfied in spirit. And most of all, she loved her baby more and more with each passing day. How could her feelings be wrong about Tim? How could he make her feel those things without feeling anything for her?

But he had set the rules and she was going to do her best to stay within them. He was Glen's best friend . . . not hers. He was just her doula and that was all.

"So you really are planning to leave your job and move to the hills and raise your baby?" he asked after she described the house.

"You make it sound like I'm talking crazy," she said. "Minx thinks it's a wonderful idea and I've all but talked her into leaving the phone company and joining me."

"You don't think you'd need a man or—"

"No!" she blurted. Tim touched her temples.

"Now you know that was not said to change your vibe," he said, shushing her to calmness. She closed her eyes, smiling as his hand ran down the side of her face cupping her under her chin. He held her face longer than intended because her eyes opened and caught him in a bottomless gaze. He audibly gulped, jerking his hand away.

Here I go again, Tim thought to himself. *Get a grip Tim,* he scolded himself.

But never once had Glenda even implied that he was moving into Glen's or Minx's place in her life. Never once had Glenda even given him a hint that she was ready to replace Simi. . . .

Never once, Tim sighed.

"Would you like to come see it before I make a bid?" Glenda asked.

"Of course I would," he answered quickly, sounding excited and boyish.

"Well, help me get up and we'll go," she giggled, reaching out her hand for him to take hold. When he did, again she felt that tingle that shot up her arm and ended with a pounding in her chest.

The drive to Half Moon Bay was very romantic as the warm breeze blew over them. He'd dropped the top on his convertible PT cruiser. Glenda laid her head back against the seat and enjoyed it. He would only imagine them on their way home after a day in the city. Glenda and the baby meeting him at the hospital after a double shift—they would go home to their beautiful house in the hills where he would have his practice now and Glenda would have started some kind of home business so that she could spend quality time with the baby.

She would have cooked a delicious dinner—since she loved to cook so much. Surely he would pick up those fifteen pounds his mother always said he needed to put on. By the way, his parents would love Glenda . . . they had a lot in common. Glenda was sharp-witted and smart and beautiful. It wasn't as if Glenda was his mother's age. Tim was a latter-born child. His mother was forty when he was born. Perhaps that was why he felt so close to Glenda. He could relate to her situation. His mother nearly died having him and so he knew how much care and consideration Glenda needed in order to carry this baby safely to term.

Again Tim's hand wandered and he found it rested on

her belly. When he looked at her, she was staring at him. Again he jerked his hand away.

How he wanted to kiss her there, on her full stomach, how he wanted to touch her swollen breast, maybe even taste her no doubt sweet milk. He was craving Glenda Dixon. No, these were no motherlike feelings he had for her. They were totally man/woman feelings. Her being a mature mother was the only connection he felt to her in comparison to his mother . . . he was sure of that.

The house was monstrously large. "You can afford this?" he asked without thinking.

"Yes, I wouldn't be looking at it if I couldn't," she answered flatly, opening the door with the key from the lock box. She hadn't hesitated to get a hold of the Realtor who, after glancing at her financial portfolio, was quick to grant her a look-see.

"I'm sorry, that was wrong of me to ask you that."

"It's okay Tim. I mean, frankly, I was a little surprised myself, but after all these years of not spending my money, thanks to my husband, I really can afford it."

"But do you think it's wise to buy during a separation?"

"Oh please honey, I have an attorney. That situation will be taken care of prior to this house-clearing escrow. Remember this is what I do for a living," she reminded him. "I teach people to think before they make life-changing decisions."

"Do you always know what you're doing?" he asked, moving close to her. It was a natural move on his part and she didn't move away.

"I like to think so, I'm mean when the situation is within my power to control, yes," she corrected.

"Unlike Jr., here," he said, patting her stomach. Glenda grinned.

"I like when you do that," she confessed, holding his hand on her stomach. The baby moved under his large palm. His other hand touched her face; his fingers ran through her hair onto the back of her neck. Her eyes closed as he pulled her into a kiss, one that engulfed his very soul. She moaned and bit on his lips hungrily giving into the passion as he pulled the thin straps of sundress she wore down her shoulders, easing her large breasts from the bra cups, kissing each tenderly, causing her to seethe with pleasure.

"Tim," she purred. "Ohhhh Tim," she repeated as he squatted before her lifting her hemline to expose her pleasure cove pulsating with life. . . .

"Tim!" she repeated, causing him to jerk back into reality. "Where did you go?" Glenda asked, noticing his vacant eyes.

"Oh . . . uh, I was uh . . . I think I'm hungry," he lied, stepping back from her. They were standing way too close to each other . . . yep, that was the problem, he realized.

"Okay, well come see the rest of this place real quick and then we'll go," she said, taking his hand from her stomach and holding it while leading the way through the rooms and then into the large backyard.

"So when did you say this was all going to happen?" he asked again, his mind still soaring from the fantasy he had yet to recover from.

"Soon," she said.

Chapter 15

Simi couldn't believe it. He was being opted out of his position. Early retirement was being offered at only a fraction of what he could make in a year. "And they call that fair!" he yelled out.

"Hey mack, you're getting too loud. Why don't cha go on home to ya wife," the bartender said.

"I don't have one any more," he growled and slurred in the bartender's face. The bartender leaned back slightly and then signaled the bouncer to extricate him from the bar.

"Heyyyy!" Simi yelled as he was tossed into the alley like the drunken bum he was turning into. Stumbling to his feet he dusted his clothes off and headed toward his car.

Chapter 16

It was Saturday morning. Minx had decided to join the group this morning on their run. Since Glenda was no longer jogging, Minx figured she would be able to keep up at this rate. She'd even bought a new outfit and gotten her nails done for the occasion.

"You are insane," Glenda said, admiring Minx's expensive manicure while waiting for Glen and Tim to arrive.

"I'm going to see what's got you smiling all big."

"What are you talking about?"

"Tim Hannon," Minx purred with her eyes closed.

"Minx, stop it," Glenda gushed and giggled. Minx gawked at the response.

"Girl look at you," she blurted and then patting Glenda's tummy she leaned in close. "Do you hear your mama acting a fool over here?"

"Do you think I'm being foolish?" Glenda asked, sounding more than serious. "Do you think it's just because I'm pregnant."

"Do I think what is because you're pregnant?" Minx asked.

"You and Glen . . . you guys miss so much," Glenda

chuckled, shaking her head and walking past Minx to gather her MP3 player and earphones.

"Miss what?" she asked.

"Let's go. Tim had to work, he's not coming," Glen blurted, sticking his head in the door before noticing Minx. "And this is so not a beauty contest," he then smarted off noticing her new haircut too.

"Thanks for the compliment, son," Minx purred.

"Why do you call me that?" Glen asked. It was as if the question had burned a hole in his head.

"What?"

"You always call me son. Why do you do that? Why can't you just call me Glen?" he growled. "That son business bothers me. I don't have a mother and so, therefore . . . yes, it bothers me."

Minx looked at Glenda who too was trying to find the root of Glen's true frustration.

"Well Glen, I'm sorry I . . ."

"No, it's me. My dad is getting divorced again. Damn, he just . . . damn it's just very frustrating."

"Oh Glen," Glenda said, stepping toward him. Glen stepped back, avoiding her embrace.

"No, I don't want to hug your . . ." he pointed at her belly. "But at least that guy is gonna have a mother."

"You're being foolish," Minx fussed now. "You are just upset. You've always needed a mother and I feel bad about that, but you can't take it out on Glenda's baby."

"How would you know how I feel? You don't have kids; you don't know."

"I so know. I know exactly how you feel. I've known you your whole life. I know you very well," Minx explained. "I . . . I know you," she stammered as if she wanted to say more but suddenly couldn't. Glenda noticed. "Your father is an idiot just like Simi. Neither of them would know a good thing if it crawled up in their drawers and bit them on their butts. Your father has had the blessing of having his son and yet he's spent your whole life trying to pawn you off on one woman after the next instead of just raising you. Men never know when they have the best, easiest life laid right out there for them."

"Life's tough, but it's tougher if you're stupid," Glenda mumbled her mantra, which seemed apropos at this juncture.

"I'm sorry Auntie," Glen said, giving her a big hug and then to Minx's surprise he pulled her into a tight embrace right after. Glenda noticed Minx hesitating before she patted his back affectionately.

Tim was speechless. He read the name over and over again. Simi Dixon. This was Glenda's husband. He wasn't dead but he was sure banged up pretty bad. He had been brought in the night before. He'd been walking while intoxicated and was hit by a car. He didn't want to be a DUI so he decided to walk home from the bar where he was drowning his troubles . . . one being the loss of his wonderful wife. He was awake now and that was all he had said over and over again, making Tim sick to his stomach. He all but wanted to tell Simi to shut up, the way he kept calling Glenda his woman, his wife . . . as if she was a possession. Glenda was a flower, a beautiful petal who only needed love to bloom. He'd seen her change so much over the last few months. Changing from an uptight corporate boss to a sensitive woman, who giggled like a little girl at the sensations of her unborn child's movement and melted under the touch of his strong hands massaging her back and shoulders and feet. Normally he never had any kind of sexual rise from a client but with Glenda he all but caught afire during their sessions. Immediately he had to turn her over to Stephanie, claiming one excuse or another for being unable to touch her. Glenda's pregnancy had her glowing and beautiful, happy and full of life. He was falling in love with her and now the fantasy was going to end. Her husband was hurt. There was no way Glenda would not come to him. She was that kind of woman . . . good and faithful.

"Have you called his wife?" the doctor asked him. Tim was snapped back into the now.

"No, uh, I haven't. I'll get right on it," he lied.

Glenda didn't mean to overdo it. Maybe it was having Glen on her mind or maybe her crazy-ass brother or perhaps it was Minx and the way she started crying after Glen hugged her, canceling the trip to the track, maybe it was all that on her mind that caused her quick walking pace to turn into a jog this morning, but after one time around she was cramping heavily and bent over in pain.

"Come on Glenda, hang on to me," Glen panicked.

"It hurts so bad Glen," Glenda cried, easing down to the ground with Glen's assistance.

"We were both really stupid today and I'm so sorry I didn't stop you."

"It's not your fault, Glen. I'm grown and knew better," she said between pants and groans. Pulling out his cell phone and dialing 911, Glen then called Minx and then his father. Glen hesitated for only a second before he next called Tim.

The ambulance came quickly, whisking her off to the closest Kaiser.

Reaching the ER, they were greeted by the triage team, one of which was Tim. This was turning into a devil of a day for him.

"What's happened?" he asked Glen, whose face was pasty in color.

"We were jogging and . . . I didn't think we were doing all that much, but she keeled over and . . ."

"Okay fine . . ." Tim said, quickly assessing the situation. "She's twenty-seven and three!" he told the triage team. "AMA," he added in case her youthful appearance hid the fact that she was, indeed, Advanced Maternal Age. Glenda cried out in pain.

"Get her up to L and D," the doctor ordered, abbreviating the name for labor and delivery. "Thanks Tim," he said patting him on the shoulder.

"I'm so sorry," Glen said to Tim as they both stood out of the way, watching Glenda loaded into the gurney preparing to be wheeled up to the labor and delivery floor.

"She knew better," answered Tim, sternly. Glen caught his expression of concern that showed beyond his harsh words.

"We all should have known better," Glen said. "And that's not what I'm sorry about."

"What does that mean?"

"I'm sorry for getting all crazy when you fell for my aunt. She's a beautiful woman and . . ."

"I . . . I didn't fall for you aunt. I'm just working with her during her pregnancy. I . . ." Tim stammered and then looked over his shoulder at the triage team disappearing into the hospital.

"Please man, you should have seen your face when they took her out of the ambulance. If you don't love her you need an Oscar."

"No, you're wrong."

Just then Minx rushed up, her expression was wild and crazed. She dropped her purse and scrambled to pick up the contents and then as if deciding nothing was as important as getting to Glenda she cursed while abandoning the rolling lipsticks and other small items. Glen and Tim hurried to meet her. Tim ran after her rolling items while Glen comforted her. She was nearly hysterical.

"The baby . . . is the baby okay?" Minx asked, nearly out of breath.

"I don't know," Glen answered. "We haven't gone up."

"We would be in the way. Trust me, the doctor knows what he's doing and . . ." Tim attempted to explain.

"Oh paaalease," Minx exclaimed, looking Tim up and down as if he was a stranger. "I'm going up there," she insisted, struggling on her high heels to continue her hurried pace into the ER, twisting her narrow hips quickly while trying to rush in her heels. It was obvious she had dressed in a hurry and hadn't planned out the outfit as well as she normally did.

"Simi's here!" Tim called out in her wake. Minx stopped dead in her tracks, spinning on her heels. Her mouth hung open.

"Don't lie to her like that," Glen said to him. "Just let her go up."

"I'm not lyin'. I forgot to tell everyone. Simi came in last night. He was all banged up. He got hit by a car last night." Tim's voice sounded sad for the first time.

"Oh my God," Minx gasped.

The three of them suddenly realized that after all these months standing by Glenda, Simi's presence at this hospital right now could now change everything.

Chapter 17

Simi couldn't believe his eyes. It was Glenda lying there in the bed. A bed in the maternity ward!

The noises coming from the monitors were a little confusing too . . . all the sounds—the quick pace of the metronome.

"Glenda," he called softly.

She slowly opened her eyes and smiled at him. Glenda always smiled when she saw him. He didn't deserve her and now, realizing she was pregnant, he knew he surely didn't deserve this.

"Why didn't you tell me?" he asked in a quiet voice. She glanced over at the monitor. She could see her baby girl clearly now. Until today they had only guessed the sex of her child but it was clear today. She was a little over six months and in labor. Because she was high risk the clinic doctors had watched her closely. She ate right, exercised, and made sure she never missed an appointment and now after all this time developing a relationship with this unborn child for it to come to this moment—she wanted to cry. But there was no way she was going to show Simi any emotions. He didn't deserve it.

"I didn't want you to know," Glenda told him flatly.

"But why? This baby is mine too," he said, almost sounding like it was a question.

"Simi, we stopped sharing things when you took what was ours and gave it to Candy," Glenda told him, her eyes narrowing to slits—more like darts from where he sat.

"Glenda, please, this is no time to talk about the past."

"The past . . . since when is a couple of months ago the past? Simi, a nearly thirty-year marriage is a past . . . phsst." She smacked her lips and turned her head away from him.

Simi grew immediately frustrated at her refusal to negotiate this situation. What was wrong with her? Never had he ever had to work this hard to get her to forgive him—for anything stupid he had done. But then again, had he ever hurt her this badly before? No.

"Glenda, I'm sorry for what I did."

"Did? Oh so Candy is gone," Glenda asked, turning quickly back to him, her eyes, staring, unnerving him. He turned away. "Look, I made a mistake. I thought something was going on with that woman that wasn't and . . ."

Glenda burst into laughter. Simi sat up straight in the chair. He was hurting. His wounds ached. Thank goodness the driver of the car was parking and he was only hit at about five miles an hour. It was all the rolling off the car into the street that had him all bruised up—all the stumbling to regain his footing while drunk as a skunk is what had sprained his wrist and twisted his knee. "Don't you give a damn about what happened to me last night? I was thinking about you when this happened."

Glenda laughed even harder now. "Simi, if you were thinking of me you would have never left home." The laughter helped but still her heart was sore. She wished he would just wheel himself back out the door that he had come in. If she wasn't hooked up to so many monitors she would have done the honors.

"I understand that now. I realize a lot of things now. I've lost my job and . . ."

The smile left Glenda's face and her laughter died away. She knew how much Simi's job meant to him. More than her job meant to her . . . that was clear. She was planning to take her maternity leave as soon as she was released and she was thinking about not going back after her daughter was born. She was going to buy that house in Half Moon Bay, make jellies, and maybe live her dream of being a clothing designer . . . maybe even fall in love with a younger man.

"Glenda, did you hear me!" Simi snapped.

"No, I wasn't listening. What did you say?" she asked.

"I said, I need to come back home. I need you to forgive me so that we can get all this behind us. We have a child to raise and . . ."

"What if I told you this baby wasn't even yours, Simi?" Glenda teased the question. She didn't really know why it came out, but now that it did she waited to see what he would answer.

"What the hell?" Simi yelped and then clutched his wrist that hung in the sling. "Whose is it, that young punk I've seen you with? I'll kill him. I'll . . ."

"You've been spyin' on me?" Glenda asked. Shock was showing. "You've had the gall to spy on me and now you accuse me of an affair? You are the biggest dog I've ever had the unfortunate fate of owning."

"Owning? Have you lost your mind! Girl I'll . . ."

"You'll what? What?" Glenda screamed. Suddenly, the monitors exploded with sound and within seconds the nurse came into the room.

"At least I was discreet!" Simi yelled.

"Mr. Dixon, we think you should leave," the nurse told him, taking hold of the back of the wheelchair.

"Yeah, take me back to my room; I don't even want

to look at this . . . this person! I can't believe you cheated on me."

Glenda was speechless. Simi was truly insane.

"Glenda, you have to calm down," her doctor said, quickly putting on his stethoscope.

"I need my doula," Glenda insisted. "Please somebody call him!"

Chapter 18

"What?" Minx asked. She was shocked at what Glenda told her about Simi and how he had acted and what he had said to her. "He's a fool. Between Simi and your brother . . ."

"Girl, I've been meaning to talk to you about this mess with my brother and his wife." Glenda began. "I know Glen is trying to pull you into it, but don't go there."

"I don't want to talk about him," Minx reneged, walking over to the monitor and touching it softly. "I always wanted a daughter," she said. Glenda noticed her melancholia while looking at the baby, whose movements were jerky and sporadic.

"Why didn't you have one?" Glenda asked. Minx turned to her.

"I'm not the mother type. You know that. I'm too selfish," she admitted.

"No you're not. Stop saying that."

"No seriously, what kind of mother gives up her baby to some man," Minx said.

"You did that?"

"Yes, Glenda, I did that. And I know how you feel

about that kind of thing. I've heard you for years talking about Glen's mother and how you felt about her."

"I never really met her. I just said what everyone said . . . and I'm wrong for that," Glenda admitted. She was young when all that happened and there was no way she was able to comprehend people making mistakes . . . acting human. But she understood it all now. Simi's affair was a human act, one done out of disregard for anything except for the moment. But it was going to cost him— a lot. It was going to cost her even more. Glancing at the monitor, Glenda realized she had learned more in the last few months than she had in years.

"You're just saying that because I just told you I gave up my baby."

"No, I'm saying it because I really am sorry for talking about that girl as if I truly knew her. I didn't know her. I only knew my brother. I knew he was scared but took on the responsibility of Glen because my parents said he had to. I understand now why he got married so many times . . . he was scared of going it on his own. Scared and weak are too different things. And maybe that girl was scared. Hell, I know I'm pretty scared right now."

Minx moved over to Glenda's bedside. "I was scared, Glenda. I was scared because I was young . . . too young to accept responsibility for both mine and someone else's mistake. He was older and had come from a good family and I felt my baby would stand a better chance if his family raised him. There were more of them than me."

"I understand, I am so scared that if I had to give that baby right there to Simi, I would die. I mean I made myself sound like a whore just to get the thought out of his mind that he has any parts of my child. It's amazing what you do when you're scared."

"You did what?" Minx laughed.

"I gave Simi the impression that I messed around on him and maybe the baby isn't his."

"Girl you are a mess . . . but I know the feeling. I allowed my baby's daddy's family to say whatever they wanted to say about me so that I could see him my way on my terms."

"Wow Minx, I never knew that. I mean, we met so many years ago, I never thought that you had a son . . . and you see him."

Minx smiled mysteriously. "Yeah, I see him just about every day."

Chapter 19

"How are you feeling?" Tim asked, sitting by her bed. She had been dozing and didn't realize he was there.

"Hi," she mumbled. Her mouth was dry and pasty. The contractions had started up again and they had medicated her in order to stop them. The baby's heartbeat was strong but Glenda's pregnancy was not going well. "They are going to give me a cerclage tomorrow." Tim nodded.

"That procedure usually works."

"Yeah, it sounds painful but then again, these contractions aren't the most enjoyable things I've ever experienced."

There was silence between them before Glenda reached out for his hand. He quickly took it and squeezed tight moving close to her, standing and placing his forehead against hers.

"I'm scared," she whispered. "I've never failed at anything and suddenly I'm failing at everything. I've failed at my marriage and now I might lose this baby."

"You won't lose this baby, Glenda. Now come on, we've been working together for months. You're not concentrating. . . ."

"I am. I can't stop thinking. . . ."

"Stop thinking . . . start concentrating. Think about the house, the playroom, little Thea's pretty pink room and . . ."

"Thea?" Glenda asked, pulling her head back a bit. Tim's eyes were still closed.

"Shhush, I'm concentrating. Now Thea is in her biggo bed in her room, sleeping, breathing sooo softly. We just checked in on her and . . ."

"We?" she asked, again trying to pull away from his head on hers. This time he put his finger against her lips and opened his eyes, swallowing her.

"Tim," Glenda began, before his lips silenced hers.

The kiss was as sweet as they both imagined, filled with a promise of a future together. Reaching up Glenda held the back of his head, holding him to the kiss as long as possible. Keeping their heads together, Tim spoke softly to her with his eyes still closed. "I've fallen in love with you, Glenda. I know it sounds crazy, but it's true."

"It sounds really crazy but wanna know something crazier?" Pulling apart, they glanced over at the monitor. "We're loving you too."

"Thea's looking at us," Tim pointed. Glenda's emotions soared as she laughed behind her tears.

Chapter 20

"Corporate is showing no mercy Glenda," her boss said, as she signed papers.

"Well, I didn't figure they would. Life goes on," she said, showing little emotion. It had been a rough night and she wasn't in the mood for all this crap. Being in this hospital bed had her about to lose her mind. However, it was worth it. Thea was hanging in and now at twenty-eight weeks, she could be born any day and stand a good chance of survival.

"I'm sorry we had to come at a time like this but it couldn't be helped."

"Well, I'm just sorry I wasn't there to take care of that little problem with Dave personally. It was more than Gerri should have had to handle on her own."

"Actually she did okay; I mean, Dave left little to quibble over. Her actions were done by the book and she fired him without any room for recourse on his part."

"Good for her. I'm proud of her and I'm glad you all agree that she should move into my position."

"You are taking this so well."

"Do you see that baby in that monitor fighting for her life . . . please, this job means very little right now. If I wasn't such a practical person I would tell you all to get out. But I know I need this money and benefits and I'll be damned if I let all the years I put into this company get taken from me when I need it the most."

Glenda's boss expected no less from Glenda. She had always been a no-nonsense woman, practical and always willing to face the inevitable head-on. Four weeks in the hospital was more than the company would allow and so she was being forced to accept a buyout at 70 percent of her year's wage. She would be forced to cash in her company's stock but could retain her 401(k) for another ten years. She would continue to have the Kaiser benefits for her and her child for an additional year as well. She took it and to hell with them.

Minx came in right after they left.

"Girl that's awful. I can't believe after all these years they pulled that on you. I wish the phone company would try some kinda crap like that," Minx said with hands on her hips.

Glenda smacked her lips. "Please I'm surprised they didn't do it sooner. They need to be glad I at least trained Gerri. I actually gave them a good employee in my place. Girl, she fired Dave. He went off and started attacking her. He sliced her tires and all that."

"Well I think you need to watch out for that fool too. He sounds dangerous."

"Taken care of already . . . I got a restraining order. You know I think about stuff like that."

"You're sounding more and more like your old self." Minx grinned.

"Please, there is no old self anymore, only a better new self."

Both women nodded affirmation of that fact. Glenda had changed, but it was all for the better. "I filed for divorce and now Simi is trying to sue me for whatever he can think of. He's broke and trying to get my money and thinking he can use this baby as a platform. He thinks he's going to get some kind of custody or whatever, so he's trying to insist on a paternity test now, before Thea is even born and . . ."

"Thea huh." Minx smiled, having heard Tim say that name too. Glenda just grinned and kept talking.

"Yeah, Thea, and that fool thinks I'm going to allow him to jeopardize her health any further with some crazy procedure now. He must be out of his mind!"

The two of them chuckled at the insanity of a desperate man. "Have you seen Glen? He's not been here in a couple of days," Glenda asked.

"He's fine. Negro has me out there trying to jog and mess."

"Did you tell him?"

"Of course not, but I did go see his father."

"You went and saw my brother? Get outta here. I told you not to let Glen pull you into that mess and now that I know, even more so. How did it go?" Glenda sat up straighter in the bed.

"It wasn't that bad. I thought it was going to be horrible after all these years and, girl, he was actually kinda happy to see me and even happier to know that I'd actually been around all this time."

"We always thought you had dropped off the face of the earth," Glenda admitted her thoughts about the mysterious girl who dropped her baby off on their porch thirty years ago.

Thinking back on their meeting, it all made sense now. How desperate she was to be friends. She was determined that they would get close. It had been easy however, as Glenda liked Minx right off. It was funny now, thinking back on it all. It was always Minx who had pushed the relationship, making sure Glen was always in her sights. Glenda laughed thinking about her and Glen's relationship all these years, the bickering, fighting, yet how much Glen loved Minx. She was his mother. The natural bond between them couldn't be denied. Minx had done what she needed to do to be next to her child—even if he didn't know it.

"I think your brother wants to date me again. Tryin' to mack after all these years, I told him . . . that's what got his butt in trouble the first time . . . foolin' with me."

"Shut up . . . girl please don't traumatize that boy any further. His parents getting back together would be way too much drama."

Minx burst into laughter.

"I get to go home this weekend," Glenda finally said, sounding serious.

"You scared?"

"Girl you know I am. No job . . . no plan. It's so not like me."

"Change is sometimes good, Glenda."

"Yeah true."

"What about Simi."

"I don't know. He's saying that he loves me out of one side of his mouth and then turning his lawyers on me at the same time. His actions are not very loving and I'm not going to deal with that two-faced stuff. I'm going through with the divorce but I'm really not ready for the ugliness."

"Damn him."

"Yeah, you'd think he'd learned how to make life easier on himself."

"What about Tim?"

"I knew you were going to ask me that next. I don't know. We haven't really spoken . . . that way . . . since that night. He's come every day to see me but I think he's just being a friend . . . trying to comfort me and . . ."

"But he kissed you . . . and you said it was a real kiss."

"I know." Glenda grinned, feeling the heat creeping to her face. Thea's heart rate increased.

"Even Thea gets excited when you think about Tim," Minx laughed.

Chapter 21

A few days later Glen ran into Tim in the lobby of the hospital. Tim was in his scrubs but off the clock and heading up to Glenda's room. Glen was on his way down.

"Hey dude," Glen greeted. They grabbed fist and embraced in a manly fashion. It had been a few weeks since they'd met . . . even by chance. Despite Glen's apology, Tim still wasn't sure if he was ready to explain his feelings about Glenda.

"Sup?" Tim asked.

"Just checking on my girls . . . well, I guess, I should change that to your girls."

"Glen," Tim began, raising his hand to end the confrontation before it started.

Glen raised his hands in surrender. "I'm just messing with you."

"I'm crazy about your aunt, I guess little Thea too but I'm just not sure . . ."

"Not sure of what?" Glen asked. "You don't plan to dump her do you? Man, that would really put a dent in our friendship. I know at first I was mad that you liked her, but I would really be mad now if you didn't. It would really be hard to . . ."

Tim shook his head. "Will you shut up for a second? You are just like that woman Minx, always running ya'lls mouths . . . sheesh. Sometime you even look like her. Anyway, no, I'm not planning to dump her. She might be dumping me. I mean, Simi has been coming to visit her and they've been talking and after he leaves she's not really ya know . . . feeling me so we haven't really talked about *us* much. I don't want to push things so soon. She's not even divorced yet."

"Please, Simi is out of the picture. He's coming to beg . . . that's all. He got served and was like," Glen shook his head as if he'd been slapped hard in the face. "So gone with the old and in with the new dude . . . you besta state ya case," Glen assured.

Tim was surprised at his words. "You're really cool with this."

"Yeah man, I'm totally cool with whatever my aunt is cool with. You hurt her though and I'ma have ta hurt you back."

Tim was bigger and stronger than Glen and could easily take him in a fistfight but Tim understood Glen's intentions. "Got cha," he agreed, stepping into the elevator with a new attitude about things.

Glenda was staring at the blank monitor with tears streaming down her face when Tim entered her room. She quickly wiped at them.

"What's wrong, Glenda? Is there something wrong with Thea?"

"No, she's beautiful." Glenda smiled, holding up the last printed picture she was given before they shut the monitor down. "They took me off the transvaginal monitor. I can only hear her heartbeat now and I miss her," she said, as the tears flowed again. Tim moved over to the bed and, kicking off his shoes, pulled back the blanket and climbed in the bed next to her. She smiled weakly at him, allowing him to snuggle close to her, laying his hand carefully on her belly avoiding the heart monitor. He laid his head on her shoulder after kissing her cheek.

"So, what kind of flowers are we planting in that biggo backyard of yours?"

Chapter 22

The new year brought about many changes and from where Glenda sat, they were all pretty good. The big issues were behind her. Thea came a few weeks early. Tim assisted in the natural childbirth. She had to stay a while in the ICU but quickly reached five pounds and was able to come home.

During that time, Glenda had managed to divorce Simi without too much trouble after Candy brought him up on sexual harassment charges—that is before she realized he had no money. She dropped the case then but not before Glenda was able to use the evidence that Candy provided to obtain a divorce on the grounds of adultery. She also managed to get full custody of Thea since Simi had insisted on a blood test . . . a blood test, which only proved beyond a shadow of a doubt that by 99.99 percent Thea was his child. Unfortunately, for him, his groundless doubt over paternity along with his own promiscuous actions just made it easy for Glenda when they went to court. Simi didn't stand a chance at getting spousal support from Glenda either, considering she was unemployed now.

As far as their joint income was concerned, Glenda had

managed to tuck nearly all of her money away in Glen's name during the separation, which was never filed as a legal separation, and so her actions were not counted as impropriety. Nevertheless, Simi demanded his share of their joint income, but he was only able to get his share of the monies that came from the selling of their assets—the house, the car, the time-share in Laughlin, of which none of that stuff Glenda had any problem relinquishing. She didn't hate Simi, and besides, she didn't want Thea to think her parents didn't once love each other. Simi wasn't a bad person—just confused. All Glenda hoped was that soon he would get over his issues and at least come see his daughter . . . but she wasn't going to push that issue either. Thea was surely loved enough.

As soon as the divorce was final Glenda bought the house in Half Moon Bay. Minx came by often enough and now with Minx and Glenda's brother getting serious it looked as if she would truly be part of the family now. Glen came by every weekend for their cross-country run and seemed excited about his father dating Minx although he still was none the wiser that Minx was his biological mother.

Funny how that all worked out, Glenda thought now, while moving the log with the fireplace utensil. She'd managed to get the fireplace insert bought just in time for the first storm of the winter season. Half Moon Bay came with plenty of gray days and cool weather and so having a cozy fire to cuddle up in front of was going to be perfect. She had often dreamed of moments like this when she would stare at that picture stuck on that corkboard . . . what seemed like years ago now.

Thinking of Gerri, Glenda realized she owed her a phone call to thank her for the beautiful flower arrangement she'd sent. Gerri felt she owed Glenda a lot, Glenda knew than and so accepted her gifts graciously, even though she always figured that Gerri could have made the upward movements on her own when ever she got around to just concentrating on the important things in life.

Thea's cries came through the monitor loud and clear, catching Glenda off guard. "I thought she was asleep."

"Please, Thea nap over ten minutes? You must have her mixed up with somebody else's baby," Tim said with a chuckle.

"Leave my sweetie alone . . . she just doesn't want to miss anything."

Pulling her into an embrace, Tim kissed her sweet and long. "I think that is a sign of a lot of intelligence."

"Just like her mommy. She's gonna go far in life," Glenda bragged playfully, stroking the back of his neck tenderly. She never tired of touching him and vice versa.

"Do you regret anything, Glenda?" he asked, looking deep in her eyes for any crack in her brave front, any fault in her contentment.

"I have Thea, and you, our friends, my house . . ." she pointed at the assortment of jellies and preserves on the table, awaiting shipment. "My little home business," she said with a chuckle, as the venture, although relaxing and fun, had yet to turn much of a profit. "Tim, I wouldn't change this life for any I've had before."

Pulling her close he inhaled the scent of her hair and kissed her temple. "Maybe we should go take a nap," he whispered, sounding a little playful.

"But I'm not tired," she whispered back in the same flirty tone.

"I can change that," he said, his words holding out a promise she could not refuse. Smiling broadly, she took his hand and allowed him to lead her up the stairs to the room they shared as newlyweds, stopping only to scoop up Thea out of her crib on their way.

Katrina Blues

Maxine Thompson

Prologue

Coleman Blue

Lower Ninth Ward,
New Orleans, Louisiana,
August 25, 2004

When a Man Loves a Woman

"Blue'll kill ya about his wife," Cantrella, his mother-in-law, an avowed alcoholic, would spout out in her slurred, Gullah speech whenever she was having a drunken brawl with her boyfriend, Tank. "I'm a tell a him you was talkin' about Mellon."

"You a lie and the truth ain't in ya," Tank would retort back, throwing a beer bottle at Cantrella. This was the rhythm of all their Fridays from as far back as Coleman had known the family. He just took it that Tank was talking about Mellon; nothing with an ounce of truth to it. That was just drunk talk.

Now he hated to think back to that moment—to the very millimeter of a second of a heartbeat before something terrible happened. Something irreversible and unthinkable. If only he hadn't gone home early that night. . . .

Perhaps it was because of the full moon, perhaps because he'd just come off the road about a week ago and it had been a while, but for some reason, that Friday night Coleman was looking forward to going home and making love to Mellon, his wife of eight years. It was as if her raven-colored body and her exotic, slate-gray eyes were calling him. He felt his member rising just thinking of her.

That night, after he finished his gig at the Moonlight Jazz Chateau, he absently whistled "Love Jones." Striking up a blunt, he hurled his saxophone into his case, grabbed his gear, and was ready to get home to his wife.

"Leaving early tonight?" Malik, the drummer, who used to be his best friend, called out. Usually, after a set, Coleman hung around the club, riffing, messing around with new tunes, sometimes until five in the morning. Sometimes, he'd get home just as the sun was coming up. Even though he stayed out all night, other than a few lapses, he basically didn't cheat on Mellon in his mind. At least, he didn't cheat with his heart.

Mellon just did it for him. She was all the woman he wanted and needed, other than now and then when a groupie could talk him into a one-night stand.

Coleman looked at him and paused. "Good night." He was in a good mood. He could even forget the beef he had had with Malik for saying that Mellon was no good for him. He loved Mellon and he didn't care what anyone else said. He could already see himself pumping his way into that pyramid V between Mellon's legs. The girl's loving was so good it needed to be bottled and sold. And she had to be born with it. She'd had this same musky sensuality since she was a young girl. The first time Coleman went sniffing around her.

It was love at first sight for Coleman when he saw Mellon. He was sixteen and she was a gum-popping, sassy girl of thirteen. It was her Creole accent that he'd fallen in love with. Although she was a project girl, and his mother had warned him against her, he didn't mind. Truth be told, he was a project child himself—that is, before his father died and his mother, accompanied by her insurance money, bought their two-bedroom bungalow outside the projects. In 1997, when he returned home from the army where he'd served a tour of duty in Bosnia, Coleman married Mellon.

When he turned the corner at the far end of his street, because of the full moon, Coleman noticed but didn't pay attention to a familiar-looking Escalade parked under his neighbor Mrs. Wall's cottonwood tree. Still whistling, he cut off the radio when he pulled into his driveway.

Suddenly an electrical charge coursed through his body. Coleman felt his pulse start to race. Why was the house dark? Generally Mellon left the living room light on, as well as the porch light.

A twinge of danger ran up his back like a sour note in jazz. Heart trotting, fear propelled him up the stairs, foot sinking into the carpet, leg pushing leg, hand reaching over hand, up the banister. By the time he made it to the top landing, he heard them. The love noises, the bed squeaking. Crack, crack, squeak, squeak. Worse, he smelled them—the love funk.

As if in a trance, he followed the dim candlelight cast from under the doorway into the hallway. Stealthily, he opened the door; they were going at it like two dogs, oblivious to anything or anyone, but that moment. That image, frozen like some grotesque octopus in a piece of amber, would forever remain emblazoned in his psyche.

Methodically, Coleman stepped back out the room,

reached in his linen closet next to the bedroom door where he kept his Glock and pulled it out. Only the shock of recognition kept him surprisingly calm. He had killed before over in the war. But those were total strangers. These were not strangers. Now he knew where he'd seen that Escalade. It not only belonged to his quartet's piano player, its owner was his first cousin, Luke. Yes, Luke, in bed with his wife. Luke who had called in sick tonight.

With a flick of the wrist, Coleman cut on the light. The coupling ended abruptly; Mellon scrambled for the blanket to cover her nakedness. However, Luke was unable to hide the evidence of his transgression. His jones was still erect and slick with Mellon's oils.

"Blue, dawg . . ." Luke stammered.

"Blue, it's not what it look like. . . ." Mellon began crying.

"Luke, naw, man," was all Coleman could utter. His voice sounded far away like a shell-shocked man.

Dazed, Coleman cocked the gun.

Chapter 1

Deni

Los Angeles, California,
August 25, 2005,
Category One Storm

> *Hurricane Katrina had just become a Category One hurricane when the Moderate Resolution Imaging Spectroradiometer (MODIS) on NASA's Terra satellite captured this image on August 25, 2005, at 12:30 P.M., Eastern Daylight Savings Time.*

"Girl, are you pregnant again?"

Covering the phone's receiver, Deni ogled the watermelon bulge under her cousin Shana's caftan, and couldn't help from blurting out her naked thoughts. As she stood in the hallway, the old-fashioned black phone's receiver balanced on her neck like a snake handler, she didn't know if she was more shocked at Shana's pregnancy, as by her cousin's nonchalant attitude. The only thing, which reeled her back, was the male voice on the other end of the line.

"Miss, are you still there?"

Wiping her brow, Deni code switched back into her professional voice. "Sir, I'm checking on a Shawn George Lockwood, date of birth 10-15-73."

"Yes, we have a Shawn George Lockwood."

"May I have his inmate number?" She turned and whispered to her little second cousin, Unique. "Cut the TV down, so I can put this number in my Blackberry."

The room was filled with the blare of some upcoming hurricane called Katrina and Deni could hardly hear the inmate clerk's voice on the other end of the phone.

The eleven-year-old scrambled to lower the dial on the old-fashioned floor model television plopped dead center in the cramped living room.

Meantime, Deni blew her bangs out of her eyes and fanned her perspiring face. She sure missed her air conditioning from her near-beachfront condo in Santa Monica. She punched the number into her Blackberry.

Although her mouth voiced words, her mind was on her cousin, Shana, who already had six children, a boisterous brood of "Be Be's kids," ranging in ages from eleven to two, one Afro-puff behind another cornrowed head, and outlandish, Afrocentric names, which would plague them the rest of their lives, as far as Deni was concerned.

"Girl, you crazy." Shana threw her head back and laughed at Deni's outburst. Her face was as clear and simple as a raindrop on a palmetto leaf—everything reflected beneath came to the surface.

What you see is what you get, Deni mused. *It doesn't seem to bother her at all.*

Here Shana was, only thirty-three and having a seventh baby. Hmmph. As if she was the world's greatest mother. As if she had a silver spoon in her mouth. As if her husband, Lionel, had more than a menial job as a school janitor. Didn't she know about birth control in this new millennium? Without knowing it, Deni twisted her lips in disgust. Shana was hopelessly lost.

As soon as Deni hung up the phone, she noticed that Shana's face had curved into waves of defiance, but she could care less. Her mind was on Shana's daughter Samari who was ferreting through her purse.

"Get out my purse!" she screeched at the five-year-old, knowing full well Shana didn't play that about her kids. Shana didn't want anyone to reprimand any of her children.

Deni didn't care. She just wanted to keep all sticky, stubby fingers off her Prada purse and her Versace suit. With a firm grip, she pried her purse out of the little girl's fingers, then clutched it to her chest. It wasn't just her money that she was worried about. It was that damned letter. Her purse contained a letter, the one she didn't want her cousin to know about. The letter from that man—that stranger, claiming to be her biological father. Right now, the letter still burned a hole into her psyche. Like kryptonite, it had the same power to blow her fragile, hard-won security out the water.

Shana rushed forth and gathered Samari in her arms. "Leave Cuda Mama alone! She didn't do nothin'!" She gave Deni a defiant glare. Shana also loved nicknaming her children in even more ridiculous names than their birth names.

Peeking from under her mother's embrace, Samari gave her a "See there!" glare.

Deni changed the subject. "Where's Mother Ticey?" She looked away, hoping to circumvent the collision she knew was coming almost as inevitably as the New Orleans Katrina hurricane they'd been warning about on the news all week. Why had she come over here anyhow?

But Deni knew the reason. Whenever she was upset,

instead of going to her immaculate condominium in Santa Monica, she came to this wall-to-wall, peopled place to draw solace. In spite of its run-down appearance, this Charoite-vine–covered stucco house, with its worn-around-the-edges look, held so much love, it oozed out of the corners like a full cherry pie. This home also held her maternal grandmother, Mama Ticey (whom Deni had recently begun calling Mother Ticey), who had a way of bringing in light, making the house have a palatial feel. Crimson bougainvilleas clustered around the sagging porch and gave the house a cozy character, even though it stood at the edge of the Jordan Down projects.

Today, Deni had come home seeking peace, but instead, found herself in the midst of what she called "the crazy farm." She'd also wanted to talk to her grandmother about this alleged father of hers.

Instead, here she was, already upset by this cursed letter, then next she'd found out her first cousin, Shawn, whom everyone called Slammer, was back in jail, facing a third strike. Then, as if to add a clincher to her day, she discovered that Shana (Slammer's twin), her silly behind cousin, was pregnant for the seventh time. Aye-yi-yi. How come you couldn't pick your own family? Her family was completely off the chain.

The next thing Deni knew, Shana had blocked her path in the hallway, feet planted firmly, arms akimbo, head waving from side to side, as she bleated, "So what's all this tom 'bout 'you-pregnant-again?' Correct me if I'm wrong, but as I recall, I am married—unlike some people who got left at the altar like a whore's panties." Shana's lips curled into a nasty slur. Shana gave the word *married* about four syllables with her verbal facility.

"Hey! Don't go getting ballistic on me!" Deni knew that Shana was intentionally making a stab at her manless, childless, weddingless state of being. This jab was also to remind Deni of her wedding fiasco from last year, at which she'd been jilted at the altar, in spite of six bridesmaids, six groomsmen, and the whole nine yards. Shana's insult was meant to crush her. *It did*.

But years of growing up with her abrasive, outspoken ghetto-ass cousins had taught her the art of "comeback."

"Besides," Deni added, deliberately holding her nose high in the air, "I don't need a man to validate my worth."

Around her roughshod relatives, she knew she had to wear a callous carapace—even if it was a facade, even if she knew she was being as fraudulent as a three-dollar-bill.

Before the two women's harsh words could escalate into the war zone of no return, as if out of nowhere Mama Ticey hobbled into the small dining room, smoothing the air with her butter-bread warmth. Several of her great-grandchildren, Ketourian, Ian, Samari aka Cuda Mama, and Miss Muff, arms hanging wreathlike around her sweet-potato-shaped waist in a hug, clustered about her. Her familiar scent of Juicy Fruit gum and sarsaparilla lingered in the air.

"You two at it again," Mama Ticey entreated. "Fightin' est cousins I ever saw. Ever since you were girls, you've been fussing. Now kiss and make up."

Just as suddenly as a summer shower will stop, the two women ceased arguing. Not only the bearer of peace, Mama Ticey knew how to smooth over dissension. Although the cousins didn't make up, they broke into welcome for Mama Ticey, each woman taking a bag out of her arms.

"Miss Emma couldn't give me any money to help get Slammer out of jail, but she sure gave me some pretty turnips and mustards. Shana, you feel like cleaning them for your old Mama Ticey?" Miss Emma was Mama Ticey's next door neighbor.

"Yes, ma'am." Shana took one of Deni's bags from her

arms, stuck out her tongue at Deni, then turned and dawdled into the adjacent kitchen.

"Deni, you hear about Shawn?" Mama Ticey asked. Her hands, which never rested, settled on Miss Muff's head. Absently, she began to replait a braid that had unraveled. Everyone called Shana's seven-year-old daughter Miss Muff. Anyhow, Deni could hardly remember what the child's real ghetto-fabulous name was. *I Let You Queen*. That was it. *Shana needed to quit.*

Deni listened for what her grandmother didn't say. Mama Ticey didn't mention the fact that Slammer already had two strikes, or felonies, and this would be his third felony—which, by California's three-strike law, could end up costing him a life sentence.

"Yes, I did, Mother Ticey. I see he's at it again. This time the charge is receiving and concealing stolen goods. The bail is fifty-five thousand, which is fifty-five hundred cash. This is ridiculous. I know you better not put this house up with the bondsman. Grandaddy left this house for you. Besides, when is Shawn ever going to learn?"

"Oh, now, Deni. The boy just made a mistake. Always was high-spirited." Mama Ticey gave a sigh mixed with part-resignation, part-love, and part-admiration.

"Mother Ticey, with all due respect, but the boy is thirty-three years old." Deni heard her usually soprano voice raise an octave and crack.

"Well, he's still a boy to me."

"Well, he's not a boy when he goes and breaks the law."

"I think I'll pawn my diamond earrings."

Suddenly all the starch left Deni's speech and she reverted to her childhood name for her grandmother. "No, you won't, Mama Ticey! I bought those for you, and I'll take them back before I see you pawn them on Slammer. He's not worth it!"

Suddenly Shana hurtled as swiftly as a quarterback out of the kitchen. Her hands, still wet from picking the greens, whirled around her head, windmill fashion, reminding Deni of the movie *The Matrix*.

"Hey, wait a minute, Miss Muckety-Muck! Don't come over here showboating. Thank you so much 'cause you got a little education. Thank you because you drive a Mercedes and don't live in the 'hood no more that you're better than us.

"But you ain't no better than nobody. You still one of us. I think we saw that at your little wedding last year, which by the way, my friends still laugh about."

Deni ignored this remark. "Wait a minute!" She stepped up to Shana, knowing her gangster-acting cousin would put her lights out if it wasn't for her pronounced pregnancy, yet emboldened by her anger, Deni pointed her finger in her face. "You had a better chance at going to college than I did. I worked my ass off for what I have, and if you didn't take advantage of your opportunities, that's your business. I'm sick and tired of this mess. Every time Slammer's ass goes to jail, I see I'm the first person y'all call on. But this time, he can rot in there for all I care." Deni crossed her arms in a "There!" symbol.

"You don't mean that, Deni," Mama Ticey interceded. "You're just upset. You know blood thicker than water."

Mama Ticey appeared so distraught that Deni threw her hands up. She definitely didn't want to run her grandmother's blood pressure up, so she stalked into the old bedroom she used to sleep in as a child. Deni looked around the room as if seeing it for the first time. Secondhand furniture and worn-out looking twin quilts, which Mother Ticey made by hand. Everything was neat and orderly. No clothes or paper on the floor. The brown carpet bore broom marks where it had received its daily sweeping. Pictures graced the walls of three generations. Her late Grandpa Amos Richards, her grandmother, Mama Ticey, her late mother, Esther, and a shipload of relatives. This is the way it had always been for her. No father in the picture. She'd never felt his absence either, so why did she need him now.

Before she could let out a scream or slam a brush down on the dresser bureau, Deni noticed that Shana's baby, Diamond, was curled up sleeping on the very same quilt she used to curl up in.

She settled for a virulent hissing through her nose and clenching of her fists until her nails left half-moon marks in her palms. Something was wrong with this whole picture, Deni decided. Here she was, supposedly part of the "Talented Tenth," which W.E.B. DuBois had regaled in *The Souls of Black Folk*.

But if anything, her gifts, her talents, her intellect, only served to alienate her from her family, her roots. "I just can't relate to Black people," she said out loud. "Even if this is my family."

And men. That was another sad story. Like a person finding bitter meat inside of a much-desired cracked nut, her mind lingered over an incident, which had taken place earlier that afternoon. Just as she was healing from what happened with her former fiancé, professional playa, Black Businessman of the Year, Trent McGee, she'd been flirting with the idea of stepping back out into the dating game.

Currently, to pass time, she was sleeping with a married accountant named Ronald McClellan, with whom she had no desire to have a long-term relationship, but who, for now, was just a "tune-up, get-through-the-hard-times" lover. Unfortunately, after each lustful encounter she felt as cheap as a two-dollar crack whore. She knew she had to end this liaison; but at this time, she just didn't have the strength to do it.

Earlier that afternoon, when Deni had headed out of the employees parking lot during the lunch break, she'd noticed the carmine red convertible Jaguar that she'd been eyeing surreptitiously for the past month. It belonged to the only other Black county counsel—in fact the only Black male attorney on the panel. Before his arrival, she'd been the only African-American dependency court attorney on the panel in their assigned courtroom.

Its owner, Hollis Winfield, was a rugged, muscular brother. They'd spoken briefly in the elevator, when he first started work about a month earlier. She wanted to invite Hollis to a casual lunch with her. Deni had started to blow her horn at him. As it turned out, she was grateful she hadn't. When she caught a glimpse of strawberry-blond hair cascading out of the window of the rider's side, she recognized the woman as his secretary.

Why did all the professional brothers feel they needed a white woman on their arm to complete their image of success? Although Deni, as a child dependency court-appointed attorney, could go do battle in a courtroom like any man, she wanted to be able to rest in someone's arms when she came home at night. She wanted to be able to nestle her head in that little spot between a man's neck and his shoulders. She wanted to lay her career down—if only for a little while. She thought about Trent, and although her public humiliation still stung after a year, this was better than if she'd wound up married to someone who didn't love her.

Glancing down at the sleeping baby, hair curlicued into about thirty circular braids, thumb stuck in her mouth, Deni felt something thawing inside of her. A debacle of denial. In its place, a new emotion, as inchoate as the first unfurling leaves of a rosebud, began to open up inside of her.

She did want a baby—exactly what other women wanted. She didn't want to miss out on her chance at motherhood, but she knew she didn't want to have a baby without a husband, even though many of her friends were doing it. Lord knows, she hadn't forgotten how hard her mother had struggled to raise her by herself. And now to find some snake, claiming to be her father, had crawled from beneath a rock thirty-four years after the fact, it was just too much to take right now!

Hell to the twentieth degree no! If she was married and settled, perhaps she'd feel different. But she kind of felt like it was this absent father's fault in the first place. If he'd stuck around, she'd know how to act with men and how not to be so independent. All she knew was being strong like her mother. Even though she had a good income, she didn't want to be responsible for a child without benefits of a mate.

She paused. Maybe, she was being a bitch about Shana's pregnancy. Maybe she was jealous. Jealous of Shana? Deni found the thought too unsettling.

Chapter 2

Coleman

August 29, 2005,
Category Five Storm

> *Breaking news. Katrina is no longer just brewing in the Gulf. New Orleans residents are warned to evacuate. We've upgraded Katrina to a Category Five storm. Please evacuate New Orleans.*

As long as he lived, he would never forget how the winds sounded like a jazz riff with a woman moaning and giving birth at the bottom of a well. The winds of God's choir were enraged; Mother Nature gone awry. Later, he regretted that he'd waited so late to get out. The next time, if there'd be a next time, when they said "run," he would run.

Faces drawn tight, fear etching every move they made, they'd thrown everything they could into his Ford Explorer.

"Daddy, can I take my skateboard?" Britton had asked

when they left their three-bedroom ranch brick house. "Can I take my Power Ranger too?"

"Okay. Just one thing."

"You still gon' buy me my own saxophone?" Britton gave Coleman a serious look.

"Not now, Britton. We'll talk about that later."

So Britton picked his metallic skateboard with the blue-black background bearing silver decals on it.

"Daddy, let me get my blankie," Blossom said. That was all Blossom wanted. That old faded, bedraggled baby blanket. He'd bought that blanket when she was a baby. Without her saying it, Coleman knew the blankie reminded Blossom of her vague memories and the smells of her mother who'd run off when she was three going on four.

Most of all, he would have never believed that Katrina would take away the levees. He'd always remember the sounds of cars crashing through the air, the roar of the muddy waters roiled by Katrina, the drenched homes and neighborhoods. At the end of the storm, over eighteen hundred were confirmed dead. Until the day he died, the dreadful roar would haunt his nightmares.

All his life he'd grown up hearing that a hurricane could hit New Orleans, but he didn't believe it. That's why he'd evacuated so late.

For the last eight hours, his vision could only see the long trail of cars ahead of him and the ones behind him, on the Interstate 10, cars he presumed like his own, which were filled with fear. He hoped his Ford Explorer would make it to Los Angeles, which was his destination. For some reason, he felt called to go to LA. He heard this was a place a saxophonist like himself could always get work.

After a while, surrounded by the darkening buffalo of

clouds, everything looked as wavy as a mirage. His eyes began to water just when the cell phone rang, interrupting the deadly silence in the car. He recognized the number as that of fellow musician Malik's.

"Y'at, Blue?" In New Orleans, they used to say, "Where you at," now it had been abbreviated to "Y'at?"

"I'm still in New Orleans, but I'm trying to get me and my babies and my mother out of here."

"Man, the storm is coming in. I made it to my sister's house in Baton Rouge. Where you headed?"

His fellow musician friend Malik and everyone he knew had scattered to the four parts of the earth. Suddenly his cell phone blanked out. Blue clicked it shut.

"I'm scared, Daddy," Britton said.

"Don't worry." Coleman didn't feel so sure himself.

His mother, whom everyone called Miss Johntrice, began to pray, holding her Bible to her lips. "Lord, please deliver us safely." A devout Catholic, she also held her rosary beads to her lips and fingered them nervously. "This reminds me of the hurricane when I was a little girl and the bridge was blown out."

"Oh, yeah?" Coleman said absently, but his mind was on when they evacuated. "What happened?"

"My mother went into labor and delivered my youngest sister, your Aunt Miracle."

"So that's how Auntie got her name?"

"That's how most Black people got their name . . . Your daddy used to say that."

Coleman chuckled nervously, remembering his father who had taught him how to play the saxophone. His late father had been a musician too. His mother, with her genteel ways, was paraphrasing how her husband, the satyr, used to say it. "Niggaz get they name catch as catch can," he used to say.

Miss Johntrice added, "It was a miracle that any of us made it through other than by prayer."

"Daddy, do you think Mommy's okay?" Blossom interrupted.

"She'll be all right."

Chapter 3

Deni

Los Angeles, California,
Category Two Storm

As she stared down at her mother's faded sepia high school graduation picture, Deni tried to remember her. Because her mother, Esther, had always worked two jobs, which had afforded Deni the privilege of attending private Catholic school as a child, she'd spent most of her time over at Mama Ticey's surrounded by a shipload of cousins. Although Esther had given birth to Deni when she was only seventeen, there were no remembrances of her mother ever being young and frivolous. Esther had been a stern, serious young woman. After Deni's birth, she had been baptized as a Catholic and just about led the life of a nun.

In spite of her relatives, Deni had been rather shielded as a child. She was a grown woman before she realized that the reason she'd worn the same two blouses every other day with her school uniform was that she had no other blouses. Her mother used to wash her blouses out by hand every night. Sifting through each precious sliver of memory of her mother—her hard-working mother—Deni knew her mother's short existence had spanned so briefly because she lived on about four hours of sleep after Deni's birth.

Following Deni's graduation from high school, her mother had a stroke and collapsed. Shortly thereafter, Esther died. So whenever Deni had wanted to give up throughout the years of struggle in undergraduate school, then later, law school, the specter of her mother's life pushed her forward. She made it on grants, scholarships, and loans until she graduated.

But thinking of her cousins, Shana and Shawn, it didn't make sense how trifling they'd both turned out. Deni was raised in the same environment and managed to pull herself up by her bootstraps, so why couldn't her cousins have done better?

As far as Deni was concerned, they'd had a better chance at making it in life than she had. Shana and Shawn were both the pampered progeny of her Aunt Martha and Uncle Earl. They had had the luxury of two parents, something Deni had never known, as well as a live-in grandmother, Mama Ticey. She didn't even know who her father was—that is until this letter came from this stranger alleging he was her biological father.

In fact, the first three years of her life, Esther had lived with her mother, Mama Ticey, and Aunt Martha and Uncle Earl, who still lived together to this day.

Deni and Shana and her twin brother had been born months apart and raised together in subtle competition. If Deni made an A on a paper in school, Aunt Martha was hell-bent that Shana would get an A, even if it meant doing the paper herself. It had always been assumed that Shana would go to college (even if Deni and her mother, Esther,

knew Shana was as learning challenged as a salt shaker),
so when Shana got married to her high school sweetheart
and began to produce baby after baby, Aunt Martha had
been devastated.

Deni knew in her heart how Aunt Martha felt. That it
was Esther's illegitimate daughter who'd turned out to
be the family's successful child. A Los Angeles County
dependency court attorney, to boot. Deni, the one who
lived in a four-bedroom, spotless condo in Santa
Monica—how could she afford it by herself?—and drove
that nice, expensive car? Hmm, mmm, mmm.

To compensate for her deflated hopes and dreams for
her daughter, Aunt Martha would make over Shana's kids
excessively. Especially in front of Deni. Her aunt even pretended to be pleased with Shana having so many children.

"Oooh, my baby Shana has another little one in the
oven," she'd coo. "When are you going to get married
and have some babies?" Aunt Martha would often chide
Deni. "You aren't getting any younger."

Remarks like this would set a conflagration smoldering
in Deni's heart. Didn't her family know that if she could find
a qualified African-American man—one with what she
considered a comparable education—who didn't already
have a harem of women, she'd get married?

Whoever she married would have to be someone of
equivalent educational standing. Her former fiancé, Trent,
had possessed the education, but he already had a full
life, one too full of himself that there was not enough
room for Deni. One that also included another woman, as
she'd found out after her aborted wedding.

The door cracked open, slanting a sliver of light into
the darkened room. Deni was surprised to see Shana
step into the room.

"Hey, girl." Shana averted her gaze from Deni. "Forget what I said. I'm just stressed out. Slammer is going to be the death of us all."

Deni couldn't believe Shana was offering an apology. She knew how hard it was for her cousin to go against the grain of her proud nature, but she also knew that Shana had an ulterior motive. Shana was only making up so that Deni could post bail for her fraternal twin, Slammer. Still—

"Hey, girl," Deni conceded. This was the way they had always made up as children. In a seamless, language-without-words communion.

Deni had an idea. "There's this new restaurant called Masquerades down in the marina. Let's run over there for dinner."

"I ain't got no restaurant money."

"No, it's on me."

Marina Del Rey

The line was so long at Masquerades that it wound around the outside of the restaurant like a boa constrictor and contracted onto the pier.

Besides the seafood being fresh, Deni had always loved how the waiters and waitresses wore masks, reminding you of the old Parisian masquerade parties. The sophisticated ambiance inside the oceanfront restaurant matched the celebratory atmosphere. Violin music decorated the air.

While the two women waited, leaning against the balustrade, Deni looked out over at the ocean. The waves capped and curved into a dark undertow. The sky had an ethereal quality, as the pink penumbra of the sunset left a lurid track following its descent into the ocean. Seagulls screamed a requiem to one another as they dived onto the ocean's surface, trying to catch fish. Turning away, Deni tried to make small talk.

"Did you have the ultrasound or get those four-D sonogram pictures?" Deni knew about 4-D sonograms because a coworker named Ashley Winbleckler had brought in her sonogram pictures, which actually showed impressions of the baby's face in the uterus.

"No, I like to be surprised."

"What do you want—a girl or a boy?"

Deni felt like a hypocrite, knowing that her first reaction had not been more diplomatic.

Shana let out a sigh and shrugged her shoulders.

"When is the baby due?"

"About the first of the year."

Deni stopped talking and decided to let the conversation die. Shana just wasn't on the same plateau with her.

As the line inched its way into the inside vestibule of the restaurant, Deni noticed that they were standing in front of a full-length mirror. Furtively, Deni studied herself and her cousin's reflections.

Without a doubt, she was the better dressed of the two women, with her matching black leather pumps, her power suit, and designer purse. She wondered which one of them looked the oldest. In all fairness, though, Shana still had some of her former youthful looks in that her arms and legs were still slim.

In fact, when she wasn't pregnant, she surprisingly had retained the figure of a teenager. Deni studied how Shana's back arched like a bow, her legs waddled, her hands placed in the small of her back.

But still, with the stresses of childbearing, the only salient feature remaining about Shana's face was her twin, blue-gray-flecked eyes. In her face, which had once been as lush and pretty as a mango, they had pronounced her to be a stunning beauty as a teen. Now, with the vestiges of all her pregnancies sagging at the corner, her face resembled a round cantaloupe. She wore her husband's name tattooed on her neck. Deni cringed inside. *Tacky.*

Even so, to talk to her, Deni felt she was still talking to the former teenager she had known. The irony of it all was that Shana seemed to be frozen in time, suspended somewhere psychologically at age nineteen or twenty, when she'd given birth to her first child. Deni decided then and there if she ever got married and had a baby, she would not vegetate and become stagnant as Shana had.

Deni wanted to tell Shana how ghettoish the cornrows looked, and that the three earrings lining each earlobe were too "teenybopperish." She thought of the jokes, "You know you're ghetto when . . ." She itched to suggest that Deni shouldn't wear the African-looking kente cloth if she ever went on an interview. And maybe she could have the tattoo *Lionel* removed from her neck. Not that Shana had ever intimated that she even wanted a job. But using her better judgment, Deni held her tongue. Why risk cracking this thin layer of peace temporarily sustained between them?

Still, but, how could Shana stand her life? Deni began to muse over all the good things about her own life, such as her credit card, which was going to pay for whatever Shana selected and her lobster dinner, when she heard Shana ask the waiter, "Excuse me, sir. How much longer do you think it'll be?"

The waiter, who was dressed in the Masquerades black jacket and tie uniform, accompanied by a Zorro mask, was brusque. "I don't know."

Shana turned back to Deni. "I've got to get back to my kids."

"It shouldn't be too much longer, Shana," Deni assured her.

Less than ten minutes later, the same waiter escorted two white women to a table. The women had arrived at the Masquerades considerably later than Deni and Shana.

"Did you see that?" Shana's voice held the threatening crackle of lightning slashing an indigo sky.

"Don't worry. I'm sure it's a mistake," Deni said, touching Shana's arm, which had tightened up in her grip.

Deni could see the beginning of the swelling look— the one she knew resembled a swelling toad, which generally preceded Shana's "going off."

"I come here all the time," Deni added. She thought of how often she had come to this restaurant with her white colleague attorneys, Jennifer and Megan, from work and had been waited on promptly. True enough, she'd never gone to Masquerades at night, but she had always thought they provided excellent service. For the first time, Deni noticed that they were the only two African-Americans in the restaurant.

The same waiter, who had brushed Shana off as one might flick a flea off his sleeve, sauntered by. It was very apparent this time that his intent was to seat the white family who stood behind them in the line. Shana tapped the maître d' on the shoulder. The man stopped in his tracks. He stared at Shana's sable hand lightly pressing against his starched white shirt, as if it were a snake.

"Hey, I think you made a mistake, mister. We were here first." Shana's voice sounded controlled.

"Miss, lower your voice or we will have to ask you to leave the premises."

"What? Tell me something, sir. Don't our money spend just as good as theirs? I always thought it was 'first come, first served.'"

"Lady," the waiter said in a condescending tone, "I will have to call security and have you put out of here if you don't stop disturbing the peace."

Deni tried to interrupt, to mediate the situation, before it got further out of hand. "This is all a misunderstanding, sir. I can explain."

Shana was not to be placated that easily. "You won't have to put us out. We are leaving. Ain't that right, cuz?"

Shana waited patiently for Deni's reply. For a moment, Deni's feet felt glued to the floor. They turned into blocks of sludge. The professional side of her wanted to apologize and explain the idiosyncrasies of her Black clients whenever she approached the bench.

Suddenly, she remembered Shana taking up for her when she was eight years old, when a gang of bullies tried to beat her up after school one day. That was one day she'd been happy that her cousin was crazy enough to go up against three older girls. They'd left her alone after that.

Deni started to tremble all over as an emotion long denied bivouacked in her heart. She was angry. Angry over the injustice that she'd witnessed in the courtroom earlier that day when an African-American mother lost all four of her children in what should have been a family law custody case. The father was married and had money. In America, money still talked and as they said, BS walked.

Outraged over the sense of rejection she'd felt when she saw the only brother down at court taking out his white secretary to lunch. Unmasking the ropes of professionalism she wore, a silver glimmer slugged her in the solar plexus, leaving her breathless. What made her think she had more sense than Shana?

What made her think she was the one better off? Was she? At least Shana didn't have to pretend she didn't know an insult when she saw one. Now what was crazier than that? Before Deni could will her feet into motion, a security guard materialized.

"Miss, I think you two will have to leave."

The words finally found a shape in her head and issued out of her mouth. "Wait a minute, mister. You don't have to put us out. We are leaving. You'll be hearing from my attorney tomorrow. And here's my card."

The security guard looked down at the card, then threw it in the trash.

Deni took Shana's arm, as they simultaneously threw their heads up with dignity. Deni felt fibers inside of her reconnecting with something quintessential that she'd lost, but which upon finding, the tapestry felt more whole.

"Yeah, sho' you right, cuzz!" Shana joined in, slamming the restaurant door with a resounding echo.

Chapter 4

Coleman

August 29, 2005

What Makes a Man?

It was funny the things you thought about while sitting in a car, inching along a crowded, gridlocked freeway, not knowing if you were going to live or die.

Coleman thought about how he'd bought the blankie for Blossom when she was a baby. How he'd learned too late that Mellon had what they called a "yellow liver." How she was a straight-out nymphomaniac. How she had the nerve to have the baby's blankie thrown across the headboard when he caught her in the act, legs straddled over Luke's shoulders.

Now that hurt. Perhaps he could've taken it better if Luke hadn't been family. No, he couldn't have. Didn't matter that now and then he'd slipped up, but at least he'd been discreet when he was creeping. Anyhow, what kind of woman would bring her man home to her own house?

So all the rumors had been true.

Thinking about it, now that was enough to make a man lose his mind or catch a case such as in Ron Isley's joint, "Contagious." The only reason he hadn't killed Mellon was because of Blossom. He had felt something tugging at his pants leg and looked down and saw his baby, rubbing the sleep out her eyes.

"Daddy, I want a drink of water."

Had it not been for Blossom, he didn't know what he would've done. He had calmly closed the bedroom door, woke up Britton, and without saying a word, drove his children over to his mother's house. When he returned to his home with his loaded gun, Mellon and Luke had disappeared. He never saw them again.

It's funny how a small thing like that could change someone's destiny. Blossom's needing a glass of water was the thing that had brought him back from the brink. But now he felt like less than a man that he didn't kill the two people he'd once loved who were defiling the marriage bed.

What was a man after all? He thought of a man from his neighborhood, Willie Ben, who had found his wife in a compromising position in a car with another man. He'd shot and killed his wife, then turned the gun on himself and committed suicide.

Underneath Coleman was glad he didn't kill either of the adulterous couple or himself. He guessed the comedians were right. You couldn't make a housewife out of a hoe. After his experience with Mellon, he didn't trust women. He'd have a woman just to release himself— almost a way of wreaking vengeance on the female gender. Just when they would get hooked on him, he'd do the old disappearing act. No, everything still felt too raw to him to expose himself. He didn't think he'd ever go there again with a woman—that is, love one like he'd loved Mellon.

Now, because of his children, he was glad he hadn't done what he wanted to do, what he still wished he'd done just for the sanguine satisfaction. The truth was he didn't want to go to penitentiary or worse, even get the chair. Secretly, he was glad it had worked out this way. Naw, Mellon wasn't worth dying for.

He still wasn't healed. Once he got back to the house, his mother moved in with him and they had built a nice life together. He worked nights and didn't have to worry about a babysitter. He had no regrets about Mellon leaving, but sometimes he fantasized he'd shot her. The pleasure he vicariously would have received in seeing her bullet-riddled body. . . . Yet, in his crazy way, he still loved Mellon; he just could never forgive her.

At the same time, he was glad that his ex-wife Mellon was no longer in his life. Here he'd finally gotten a little safety net going for his children, and Mellon had moved away with Luke and then, just when he was finally able to exhale a little, life dealt this blow—Katrina, which hit, knocking the wind out of his epicenter. Just when he thought everything was finally getting under control. . . .

He'd never been more afraid in his life. Would he and his family live? Would they make it to safety? Never in a million years did he believe that the levees would break. Somehow, he'd have to keep his mother, Miss Johntrice, his eight-year-old son, Britton, and five-year-old daughter, Blossom, safe.

Driving, heart pounding, and the deafening silence in the car, made him make a vow to God. If he lived, he'd give up smoking blunt. He'd give up sleeping with women who he didn't have any feelings for. His thoughts turned to all the old albums he'd listened to that taught him to play the saxophone. Coleman "Hawk" Hawkins, Charlie "Bird"

Parker, Cannonball Adderley, John Coltrane. He had left them behind. That was what he would miss the most.

Why didn't he get his family out sooner? Why didn't he keep an emergency disaster kit in the house? Regret washed over him as he inched along the highway.

His only consolation was this. At least they were in better shape than many of the residents. Hopefully, his friends and fans from the nightclub would be able to get out.

Chapter 5

Deni

Los Angeles, California
August 29, 2005
Category Three Storm

> *People pay for what they do. And still more, for what they allow themselves to become. Moreover, they pay for it simply by the lives they lead.*
>
> —James Baldwin

"I swear, Shawn, this is the last time I'm getting you out," Deni fussed as Slammer slid into the buttercream leather seats next to her in her Mercedes. They were sitting in front of the Los Angeles County Correctional Twin Towers Jail. The Los Angeles smog had just lifted at noon and sun rays were finally piercing the clouds. The August day was not sweltering; in fact, it had been a somewhat chilly month for August. She didn't know herself what had changed her mind about Slammer, but something about what happened at the restaurant when she was with Shana had stirred the fight up in her. After all, he was family.

"Yeah, yeah, yeah." Slammer clicked on his seat belt.

"Don't get smart. I'll get you locked back up."

"Okay, cuz."

Deni revved up her engine. As she pulled off, she switched the radio to 92.3 the Beat. She had been listening to the classical music station, but because she didn't want Slammer to know, she cut the radio off when he got in the car. She headed for the 101 Interchange Freeway. The palm trees sped backward in a blur as she merged onto the freeway.

"Now, the first thing I want you to do is go find a job. It will look good when you go back before the judge." Deni switched over to the fast lane where she could drive at her usual 70 MPH speed.

"Look, when you've been locked up, it's hard to get a job," Slammer protested.

"Save it. I know one thing. You better get a job so you can pay me back my money."

Deni began to mumble as though her cousin wasn't present. She wanted him to hear her thoughts. "One thing I know for sure. When you around seven broke nuccas, you're going to be the eighth one." Deni began mentally balancing her checkbook.

She'd wound up taking 5,000 dollars out of her personal checking account to pay Slammer's bail.

"Look, cuz, I really appreciate what you did for me."

"Why don't you do something productive with your life?"

"When did you start talking so proper?"

"Oh, because I speak standard English I'm speaking proper. If you spoke it, perhaps you could find a job."

"Society doesn't want me to rehabilitate. Every time I put in for a job, they say you're an ex-con."

"Well, you know you have to see your probation officer and you also have to find a job. I pulled some strings to get you out. You know you got two strikes now." Ever since Deni's ordeal, as she now preferred to call her waltz down the wedding aisle, she had thrown herself into her work. As a result, she'd covered a lot of cases for other attorneys who now owed her favors.

"I know, I know. The system is set, Deni. They make money every time they lock a brother up—just like in slavery. They get free labor."

"I don't want to hear your excuses. You mess up again, I'll help you get that third strike."

"Don't be sweatin' me. All I know how to do is hustle and that's always been my thing."

"Well, it doesn't seem to be working too well."

"You think I wanna work at McDonald's or some hamburger joint at my age?"

"Why not? It's an honest living."

"Well, I was tryin' to get my entrepreneur hustle going. I was selling clothes and things like in John Singleton's movie *Baby Boy*."

"Shawn, you can't be selling hot clothes."

"It's easy for you to say, laying up there in Santa Monica in your nice condo with your swimming pool and shit."

"I earned it, fool."

"Well, I just don't want to be a sellout."

"Sellout?"

"Yeah."

"Oh, you're trying to say I'm a sellout?"

Slammer didn't say anything, as if he knew he'd gone too far as it was.

After they drove off the Harbor Freeway, Slammer

changed the subject. "Hey, cuz. Could you stop over at Mama Cheng's store and get me some hog headcheese? That's all I've been craving. They don't have that in the joint."

"Well, where did you think you were? In a country club?"

"Aw, cuz, don't be like that," Slammer laughed as Deni pulled over to a corner store at Crenshaw and Stocker. A group of men clustered around the corner store, holding bottles of forty-ounce malt liquors and smoking blunts. The smell of marijuana permeated the air.

Beauty salons, Jamaican restaurants, candle shops huddled on the main thoroughfare. Black Muslim brothers selling bean pies, and young men selling "bootleg" DVDs stood on the corners and in the medians by the red lights. Everyone was selling or buying.

Suddenly Slammer stuck his head out the window and threw out both hands in the "gimme five" sign.

A man with his hair braided in cornrows called out, "Hey, Killah. Wassup?"

"It's all copacetic."

"Attitude, dawg, when did you get out?" Slammer called out. Deni cringed. Slammer acted as though he was at some type of class reunion.

"Last week." Deni observed that the man called Attitude also looked as if he had a bad one at that. Unconsciously, Deni moved her purse closer to her chest. Where did her cousin meet all these renegades?

Another man wearing a black scarf on his head and sagging pants, who sat in a wheelchair, questioned Slammer, "Man, when you get out?"

Slammer stayed in the car, bellowing out words as though he was on a loudspeaker. "Yeah, P Dog, they let a nigga out this morning."

Deni couldn't take it anymore. "Can't you try to change, Shawn? You're about to kill your parents. You need to get off the chitlin' circuit." Deni sucked her teeth in disgust.

"Yeah, I'm gonna do better, counselor." Slammer spoke in a placating voice.

The words from the street-corner men flew through the window like jackals. "Dig this, mahfucker."

"Check this out, dawg."

"Stay up, baby boy."

"Hey so you out?"

Deni couldn't believe it. The men gathered around her car and carried on as though Slammer was some hero returned from the Iraq War. Was jail the new graduation system? Deni smirked.

Three hood rat-looking girls with attached individual braids, large hoop earrings, and small hoops in their noses and lips, large tattoos emblazoned on their arms and revealed bosoms, hovered around the cluster of men. One woman had a definite razor cut across her face. Each woman drank from a 40-ounce malt liquor bottle and, as if in imitation of each other, had cigarettes hanging dangerously off the edge of their lips.

"Who that fine shorty with you?" Attitude inquired.

Slammer threw his palms up in protest. "Aw right now. This my cuz."

One of the girls glared at Attitude. Deni presumed she was his girlfriend.

"Who that you tryin' to get to holler at you, 'Tude?" the girl with the razor cut quipped, her hands placed on her hip.

"Excuse me, Miss Ma'am," Attitude did a bow from his waist toward Deni. He turned to his girlfriend. "Aw, l'il mama, don't trip. I'm just being polite."

Deni said under her breath, "Stay away from him. He looks like a Blood."

"No, he's not. He's an O.G."

"What's that?

"An original gangster."

"You say that like that's something to be proud of."

"It is. Most of them don't live to get old or either they are crippled or up in somebody's jail."

"Is that what you want to happen to you?"

"Aw, cuz. Don't worry about me. I'm not going to be a sellout like you."

Slammer bounded out the car and ran into the store before she could retaliate.

Without wasting a second, Deni used her electronic buttons to lock her doors, roll up her windows, and switch the channel to the local news channel.

Absently, she listened to the news. "Hurricane Katrina has hit New Orleans. Everyone has been told to evacuate, but we're afraid for the sick, the shut-in, the elderly. Blah, blah, blah."

Within seconds her mind tuned out the news. Sitting in the middle of the hood, somehow the danger of the hurricane in the Gulf did not register on Deni's radar. Although she had grown up in what used to be called South Central but now was more politically correctly renamed South LA, drive-by shootings were becoming so rampant, she was more concerned about getting hit by a stray bullet than she was about some hurricane a thousand miles away. If anything, she could kill Slammer herself for putting her in harm's way. She felt her hands getting clammy and her heart begin to pound with a loud thud.

When Slammer finally loped back to the car, Deni unlocked the doors. She didn't breathe easily until Slammer slid in the seat next to her.

Just before she could pull off, out of nowhere, a white-and-black LAPD patrol car fishtailed, screeched, and belched to a stop. The police car siren wailed mercilessly.

Before Deni knew what happened, an officer came over to her car, looking as if he was going to draw his gun.

The crowds began to scatter and disperse. "Five-Oh. Let's book."

"Run, Primo. Get P-Dog. The PO-Po!"

Four more police cars pulled up, sirens whirring. Several of the street-corner men were collared before they could get away.

Protests rose from the throngs. "Officer, we didn't do nothin'."

"This is bullshit! We just mindin' our own business."

"Ain't gon' be no Rodney King shit going on here."

Deni took a deep breath as she studied the white law enforcement officer swaggering towards her. She noticed he had scarlet pimples on his face and he looked rather young.

"Miss, keep your hands on the steering wheel," the officer commanded. "Now, we want to see your license, your insurance, and registration."

Slowly, Deni reached into her dashboard and took out her insurance and registration. Before she could hand over her ID, another police officer snatched opened the rider's side door, reached inside, and grabbed Slammer out and flung him up against the car's hood. One policeman beat him over the head with his billy club.

"What the—" Deni was flabbergasted.

Within minutes, several more patrol cars arrived and began to rush after the crowd in front of the liquor store. Before Deni knew what was happening, the police had her door opened, and had thrown her out of her car and up against her hood. The next thing she knew, she felt white hands groping all between her legs and on her breast. She was so humiliated, she wanted to scream. She was able to see the badge of the officer who was fondling her. Officer Charles Malloy.

Out of the corner of her eye, she could see two officers hitting Slammer and throwing Slammer on the ground. She was livid, but she didn't know what to do.

Deni tried to remain calm. "Officer, what did we do? You don't have any probable cause to be pulling us over. That's my cousin you're beating on. I have his release papers in my purse."

Deni could see them handcuffing several of the guys, and laying them on the ground like they were so many sardines.

"What did they do?" she cried out.

"Miss, shut up, or we'll arrest you too."

When Deni pulled her court badge from under her suit jacket, the officer threw his partner a strange look. He was silent for a moment, a twitch tugging at the corner of his mouth. "The store owner complained that they were selling drugs on this corner."

"Do I look like a drug dealer to you, sir?"

"Let them go," he said to his partner. He wrote down Deni's license plate, her information, and Slammer's information, off his release papers.

When Slammer got back in the car, Deni noticed his head was beginning to swell.

She knew they had been loitering but didn't see any of the crowd particularly breaking the law. Hadn't LAPD had enough police brutality lawsuits against them? When would they learn?

"You give a fool a gun and a badge, an immature fool at that, and they feel they can come down here and trample on people," she mumbled. For the first time in a long time, she felt some connection to her people—even if these people weren't up to her standards.

Deni knew she was up for a promotion, so she had to think first before she put in a charge against the city. The next thing she knew, she began to hyperventilate.

"Sorry about that, cuz," Slammer said. He dabbed at his forehead, which had a trickle of blood running down it.

"Are you okay?" For the first time, Deni felt an allegiance with her cousin.

Slammer sounded angry. "We should file a complaint at the station."

Deni thought about how it would affect the strings she'd pulled to get Slammer out. "Yeah, don't worry. I will."

When she dropped Slammer off at Mama Ticey's house, she shook her head in disgust. Why did everyone feel if you had made it in the black family, you had to help everyone? None of this would have happened if she hadn't stuck out her neck. She was sick of it.

When she got home, she looked around at her French Provincial furniture, her white carpet, and her white entertainment center. Everything looked so white, so sterile. Her schedule was posted on her refrigerator, in her bathroom, and in her guest bathroom. She lived by her to-do list.

"It's not you, it's me." Trent's words came back to haunt her. A man's classic "I'm dumping you" words. That's what he told her as to why he didn't show up at the church in front of two hundred guests.

Downing a glass of sherry, Deni played a song by Cherish called "Unappreciated," thought about the signs that led up to her public shame, and had a good cry over her broken wedding, her broken heart, her broken life.

Chapter 6

Coleman

(CNN)—New Orleans Mayor Ray Nagin blasted the slow pace of federal and state relief efforts in an expletive-laced interview with local radio station WWL-AM.

Defining Moment

"Ma, turn the TV up," Coleman said.

They were living in a motel room in Austin, Texas. Nothing much to look at. Twin beds. Faded carpet and dingy tea-colored bedspreads, but this was the best he could afford with what was left of his 4,000 dollars he'd taken out the bank. This had been one of many nameless motels they had stayed in on the trek to California.

"Coleman, perhaps you shouldn't watch this. It seems to keep you more upset." Miss Johntrice's voice was gentle, calm. She'd remained calm through the whole ordeal.

"No, I want to know what happened to our friends, to our house."

From what the news reported, the system had failed,

plain and simple. The system was only designed to protect at a category three–level storm. Already below sea level, New Orleans was a prime target.

August 29 would always be a watershed for him—it was the day that had changed his whole life. It was the pictures he missed the most. His home had been destroyed. He hoped he could find work as a saxophonist in Cali. He was going to miss the French Quarter and Congo Square.

His thoughts turned back to the Superdome. They'd made it to the Superdome, which was the closest thing to the Middle Passage that America had seen in recent history. He would never forget the stench, the feces, the urine, the soiled Pampers, and even the violence. After a week, he'd started on the next leg of his journey to Los Angeles.

Afterwards, he had hoped his car would make it to Los Angeles and then it did.

One of his first calls in Los Angeles came from Malik. "Blue, I've got bad news for you. Your house was totally destroyed."

"That's all right. I was planning on not coming back anyhow. I'm staying in Cali."

Chapter 7

Deni

September 2005,
Category Four Storm

A week later, when Deni made it in late from work, the strong scent of hyacinth, jasmine, and oleander scented the air, and instead of uplifting her mood, it made her feel more melancholic. She almost hated to come into her house, it was so filled with longing. Yearning. Loneliness. She still had her wedding dress hanging up in her closet, where it stood, a mock reminder of her dashed hopes and dreams for marriage. For years she'd bought wedding magazines. She had planned to have the perfect wedding.

"If I'm so fuckin' gorgeous, how come I can't find a man?" she thought.

She grimaced when she looked at her old violin, which she showcased in a glass menagerie. She'd had this violin since she was twelve years old. This was the last of three violins, which her mother had struggled to pay for, and which seemed like a condemnation of all the hopes and dreams her mother had had for her.

She was in a crappy mood because she'd found out that Trent, her former fiancé, had eloped with his white secretary Margaret. The nerve of that no-good bastard. She was also depressed because Mr. Ryan, her supervisor, had called her in and reprimanded her because of the report that she had put in a complaint against the LAPD.

"This doesn't look good, Miss Richards. I received a report from the police department saying you were consorting with a felon. I'm going to have to reprimand you."

"But this Officer Malloy showed inappropriate behavior to me. Did you see my report against him?"

"Miss Richards, there definitely seems to be a conflict of interest here. Would you consider dropping the allegations?"

Although Mr. Ryan didn't say it, it was implied that they would not reprimand her if she dropped the charges.

Deni didn't want to report that the felon was her first cousin, so she decided to drop her charges. But what about her dignity? she'd wanted to say. So some young punk wearing a uniform had the right to fondle her?

Halfheartedly, Deni looked at her voice message machine. She saw her message light flashing green. Putting her briefcase on the desk, she pushed the button and listened to her messages. The first message perturbed her. It was from the man claiming to be her father.

"Attorney Deni Richards. Robert Franklin here. I was just wondering if you received my letter. I'd like to know if we could meet for lunch soon."

"The name is Den-I such as in Deny," she snapped at

the answering machine. She already disliked this Robert Franklin for how he mispronounced her name.

Suddenly her phone rang, getting her the much-needed relief from her turbulent emotions. It was her liberal white girlfriend, Jean Allen. They'd met at UCLA as roommates and were now in an interracial book club together. Jean started right in on her. "Did you contact the discrimination lawyer about the restaurant?"

"No, I changed my mind."

"Why?"

As close as Deni was to her girlfriend Jean, she didn't want to disclose what had really happened to some of her money or about the incident that had transpired earlier last week with the LAPD. Her white friends could never understand racism. It was like trying to translate Chinese to a Russian person. Her white friends always felt she was too sensitive, anyway. "Well, something came up."

"Anyhow, you remember what happened to the discrimination case against Denny's?"

"I know, but if Black people went around charging discrimination suits we could never get any work done."

"Okay, counselor. I know you don't want to rock the boat."

Deni didn't tell her, but she'd contacted her private attorney, but failed to follow up because she was too stressed out with filing her complaint against LAPD. "Yes, I'm up for a promotion. I had to think about that too. How did your test come out?"

"Negative." Jean was referring to her and her husband Abe's five-year attempt to get pregnant. They were what demographers called DINKS—double income, no kids. Jean wanted a baby in the worst way, though.

Obviously, last month's fertilized embryo eggs didn't implant.

"Oh, well. I'm sorry to hear that. Maybe next month."

"No, I'm sick of this." Jean's voice faltered.

"Why don't you try adoption?"

Jean changed the subject and didn't answer. "Well, guess what happened today?"

Jean taught at Fifty-Fourth Street Elementary, one of the local Los Angeles primary schools. She loved her fourth-graders, and seemed to especially love Black children. For a white girl from the Valley, she didn't seem to mind working in the hood.

"What?"

"A crack addict walked into our school butt naked in front of my class of third-graders."

"What did you do?"

"I kept the children calm. I was able to get security down to the room and take care of them, though. We had to have the police come out."

"You poor thing," Deni empathized with Jean. She changed the subject. "How's your mother doing?" Jean's mother, a thirtysomething-year chain smoker, often suffered with emphysema attacks now. She still tried to smoke and was in an oxygen tent. "She's doing fine—that is, if she doesn't blow up her oxygen tank trying to sneak a cigarette. I hope I don't have to go up to San Francisco and see her anytime soon."

Deni laughed. "I hear it's hard to quit."

"Anyhow," Jean went on, "by the way, did you ever contact the man who wrote you?"

Now it was Deni's turn to be uncomfortable. "No." She didn't want to talk about this putative father right now. An awkward silence ensued.

"Did you hear about that hurricane hitting New Orleans?"

"Yes. I'm going to turn on the news. I'll call you later."

Deni hung up the phone and went over to her big-screen TV in her great room and turned on the news. So much had happened this past week, she'd hardly kept up with the news about Hurricane Katrina. When she turned on the news, she was shocked. She couldn't believe what she saw.

What she saw shocked her. It was as if she was in a time warp. She couldn't believe all the black families she saw standing on the oases of their roofs with floodwaters surrounding them. Survivors held up signs, HELP! Then the cameras shot over to the Superdome. She couldn't believe it. Most of the people who were trapped were poor and black. It looked like a modern-day slave ship. What was the world coming to? She saw a few whites, but most of whom the news captured were black people. People who looked like her.

The people that the newscaster interviewed reported, "We're hungry."

"We're cold and wet."

"We're thirsty."

Deni wanted to help, but what could she do? After all, it wasn't her problem. Or was it? Afterwards, it depressed her so she poured a large wine goblet of Chardonnay. She didn't like to drink alone, but since her aborted wedding, she'd found this to happen more and more. She hated that she was forced to drop her complaint against the police department, but she knew all the departments were interconnected and this might interfere with her promotion. Was she a sellout like Shawn said?

As she sipped on her wine, her thoughts turned to the letter from Robert Franklin.

How did he get her phone number? Then, she realized that if he was a former FBI agent, he had access to all types of private records.

That night, she read for the second time Robert Franklin's letter.

Dear Deni,

My name is Robert Franklin. I believe I'm your biological father. Enclosed is my picture. Your mother and I were high school sweethearts. I went away to the Navy and I lost touch with her. She never returned any of my letters and she never let me know that she had given birth to you.

I later joined the FBI. I have since retired and I was looking Esther Richards up and found out that she had passed.

I'm so sorry to hear that. She was a wonderful young woman. So full of life and dreams. She was my first love. We had something special. Somehow we lost touch after I did my tour of duty in Vietnam. Although I married someone after I got out of the service, I always thought of Esther.

My wife died three years ago. I saw a program on lost loves and I thought of Esther. That's how I found out about you.

Esther never had any other boyfriend who I knew of at that time, and that's why I think I could be your father. Please contact me at 805-555-5622.

Robert Franklin,
Santa Barbara

She looked at the picture of the man enclosed in the envelope. She did look a lot like him. She had the same thick eyebrows, the same almond-shaped eyes. The only difference was in their complexion. She was a medium cappuccino color, and her father was the color of deep espresso.

Stunned, Deni curled up in her Queen Anne chair. First, she had to wrap her mind around the idea that there was this man her mother had loved, because she'd never seen Esther date anyone in her life while she was growing up. And if Robert Franklin was indeed her father, she thought about how her mother could have gotten child support and her life could have been easier. Perhaps even her mother could still be alive. Deni's cheeks burned and she grew full of rage. No, she didn't think she wanted to contact this fool. He was a day late and a dollar short. Who needed a father after all this time?

What she needed was a tune-up. She picked up the phone and called her married lover.

Chapter 8

Coleman

October 2005

Internet

"Passivity did the most damage," says the 520-page report, *entitled* A Failure of Initiative:

"The failure of initiative cost lives, prolonged suffering, and left all Americans justifiably concerned our government is no better prepared to protect its people than it was before 9/11."

From Sheltered to Homeless Shelter

Los Angeles was nothing like he thought it would be. He didn't even want to think over the last few weeks. It had been a nightmare, hell-on-earth experience.

Finally, he had settled in Los Angeles. When his car, overheated radiator and all, arrived with his mother,

Miss Johntrice, Britton, and Blossom, he had one goal. An apartment for his family.

The first thing he did was find a gig playing in Redondo Beach at a jazz club on Fisherman's Wharf.

He missed the Big Easy, but he knew now that home as he knew it would never be the same. He couldn't look back. He could only go forward. But now here he was living in a homeless shelter. Him—a former homeowner—now reduced to being indigent, a homeless man, asking for handouts. He had to work hard to maintain his dignity, though. He couldn't believe how many of his friends had been scattered.

When he called FEMA, it was always the same thing.

"Oh, we lost your application."

"We called you and you didn't respond."

His house insurance was a joke. They wouldn't pay enough to replace anything hardly. He needed his mortgage papers and insurance papers and he had to write back to New Orleans to get the papers.

He heard reports on the news saying, "This is a signature moment in history," but it didn't feel like it when it was happening to you.

Images haunted his sleep after watching different New Orleans residents. He still recalled the stench at the Superdome, and the sights of animal carcasses and even human beings floating down the street. He really got upset when he saw anyone on the news from the Lower Ninth Ward and how demolished that area was.

He was watching TV to see the aftermath. "There was a boat in his backyard."

"The president doesn't think he has to do anything for this area."

"We need a different government."

He would miss Bourbon Street, and all the New Orleans

music, but something in Los Angeles called to him. It felt like an adventure. He wanted to try, even if he failed.

His cousin told him that his home and his mother's home had been destroyed. That was another problem. Fighting with the insurance, and trying to get the money.

His mother took care of the children while he did temporary work during the day at Labor Ready—anything he could find. He hadn't enrolled Blossom or Britton in school yet, but his mother did home schooling with them. One night when he came in, Miss Johntrice couldn't find Blossom. When they found her over in another family's cubicle, he couldn't take anymore.

"Blossom, come out. Where are you? You're starting to scare me."

Blossom finally showed up from one of the other family's cubicle. "Here I am, Daddy."

Coleman grabbed her and hugged her. "Don't ever go off with strangers, you hear me, Blossom?"

Blossom broke into tears. "I'm sorry, Daddy."

"I'm not mad at you. Daddy is just—" His voice broke off. He was mad at himself for putting his family in this situation. But what could he do? He wanted a shot at the LA market. He had so many bad memories in New Orleans and this was his chance to get away.

He needed an apartment, but he couldn't get it without the FEMA. He'd used up his savings paying for hotels before he made it to LA. To move into an apartment took almost 5,000 dollars.

When he heard about the adopt-a-family program at the Archdiocese of Los Angeles, which took in families into other's homes, he decided to swallow his pride and to sign up until he could save enough money to get an apartment.

Chapter 9

Deni

Category Five Storm

Often the voice of conscience whispers
Often we silence it
Always we will have to pay

—Anonymous

Although she'd just experienced one of the deepest, toe curling, snatch-your-wig-off-your-head orgasms she'd ever had, when Deni turned over, she glared at her lover with disgust. Ronald didn't seem to notice. He had already turned away and was lighting a cigarette. Ronald was an accountant with Los Angeles County and she'd known him for the last five years, but the affair just happened after "the Trent Debacle," as she now referred to it.

Deni couldn't take it anymore. Luxurious silk sheets. Five-star-hotel. It still felt wrong. The fact that this was sex without love left her running on empty. Inside, Deni knew it was her own self she was disgusted with, not Ronald, but he just seemed so content with this coupling of bodies and not of their spirits. And what about how he was cheating on his wife? For the first time, she gave the wife a thought. Without a word, she went into the hotel's posh bathroom and cut on the shower jets. As she sponged down her body in the shower, no matter how much water ran down the drain, no matter how much soap she used on her body, she felt filthy. How many more times was she going to sleep with him? In her spirit, she knew she had to stop. Something inside of her was changing. "This is it," she said out loud as she cut off the jets to the shower.

"This is it, Ronald," she announced with finality after she came out the shower, a towel draped under her armpits. "Party's over."

"What d'you mean?" Ronald, who was buttoning his shirt, lifted his eyebrow in disbelief.

"I said it's over."

"Yeah, that wasn't what you said when you were hollering just a few minutes ago."

"True. But this is going nowhere."

"I told you I'd be leaving my wife."

Deni smiled. To his benefit, Ronald put on a good act.

"Save it. I don't want you to leave your wife." Deni's voice was firm. Her mind was made up. Finally she was strong enough to face the truth. This had just been a rebound relationship to help her get through her shame and humiliation at being stood up at her wedding. She'd broken one of her cardinal rules—never to have an affair with a married man. However, in that twilight zone–state of being after her farce of a wedding, she found herself doing a lot of things she never dreamed she would do. Such as drinking alone. She'd even tried Ecstasy once, but never again. . . . Deep inside, she knew she had to take back control of her life. She had to.

Suddenly Deni watched anger transmogrify Ronald's

features. She'd never seen such a nasty leer on his face when he spoke. "The white man had all the punanny he wanted and we were told we could only have sex when they said it. Well, I'm telling you, there is no such thing as adultery. This is a black thing—for men to have more than one woman."

Deni gasped, feeling like he'd slapped her. "I can't believe you said that."

"Don't get all high and mighty, counselor. You weren't saying that over the past few months. You knew the deal."

Deni couldn't argue the fact. She knew he was right. She had compromised her morals and now he was looking at her like dirt. She wanted out of this place—out of this hotel room. She gathered up her clothes and purse and rushed back into the bathroom.

"You can let yourself out," she called over her shoulder. "And another thing—you were never in any danger of leaving your wife."

She knew there was no future with Ronald, who considered himself quite the Lothario. She thought of Trent again. He'd been single, a couple of years younger, and a top real estate businessman in Beverly Hills. She'd thought he'd been a great catch.

Would she ever find love? She'd just read in *Ebony* where 90 percent of the Black beauty queens from the 1990 campuses were still single. Here she was, nice enough looking yet, and even she was thinking about signing up for an Internet dating service, but she didn't like the randomness of it all.

As if something inside of her had metamorphosed, she had a moment of clarity. Sure, for the time being, Ronald had kept her "dick-ti-fied," but now she knew one thing for sure. She could never sleep with him again without remembering the malicious hate in Ronald's eyes. This would be the last time she'd sleep with her lover. It had been a Pyrrhic victory. She'd won in terms of getting over Trent, but she'd lost her self-respect in the process.

She knew Ronald didn't believe it, but she knew it deep in her bone marrow, it was over.

In fact, she was swearing off men. She decided she would give celibacy a try.

Chapter 10

Deni

Social Responsibility

"Ladies, what can we do to help the poor victims of Katrina?"

Dorothy Burns, the founder of the Avid Readers Book Club, Los Angeles chapter, which met in her home in Silver Lake, pounded her gavel. "May I have your attention?"

Deni was sitting next to Jean, who raised her hand and spoke up. "Well, some groups on the Internet are sending books to the Katrina victims—"

Dorothy cut Jean off. "We've already participated in that initiative. That's good, but we need to do more. I feel like we're doing what the hypocrites did in the Bible where the rich man told the poor hungry person, 'Go, be fed,' but didn't offer him a crumb."

The most radical woman in the group, Sankofa, who wore dreadlocks that kissed her waistline, spoke up. "Katrina is living proof that racism is alive and well here in the new millennium. It's pitiful what they are doing to my people. They don't think of us as human beings. They don't care that people have lost their treasures, their pictures, or their missing children. Whole families have been displaced.

"We all know the government's slow response was based on race and class. Here we are, the richest country in the earth and we have people who live like a third-world country. I couldn't believe what I saw on TV."

The room grew silent.

Finally a Chinese yoga instructor named Suri raised her hand. "We can connect with one of the social service agencies and open our homes to take a family in until they get back on their feet."

"Who will second the motion?" Dorothy asked.

Deni didn't answer because she didn't give the suggestion a second thought. Her life was too filled now. She wanted her home to be her sanctuary, her private place.

That night when she made it home, Deni popped a TV dinner into the microwave, then settled down to watch her favorite movie, an adaptation of John Grisham's *Time to Kill*, with one of her favorite African-American actors, Samuel Jackson. She loved the protagonist, Jake Brigance, who was also an attorney. It made her realize why attorneys get such a bad rap as she saw the unpleasant stands they often had to take. Just like the one she had to take about dropping the police brutality charges against LAPD. Just like the children she took from parents, who if they knew their rights, would be able to keep their children. Or just like the rich parents who knew their rights and were able to stay in the home with Munchausen syndrome or molestation going on.

Watching the movie, she liked how Jake did take a stand before it was over. She wondered what she would have done in that case, if she had been white. . . .

Deni's head nodded, but she decided to fend off the blanket of sleep.

The next thing she knew she is standing at the altar, but somehow she gets whisked away from it all. When she looks up, she is on a train.

"Where am I going?" she asks the ticket conductor.

"Next stop, New Orleans."

"I guess I'll visit the French Quarter," she says, but she winds up in the Superdome.

A big, Gestapo-looking white man in a uniform with a swastika stands before the door.

"No, I can't go through that door. I'm an attorney."

"You're still black," he tells her. He directs her in.

While in this level of purgatory, she sees people who were wet, hungry, and cold. She takes a video camera and tries to capture this moment of history.

Someone stops her. "This is only for the white media to show what they want to show." The white media shows the blacks as looters; the whites as foragers.

Something else stops her. "I'm hungry," she says, feeling her stomach growl. "I'm cold. I'm wet."

Next, she falls into a deeper level and sees a black man swinging from trees, being lynched. She even witnesses a black woman hanging from a tree with a white crowd of men cheering as they surround the swinging body.

Next, she hears a white man named Willie Lynch standing on Virginia colony shore of the James River preaching. "We will keep them pitted against each other for the next three hundred years. Light-skinned against dark-skinned." The year is 1712.

Like Dante descending into the Inferno, she feels herself plunging farther down into an abyss. In the next level, she stands on an auction block in New Orleans, naked to her waist. The auctioneer says in a stentorian voice, "This fine wench goes for one thousand dollars. She'll be a breeder, bringing you plenty of pickaninnies to help take care of your plantation."

In the last level, she is on a ship. She is lying face to feet, sardine-fashion, crowded next to a man. The man speaks in a strange tongue. The word Wolof *pops in her head. This man is handsome and in a crazy way, she feels attracted to him. She is in the Middle Passage.*

Suddenly a deep booming voice says, "We convict you for not being willing to help the bottom of the economic pyramid. To whom much is given, much is required. You are to give back, Deni."

Deni woke up with a start. A white snow screen shimmered from her TV into her bedroom. She looked at the clock. It was four-thirty in the morning.

She couldn't go back to sleep because she had to process this strange dream. What was the meaning? It was as if the whole history in this country before now had flashed before her.

The word *peripeteia* flashed in her mind. The moment in Greek tragedy where everything the she-ro thought she knew about her life was wrong. Then something occurred to her. How had she ever thought she wasn't linked to her people?

How had she thought that if she obtained an education that would make her fit in to white America? Was Slammer right? Was she a sellout?

The next morning, she picked up the phone and called Catholic Social Services.

Chapter 11

Coleman

Santa Monica, California,
November 2005

Colliding Worlds

"Daddy, is this where we're going live?" Blossom asked as Coleman and his family pulled up in front of a two-story English Tudor with its rounded arches, turrets, and shallow moldings. Although it was in a condominium complex, each house looked different and was painted a different color. The house belonging to Deni Richards was painted in a muted harvest green trimmed in a crème de menthe.

"Boy, this family must be rich!" Britton blurted out.

"I hope they are Christian," Miss Johntrice said, kissing her rosary.

Coleman stared at the two-story condominium and wondered what had he gotten himself into, but then he thought back to the shelter and said, whatever it took until he could get his own apartment.

His first impression of Deni Richards was that she was uptight. Her white, high-collar blouse was buttoned up to the top. Once he stepped inside, her house looked like a museum, like no one even lived in it. Her carpet was white; all her furniture was white. Would his children be comfortable here?

"Hello, I'm Coleman Blue." Coleman reached out his hand. Deni looked at him strangely. "Hello, pleased to meet you. I'm Deni Richards."

He noticed she didn't shake his hand. He turned to his mother, "This is my mother, Mrs. Johntrice Blue, my son, Britton, and my daughter, Blossom."

Deni shook his mother's and the children's hand. "Come in," she said. "You really have beautiful children. I'll show you to your rooms."

"Does anyone else live here?" Miss Johntrice asked.

"No, I live alone."

A look of surprise crossed Miss Johntrice as if to say, what does a single woman need with all this space?

Deni showed the family around her house, which included four bedrooms, one of which she used for her home office. She'd decided to give the Blue family two of them. Her bedroom was on the first floor. Coleman and his mother and the children were to reside in the two bedrooms that were on the second floor. She had two full bathrooms on one floor and a half a bath on the other.

"We also have access to a community swimming pool and gym that belongs to the entire condominium complex."

Coleman looked at her bookshelf that was in her family room off the entrance hallway. *The Isis Papers* by Dr. Frances Cress Welsing.

"I don't see no Bible," his mother commented.

"It may be in her bedroom," Coleman said under his breath. "Mama, beggars can't be choosy. She must be good people. She's taking us in."

Miss Johntrice just grunted under her breath.

Chapter 12

Am I My Brother's Keeper?

"Daddy, do you think Mommy left because of us?" Britton asked.

The first night when Deni heard Coleman saying prayers with his children, something struck a chord inside of her. She was on her way to her upstairs office to pick up the briefs for a case she had in court the next morning. She tried to remember when she last prayed herself. Suddenly she felt embarrassed.

Deni paused and listened for Coleman's answer. "No. It had nothing to do with you. It was a problem between your mom and me, but never you. It was not your fault. Now bless Mommy and bless the whole wide world."

Deni didn't mean to eavesdrop, but she found this family interesting. She had wondered what happened to his wife, or to the mother of the two children. Were they ever married or was it a baby mama drama sort of thing?

The strangest thing was that now she looked forward to coming home at night. The first time she saw Coleman he seemed familiar. Like she had known him from somewhere before. Déjà vu. She had such a strange feeling. She hadn't meant to not shake his hand, but he had shocked her in his familiarity.

Coleman donned a clean-shaven head, was of medium height, the color of a paper bag, and handsome in a rugged sort of way. When he'd reached out his hand to shake hers, Deni hadn't responded, because a chill was caterpillaring through her. Coleman looked familiar—like she had met him somewhere before.

His hands were muscular, yet soft-looking. She'd read in his profile that he was a musician, a soprano saxophonist.

His children were both very attractive. Blossom's two thick natural braids swung down her back and she reminded her of Keshia Knight Pulliam who used to play the youngest child Rudy on the old *Cosby Show*. Although she was only five, Blossom's slate-gray eyes, which stood in stark contrast to her sable complexion, gave her an exotic look. Britton wore dreadlocks that looked nice, clean, and neatly trimmed. Both children were very well behaved and loveable children.

Blossom hugged Deni as soon as she saw her, which made something soften in her heart.

That night Deni lay in bed and tried to pray. She'd almost forgotten the words. In her mind, she reviewed the events that had led up to her opening her home. The discrimination at the restaurant. The humiliation of being frisked by the police. Seeing her cousin being the victim of police brutality. Seeing what happened to the victims of Katrina. Hearing about Trent getting married to someone else—a white woman at that. Waking up to her dead-end affair with Ronald. And now sticking out her neck to help this family of strangers. Was she doing the right thing? After all, was she her brother's keeper?

The words finally came to her. "Lord, help me do the right thing by this family."

* * *

The first Sunday morning after the Blue family moved into Deni's home, they attended a local Catholic church. Deni declined their offer to go worship with them, pulled her covers back over her head, and slept in, as she usually did on Sundays. When the family returned, though, she offered to take them to the Santa Monica Pier and the Venice Beach. Most people who were from other states couldn't wait to see these sights made famous through the Hollywood movies.

The beach was so close and the weather was still in the seventies, so it was typically warm for December and Deni decided they should walk so they could take in the sights and sounds of Santa Monica. As they strolled down the street, the expanse of the sky rolled before them like a clear azure crown. The ocean looked like a quiet glass whisper; the waves were so low.

Before they left the house, Britton grabbed his skateboard to take to the boardwalk with him. As he pushed with one foot on the skateboard, he used the other one to build his momentum. Sheer bliss spread over his face as he jumped on the board with both feet and pop ollied up in the air and turned around in a circle.

"You're really good," Deni said.

Britton grinned smugly, and said, "Yes, ma'am." He turned, skeeted spit out the corner of his teeth, then stood posed like the king of the mountain.

"Stop that," Miss Johntrice said. "That's not gentlemanly."

"All right, grandmere."

Legs moving up and down like a locomotive, Britton sped up ahead of the group. He crossed the corner at the streetlight at breakneck speed, let his skateboard hit the curb, then jumped up onto the sidewalk and then he leaped back onto the skateboard, never missing a beat. It was as if he was riding on the wind. When he realized he was too far ahead of them, he brought the skateboard to a screeching halt by putting both feet at the back.

"Amazing," Deni said. She couldn't believe the physical agility this child possessed. Perhaps he could join one of the local skateboard competitions.

As he walked beside Deni, Coleman held his head to the side and began to hum a be-bop-de-bop tune with his mouth.

"This is the sounds of the ocean. I can see the colors. Hear the cadence of the season in it. This is what built up to Katrina."

"Is this how your songs come to you?" Deni asked.

"Yes, I can hear the start of this one in my head. I can't wait to get back and play it. It's just the beginning of a song. I don't know exactly what it will wind up being though."

"Did you ever take lessons?"

"No, my father and I both were just born with the ear. We play what's in our head."

Later, the group wolfed down hot dogs, watched the snake charmers, the fortune tellers, the man playing instruments on his body.

When Deni had a stranger take a picture of her and the Blue family as a group and individually, she noticed people staring at them. She could tell they thought they were a family. And, for the first time since her mother's death, she felt like she *did* have a family.

After that night at the ocean, Deni woke up to loud screams. She sprung out of her bed, dragging her Egyptian cotton sheet with her. Padding across her plush carpet, she threw her silk robe over her Victoria's Secret gown and pounced up the stairs.

The cries were coming from Blossom's room. Deni tapped softly on the bedroom door. "Is everything all right? May I come in?"

"Come in," Miss Johntrice said.

When Deni walked in she saw Miss Johntrice cuddling and soothing Blossom. A piece of worn-looking blanket was wrapped in Blossom's arm between her and her grandmother.

"What's the matter?"

"Blossom's had a nightmare. Hush, little sugar dumplin'. Everything's going to be all right."

Blossom continued to thrash about and wail. "I see the flood. I see bodies. I see my mom."

"Your mother's okay. Don't worry."

Deni walked over, sat on the side of the bed with Miss Johntrice, and hugged Blossom. "You're safe now, Blossom. Don't worry."

Chapter 13

Unrest

The following Saturday Coleman watched Deni as she prepared the salad in her large open-space country kitchen. Coleman thought about the last four months he'd spent without having a woman and for the first time since Katrina, he felt slightly aroused. This was the first time he and Deni had been alone in the house together. Miss Johntrice had taken Britton and Blossom Christmas shopping. But intuitively, Coleman knew he had to keep his distance since he had to live here. Even a dog knew you don't shit where you had to eat.

He was glad he'd been too stressed worrying about survival to even consider having sex. He felt his thinking was a lot clearer now anyhow. Life was too important to have a mate you only knew sexually. Since Katrina, he'd even left his weed alone. After Mellon's betrayal, Coleman never thought he'd be interested in someone but Deni was waking up emotions in him that he'd thought he'd buried that night he caught Mellon in bed with Luke. Also he was curious about Deni.

For some reason he felt protective of her. He knew that that was crazy. Deni was a professional, independent woman. Her whole persona said she didn't need anybody, especially a man. She drove a nicer car than he did. How many women, even married couples, could afford a Mercedes? Yes, Deni could take care of herself. Yet there was something so vulnerable about her.

Deni was different than any woman he'd known. She liked to listen to Tchaikovsky, and sometimes the sounds of opera would float from under her bedroom door. And she always smelled so good. Chanel, was it?

"It's the weekend," Coleman commented to her. "I'm curious. Why aren't you out on a date?"

Deni's light faun eyes flashed with anger. "What makes you think that is any of your business?"

Coleman didn't answer her. He looked at her for an uncomfortable moment. Finally he spoke up. "Do you ever relax?"

"Why do you ask that?"

"I notice your schedule is in your kitchen, and in your bathroom."

"Just say I'm goal-oriented."

"Well, how about spontaneity? Don't you ever believe in the magic of life? That good things can happen that have nothing to do with planning?"

"I guess so. But maybe too many of us are planning on magic to take care of everything. I think that's what's wrong with so many Black people."

Coleman had an amused grin on his face. "So tell me, what's wrong with Black people?"

"Don't say it like that. I just know the ones I grew up with. They just live from day to day, never planning anything. Such as my relatives. I have a cousin who's having her seventh baby. Does that make sense in this day and age? Her husband only has a janitor job."

"Is she happy with her husband?"

Deni paused. She thought of all the times she'd seen Shana and Lionel together, laughing, playing bid whist, taking the children to church and on picnics.

"Yes, I guess so, from what I see, she is." She almost hated to admit it herself.

"Well, then, who are we to judge?"

For a moment, Deni started to get defensive. "I'm not judging her."

Coleman gave her a strange look. "You sound as if you feel like you can't relate to most Black people. I guess that includes me too."

"You think because I live in a nice home, I don't know what it is to be Black in America?"

Coleman was quiet for a moment. "Could I ask you a question?"

"What?"

"Are you getting married?"

"Why?"

"I was just wondering."

"Wondering why?"

"Oh, I was wondering about the wedding dress I saw in your closet."

"Are you snooping around when I'm at work? I didn't think I had to lock my room. I open my home and this is what I get?"

"No, I'm sorry, but I couldn't find Blossom one day and I found her in your room. She was playing in your closet. She has a bad habit of disappearing and hiding from us. I told her never to go in your room again without permission."

"Well, if you must know, I was supposed to get married last year."

"And what happened?"

Deni sighed. "Just say it didn't work out." Now, she'd

said it. Coleman could see the freeing relief in her eyes. She laughed.

Deni felt herself relaxing. "Can you tell me what happened to the children's mother?"

A cloud crossed his face, but he answered. "Her name was Mellon. All I can say is it just didn't work out." Coleman looked away.

"Were you married?"

"We're divorced now."

"Can I ask you something? Are you always this uptight?"

"What do you mean? Uptight?"

"Well, the way you dress."

Coleman watched Deni cringe. "What's wrong with the way I dress? You must be used to the bimbos that hang off you in the nightclubs."

"I've got to tell you something. My music has always been my first love."

"Well, as you know, I'm an attorney. I don't win my cases even in children's court because I wear my boobs hanging out."

Stunned, Coleman retreated to his bedroom upstairs. Britton and Blossom had gone Christmas shopping with Miss Johntrice.

There was so much he didn't understand about Deni. She seemed like a good woman, but he wondered why she was so emotionally guarded.

Absently, he picked up his sax and began to play. Life's puzzles he couldn't comprehend began to fall into place as he held his saxophone under his sway. He began to improvise.

It gave him a communion with his spirit.

Music came to him unconsciously at the strangest times. Inside he felt like crying over all the loss from Katrina. The music had a way of soothing him. It helped him to find his center, which he'd felt had been knocked out from under him. When he heard the music inside of him, he had to play what he heard. It was as if an angel whispered the notes into his ear.

The notes came so clear to him, he had to play it right then or he might lose it. His mind would never remember.

Lord, life was uncomplicated when he played his sax. Only the truth flowed through his fingers. This truth caused women to throw their panties on the stage, to slip room keys in his hand, and phone numbers (even married women did this), so he'd never wanted for a woman. He tried to be selective though.

He remembered how the older musicians often talked about shedding. He had to mature to understand they were referring to getting to the woodshed, to practice to learn the craft. The alone time necessary to concentrate just on the music and develop your own technique. This was part of the dues you paid to be in the inner circle of the hip jazz musicians circle. No getting around it if you truly wanted to be a musician.

The spellbinding sounds of jazz music began drifting throughout the house like the smell of cinnamon just before Christmas. It imbued the house with the same love she felt in Mother Ticey's home. Absently, Deni listened as she typed on a court report on her laptop. She tried to ignore the sounds that brought colorful images to her mind. At first she couldn't comprehend what she was seeing or feeling. She felt like she was eavesdropping on an intimate moment between a man and his saxophone. So different was the sound, it was intriguing.

She tried to put words to the sounds. Romantic?

Lonely? Fearful? All the sounds must be what he was feeling, Deni decided.

This was the sound of a person with a fulfilled life— someone who had lost everything he owned, yet he had retained his spirit. She suddenly realized she was sharing his truth. It included his joy, his raw pain, his fear, and his excitement at starting over. He was composing a sound. Although she'd heard him practice before, up until now she'd never noticed how talented he was.

Chapter 14

Deni

Change

"A man named Mr. Robert Franklin called today," Miss Johntrice told Deni when she came in from work one evening. "I wrote his number down by the phone."

Deni couldn't help it. "I wish he would stop calling."

Miss Johntrice looked puzzled. "Why? Who is he? He sounded like a gentleman."

For some reason, Deni opened up and told the older woman about the letter and about the calls.

Miss Johntrice listened patiently. When Deni was through, she gave her opinion. "If this man is indeed your father, you have a right to know him."

"Why? I lived all these years without a father. I don't need a father now."

"Believe it or not, women need their fathers just as much as men do. I know I'm glad I had my late husband to help raise up Coleman. It kept him out of a lot of trouble . . . except when it came to that Mellon. But, oh well, they did have two beautiful children together."

"Well, Coleman was a male child. I think it works out when a woman raises her daughter alone—even if it's not an ideal situation. I turned out all right."

"Yes, from what you've told me, your mother was a wonderful mother. But if this is your father, I'm sure she would want you to at least find out. She never told you who your father was?"

"Never. She only said I was her child and that was all that mattered."

"Well, think about it. You see how crazy Blossom is about Coleman. I think a girl really needs her father."

Deni didn't answer.

For the first time in years, Deni looked forward to coming home from work. She would come home to the most scrumptiously prepared meals. Miss Johntrice used to work as a chef. The smells of crawfish étoufée, shrimp jambalaya, turtle soup, and *bouidin,* a rice sausage, wafted on the air as soon as she opened the door. And Miss Johntrice's gumbo was to die for. Miss Johntrice showed Deni how to eat crawfish.

"You take the head off and suck the juice off of them."

Although she thought the little creatures looked gross, Deni was surprised how she liked the taste of the crawfish.

Sometimes, when she came in from work, Deni would hear the sounds of Billie Holiday, Ma Rainey and other old blues singers floating down on his old albums. And others she would hear the sound of old jazz musicians such as Miles Davis, Kenny G, Grover Washington, and Herb Alpert.

One day she even heard him trying to teach Britton how to play the sax and it reminded her of the two cats who often mated over at Grandmother Ticey's house. Blossom didn't seem to have any musical talents, but she liked to make up stories and play hide and seek all over the house. Once Deni realized this, she would let her come in her room and dress up in her clothes and have pretend tea parties.

That Christmas Deni decided to invite Jean and Abe over and have a small Christmas gathering. She decided not to invite her relatives this Christmas—not since they cut up so bad last Christmas the neighbors had called the police.

Jean and Abe were both dressed in Christmas colors: red and green plaids. Jean wore her blond hair pulled up on top of her head and had on emerald earrings. As soon as Jean saw Blossom her eyes lit up. "You're such a beautiful little girl," she said to Blossom. Then, as if remembering Britton, she added, "You're a handsome young man."

"What is that under your arm?" Jean asked Blossom.

"My blankie."

"Well, I have a doll you can wrap up in your blankie." Jean gave Blossom a little black doll, and the two seemed to click right away.

"We have gumbo, straight out of New Orleans," Deni announced, and everyone's eyes lit up.

The dinner party went smoothly. Miss Johntrice cooked turkey, dressing, macaroni and cheese, mustard and turnip greens, dirty rice, gumbo, and several sweet potato pies and seven-layer cakes.

Abe and Jean were comfortable with Deni's newfound family.

Afterwards, they played charades. Coleman had never played, yet he and Deni, who were on the same team, won.

At the end of the evening, Coleman played various

tunes on his saxophone and everyone agreed this was the best Christmas they'd had in a while. He played a little Miles Davis, and finally, he ended up doing that haunting tune he was working on that evening they'd talked. "Katrina Blues."

Two mornings after Christmas, the blare of her house phone's ring woke up Deni.

"What's this about you taking in a family when you won't even help family?" It was Shana on the other end of the phone line. Her voice had taken on a teasing tone.

"Girl, what are you doing calling so early in the morning? Did you have the baby yet?"

"Yes."

Suddenly Deni was wide awake. "What did you have?"

"Another girl."

"What's her name?"

"Deni Niveah Williams."

"What?" Deni couldn't believe it.

Shana paused. "I named her after you. I guess I want her to turn out to be just like you. Thanks for what you did for Shawn."

"What?" Deni was still in shock. "You know I'm going to be her godmother. I'll be over there when I get off work."

Deni hung up, a smile curving her lips. She was pleased. Deni knew Shana was kidding about her not helping family. Perhaps in the past she hadn't helped her family members much, but recently, things had changed.

For one, Shana was ever grateful for Deni having gotten Shawn out of jail. Shawn was even working now at Black Butterfly Press, a small black publishing company in Inglewood, and he had discovered he had writing skills. He was writing a street fiction book about the travails of growing up Black in South Los Angeles. Everyone felt Deni had helped turned Shawn's life around by getting him a second chance.

That evening, after work, she would stop by JCPenney and pick up 200 dollars' worth of baby clothes.

Chapter 15

Coleman

Redondo Beach on the Pier,
New Year's 2006

Coleman was so excited that they'd hired him as a regular at a jazz club, the Jazz Aft Board Club, in Redondo Beach at the Fisherman's Wharf, he wanted to share his joy with someone.

"I know it's rather at the last minute. Would you like to go with me to the club and hear me play on New Year's Eve?" he asked Deni five days before New Year's Eve.

Even though he hated to admit it, Coleman was beginning to look forward to seeing Deni when she came home from work. Often he was coming in from his second job at Labor Ready.

Coleman played the best set he had ever played. He played a solo, which stood out against his drummer, Ricki, the trumpet player, Victor, and the pianist, Jimmy T. It seemed knowing Deni was in the audience made him play better than ever before. He played about the heartbreak from the main women in his life. All the pain of Mellon's infidelity, all the fear of getting safely through Katrina, and all the ecstasy and the agony he'd discovered in Cali, he poured into his music.

Sitting at one of the front tables, Deni looked around. A high voltage of excitement rippled throughout the room. The room was crowded with young and old, white and black, Hispanic and Asian, all looking like they were jazz aficionados. When Coleman took the stand and put his lips to his saxophone, the notes were so pure, they made her body pulsate with desire. The slow, sensuous music filled the room. Sometimes it crescendoed and sometimes it diminished. With each note he played, Deni could feel the sexual tension growing between the two of them. She felt like Coleman was playing to her.

How could she have missed someone so beautiful? It was like an ancestral drum was calling her body and spirit with each note played.

Then she remembered. It was as if a primordial veil lifted from her eyes. Coleman looked like the man in her dreams, the man on the middle passage ship, so much, it was eerie.

"This is the man I dreamed about long before I met him. This was that middle passage dream," she murmured to herself.

Coleman was nothing like Trent, who was totally self-absorbed. "I'd thought we'd be the perfect professional couple. He met all my requirements, he was professional, owned his own business and knew how to be charming. But it was all a facade. Just a game. He said all the right things, wanted family and children, but he didn't mean one word of it. What a liar."

Maybe what I've deemed is important is the problem.

The arresting sounds made Deni begin to really see Coleman.

She began to evaluate her feelings. No, he didn't fit her ideal of a professional Brother. She would just push her feelings aside and go with the flow.

When Coleman sat down to the table, he turned to Deni. "Would you like a drink?"

"No. I've decided to stop drinking."

"Why, is drinking a problem for you?"

"No. I don't mind having a drink now and then. I just don't want to need a drink."

"I know. I've been there before." Coleman turned to the waitress. "Miss, may we have two Seven-Ups?"

Afterwards, they ate lobster at Luigi's Seafood restaurant on the Wharf. Deni liked watching Coleman eat; he had a hearty man's appetite. She could tell the way he sensuously chewed his meat, he was an epicurean man; a man of sensuous pleasures.

When they made it home, Coleman looked as if he wanted to kiss her but didn't. Actually Deni didn't consider their New Year's Eve outing a date, since they both lived in the same house. But she didn't know what to call what she was feeling.

"Good night, Miss Deni," Coleman said, going up the stairs to his room.

"Good night, Mr. Coleman," Deni said. "I really enjoyed tonight. You really can blow."

Coleman looked over his shoulder, cracked a half-smile, then clambered up the stairs.

Chapter 16

The Abyss

January started out with Coleman and Miss Johntrice enrolling the children into the local elementary school. Britton was enrolled in the third grade and Blossom in kindergarten. Blossom only attended school a half a day, but Miss Johntrice enrolled her in afternoon day care so that she could go find a job. Within a week, Miss Johntrice landed a job as a cook at a Kizzy's Soul Food Restaurant in Marina Del Ray.

Over the next four weekends, Deni, in an effort to show Coleman her world, had taken him to the J. Paul Getty Museum to see Van Gogh's famous painting *Irises*, and to an opera—*Porgy and Bess*, since she'd already seen *Tristan and Isolde*, *Phantom of the Opera*, and many other favorites. She figured Gershwin's opera was more Black and Coleman would relate to it more. One thing she realized was that Coleman, being a musician, could hold a decent conversation when it came to the arts.

Just at the beginning of February, when the news of Hurricane Katrina and its devastating effects was dying down, Deni was getting out of juvenile court at 5:30. It was Friday evening and she was thinking, "Thank God it's Friday," when her cell phone rang.

It was Coleman. "Deni, did you pick up Blossom?" His generally molasses-coated voice spurted out in terse jerks.

"Why? Is anything the matter?"

"I went to the after-school day-care program and she wasn't there. The staff doesn't have any evidence of anyone signing her out. Her blankie is still here, but her jacket is gone."

Deni could hear the bottomless dread and fear in Coleman's voice.

"Maybe Blossom was hiding from you. You know how she likes to play."

"No, we've looked all over the school. People are beginning to scour the neighborhood."

"Did you check with Miss Johntrice?"

"Yes, I checked with her. She didn't pick her up. She's on her way to the police station now. She has Britton, though."

"Which station are you at? We need to put in a police report."

Deni's heart pounded as loudly as the surf as she drove west on the Santa Monica Freeway, heading to the police precinct. It was already dark. She got afraid just thinking of Blossom out wandering in the cold. It even began to drizzle, and Deni found herself crying at the thought of Blossom cold and wet.

At the police station, Deni wiped her eyes and tried to remain composed as they gave all that they could remember. She hated she hadn't had the children fingerprinted when they first moved in with her.

"What was she last wearing?" the officer at the front desk asked.

Miss Johntrice had dressed Blossom for school. "Blossom

had on overalls with pockets that matched her ribbons and her plaid shirt."

They had to go through a profile, but each minute that passed made it look bleaker and bleaker. Someone at the school thought they had seen a white woman with dark hair and sunglasses talking to Blossom on the playground, but they couldn't be sure when they last saw her.

Deni thought about the statistics and she shuddered.

"Most children who are missing over forty-eight hours are found dead."

Somehow the Channel 5 news roving reporter showed up at the Santa Monica police department. Alisa Mendez, a Latina reporter, was on the case.

"Could you tell us what happened to your little girl, Blossom Blue?"

Deni felt like she was in the midst of a nightmare as she looked on and saw Coleman blink into the camera, fighting back tears.

Coleman had a copy of the picture they took at the Santa Monica Pier blown up. Blossom had never looked so happy. Her front snaggle teeth were broken into a happy jack-o'-lantern grin.

"I went to the school to pick her up and she was gone. Just like that.

"You see the little kids on the milk carton. Well, Blossom has a face. I hear that to lose a child to death is the worst thing, but not knowing where your child is, is a worse kind of death. Please, if you have any information, you can contact the station here. Blossom, wherever you are, we love you. Please, whoever took her, bring her back safely."

* * *

That night when they got home, Miss Johntrice's face was screwed into knots of worry. She kept fingering her rosary. Her lips silently mouthed the Hail Mary's "Pray for us sinners now and at the hour of our death."

Britton broke down crying. "I should have picked her up from school. Do you think they'll find my baby sister?"

Coleman was so distraught he couldn't speak or eat. He stayed in Deni's living room, pacing up and down the floor.

"Don't worry. We'll find her." Deni tried to be comforting to the family by hugging them, yet at the same time, she tried to hide her own anguish. She couldn't believe how attached she had become to Blossom, to the whole family.

The house had never felt so empty in Blossom's absence. She'd never noticed how silence could engulf you, swallow you whole, make you want to die. Everywhere they looked was something of Blossom's, such as the doll that Jean had given her, to decry her missing status. Every place Blossom was not was a source of recrimination. As if they had failed her—had not kept her safe.

Suddenly she had an idea. She grabbed up her purse, found the letter from Robert Franklin, which she had been carrying around for months, and dialed his number for the first time.

Chapter 17

Redemption

Santa Barbara, California

That Saturday morning, driving along the Pacific Coast Highway 1, Deni thought of the man who claimed to be her father, Robert Franklin. The sun rising in the east warmed her right side, and the fresh smells of the ocean to her left lulled her into drowsiness. She turned up the FM classic music radio station to keep herself awake.

She understood Coleman's need to be near the phone and stay at the police station. She told him where and why she was going to Santa Barbara to try to help get Blossom back. "I'll be back. You need to be here if there's any news on Blossom."

Robert Franklin. Up until now, she had felt no reason to return his calls, even after her conversation with Miss Johntrice who told her "Every girl needs her father," Deni stubbornly refused to call.

However, with Blossom missing and no leads as to where she could be, Deni felt responsible to help get her back home. After all, she was the one who opened her home to the Blue family. This would have never happened if . . . if what? She knew it was senseless to pound herself over the head with shoulda, coulda, woulda. She knew each family member was blaming him- or herself.

Deni worried about Blossom not having her beloved "blankie" with her. She would never go anywhere without it. She slept with that thing. Miss Johntrice said it not only was her security blanket, it still had smells in it, which reminded her of her mother. Blossom took her blankie to school with her every day and she rubbed it against her face in order to fall asleep, even at naptime.

Deni's heart ached, just thinking of the little girl, out there alone and lost. She knew this was a long shot, but FBI agents were known to be able to track down anybody.

Deni looked at the highway sign, which read SANTA BARBARA NEXT EXIT. She knew in a matter of minutes she would be meeting her putative, biological father for the first time in her thirty-five-year life. Her heart somersaulted and palpitated back and forth from between resentment, excitement, and fear.

Robert Franklin had sounded pleasant enough on the telephone. *But why would he show up in my life now?* Suddenly a voice inside her answered. *Maybe this is a sign that Blossom will be all right.*

Deni arrived at Crossroads Restaurant and took a seat, facing the door. Fresh orchids graced each table with a white cotton tablecloth. This early in the morning the restaurant wasn't crowded.

Suddenly a tall, dark-skinned man with gray hair and very clean-cut features shadowed the doorway. Right away, Deni knew that this was her father. She knew it in her blood. It was as if blood was calling to blood. That visceral recognition.

When he scanned the restaurant, at first, Franklin

didn't seem to see her. But when he did, his eyes blazed with the fire of recognition.

He came over and gave her a strong hug. "You look just like your mother did in her teens."

Deni had only meant to shake his hand, but his hug felt so natural and warm, all her resistance melted.

Right away, Robert Franklin handed her a letter in a familiar, lacy handwriting. "Just in case you don't believe I knew your mother."

Inside, the letter was yellowed and faded. It was dated January 17, 1971.

Deni scanned the letter greedily, so happy to see her late mother's handwriting.

Clearly, it was a love letter:

Dearest Robert,

I miss you so much. I really enjoyed your leave of absence at Christmas, and even though we spent every day together, I wished the time would have never come to an end. Now I wish I had married you when you proposed, but I felt so afraid, I couldn't make up my mind. I know they say the Vietnam War is almost over, but be careful.

You will always be my first and only love. I feel we have a love that knows no bounds. Neither life nor death will ever separate us,

Love Always,

Esther

Inside, there was a picture of a young Franklin and Esther. They were a good-looking couple and anyone could see they were deeply in love. Her mother's eyes shone with desire and hope.

Deni had never seen her mother look as happy in her entire childhood.

"I take it your mother got pregnant that Christmas while I was on leave."

"Yes, I was born September twenty-fifth, 1971." Deni thought about it. "Well, why did you marry someone else?"

"I wrote Esther until I got captured by the Vietnamese, which happened shortly after I got over there. I was a prisoner of war for a couple of years before I escaped. Suong, the young woman who helped me to escape, later became my wife. I loved my wife, but I never got over your mother. And now to find Esther had a child, and looking at you, you look just like my mother—you are definitely my child. I wonder why Esther never told me she was pregnant."

"Who knows? Mother was very proud like that. I can only guess she was ashamed to be pregnant and unmarried at seventeen, so she didn't want you to marry her because of me."

The two continued to converse, and Franklin offered to buy Deni a meal.

"No, I'm not hungry. I haven't been able to eat since Blossom came up missing last night. If there's anything you can do to help, I would be forever grateful to you. Let's get started on that. I can't believe this is happening."

They drove to his house, which was an old Victorian colonial facing the ocean. When he opened the stained glass door, Deni took in the glistening hardwood floors, the high ceilings, and the moldings, and realized Franklin had good taste just like she did; however, she was too upset to savor his paintings or any of his other antique furniture.

They walked straight to his office, which was encased in glass and faced the ocean.

"Did they put in an amber alert on Blossom?" Franklin asked.

"What's that?" Deni shook her head, clueless.
Franklin Googled amber alert system.

A parent's worst nightmare is a child abduction. According to the U.S. Department of Justice, 74 percent of children who were abducted and later found murdered were killed within three hours of being taken. Quick response is vital.

What is an AMBER ALERT?

AMBER ALERT *empowers law enforcement, the media and the public to combat abduction by sending out immediate, up-to-date information that aids in the child's safe recovery.*

The **AMBER ALERT** *Program has helped in successfully recovering over one hundred children since it was established statewide in California on July 31, 2002.*

Next, Franklin picked up the phone and placed calls to several of his old FBI contacts. Before the next hour passed, the amber alert was issued.

"Now, this will be over all the freeways, on cable TV, and regular TV."

When Deni left her father's home, Franklin gave her another hug. "I can't express how much I regret not knowing you. You are quite some woman. Your mother raised you well. We've got a lot of time to make up for."

Deni felt tears scorch her eyes. "I've been searching all my life, and didn't know why. I'm glad to know I have a father."

Chapter 18

The Wilderness

That evening when Deni drove in from Santa Barbara, she saw a crowd of people circling around her house, holding a candlelight vigil. People of all races had placed candles in glasses and bunches of flowers for Blossom, the missing child. They were singing a threnody she couldn't quite recognize, but it sounded soothing. As she pushed through the swarms of supporters and well-wishers, strangers shook her hand and hugged her. She even saw several of her neighbors whom she'd never had a chance to get to know.

As soon as she got inside, Deni noticed no one was at home. She put on the news.

"The civil authorities have issued a child abduction emergency for LA County, beginning at eleven-oh-one A.M. to eleven-oh-one P.M. tomorrow. The child was last seen at her day care in Santa Monica."

Next, she called Jean, to let her know what had happened. Abe answered the phone. "Jean had to go out of town yesterday on an emergency. I think her mother is sick again. I heard about Blossom on the news. I'm so sorry. If there's anything I can do, let me know."

Jean's mother obviously had had another emphysema crisis and she had gone to see her in San Francisco.

Next, Deni called Coleman on his new cell phone.

"Any news yet?"

"No, we're at the police station. I heard about the Amber alert, which Mr. Franklin was able to get into effect. Now there are all-points bulletins everywhere. I can't thank you enough, Deni."

That night after everyone had gone to sleep, Deni lay in her bed, still trying to go to sleep but unable to. She was excited about the amber alert, but still afraid. Was it too late? Would it help find Blossom?

Suddenly she heard a soft tapping on the door.

"Who is it?" Deni said, but she had a feeling who it was.

A hushed voice answered, "Coleman. Can I come in?"

Deni pulled her sheets up around her. Coleman eased into the room, looking like a broken man. His shoulders slumped in, his eyes were red from not sleeping.

Deni looked on as he paced in a circle around the room.

"I just needed to talk. I just feel so overwhelmed and so helpless. I keep thinking maybe she won't get to come back home. I have to blank it out. It gets too scary to think about—what could be happening to her. Then I just have to pray."

Deni patted the bed. "Come sit over here and just rest your feet for a moment."

Coleman heaved a deep sigh, but then complied. Plopping down on the bed, he dropped his head in both of his hands.

"This is all my fault. Oh, God, I'd do anything to have

Blossom back." Before Deni knew it, Coleman was in her arms, sobbing like a baby.

"This is all my fault. I wanted to come to LA, to get away from the past. It wasn't just Katrina. I needed a new life."

"What happened?"

"Nothing. It was just too much of my ex-wife there . . . then so much mess."

"Did you love her?"

Coleman shut down and wouldn't talk anymore.

As he heaved deep sobs wracking from within his chest, Deni rubbed his back like a child's. All of a sudden he wrapped his arms around her waist and held on to her like a life support, as if he let go of her, he wouldn't know what would happen to him.

Finally, he dozed off, arms still wrapped tightly around Deni's waist.

Coleman woke up to the morning light slanting into the room. At first, he didn't remember where he was. Then he remembered coming to Deni's room last night, but he didn't remember falling asleep, he'd been so zonked. It was as if he'd stepped inside the sacred warmth of the womb when he stepped into her white-on-white boudoir. He'd never been inside of her bedroom when she was at home. Her four-postered bed with its sheer canopy cover filled one end of her large room. Ivory silk valances hung from her ceiling to floor windows and a matching silk comforter covered her king-sized bed. Her room smelt of a combination of talcum and fresh flowers.

Without realizing it, Coleman felt better than he'd felt in two days. Waking up with his arms around Deni's waist, he also smelled her soft woman scent.

The memory of Blossom's kidnapping no longer had

him as stressed. Perhaps he had needed sleep. Now he was more hopeful. He remembered some of Deni's soothing words from last night. She had reminded him that there hadn't been a ransom note, so Blossom could have wandered away from the school and just got lost. With her winning personality, someone had probably taken her in.

He had to hold on to Deni's words of solace. "Everything is going to work out."

"Let's go to the early mass," Coleman suggested, a renewed strength and hope in his heart. He knew if God would just give him another chance with Blossom, he'd never worry about her paternity again. It didn't matter if she was his biological child or not. He'd raised her since she was a baby and since he'd fed her and bonded to her, Blossom was his daughter. Period. He also knew he had to forgive Mellon in order for him to move on.

Deni nodded. For the first time, in years, she felt like returning to the Catholic church where she had attended private school all those years ago. She decided she would light a candle for Blossom when she got there.

Chapter 19

Reunion

When Deni, Coleman, Miss Johntrice, and Britton walked out of the large Catholic cathedral on Wilshire Blvd., Deni's cell phone began to vibrate. She'd turned it on vibrate, just in case there was any news about Blossom while they were in mass.

As she frisked through her purse, Deni's hands trembled. What if it was bad news? She didn't even want to think about it.

Coleman and Miss Johntrice looked at her eagerly.

"Deni." A strange baritone voice spoke up.

At first, Deni didn't recognize the voice. "Who is it?"

"This is Robert Franklin, your father. Deni, we have good news."

"What?"

"We've found Blossom."

"What? Where? Is she all right?"

Coleman, Miss Johntrice, and Britton began to clamor around her with questions. "Who is it? Where's Blossom? Is she safe?"

Deni held up her hand. "Hold on. She's safe. It's Robert Franklin." She turned back to her cell phone. "What happened?"

"We found Blossom up in San Luis Obispo. She was in a convenience store with her kidnapper. A lady named Louise Stubbs noticed Blossom because she was looking so sad. She was also taken in by Blossom's unusual eye coloring.

"In the first place, there aren't many black people up in San Luis Obispo. This is a central coastal college town. This lady hadn't seen the news either. It was really a miracle how we found Blossom. Ms. Stubbs says there was just something about how sad the child looked that caught her attention.

"When she asked Blossom if she was okay, the lady whom she was with snatched her up so fast, it threw up red flags in Ms. Stubbs's mind. Plus, Blossom kept looking back at her with these sad gray eyes."

"So being a good citizen and living in a small town like that, Ms. Stubbs followed the car when it pulled off with Blossom. As her suspicions grew, she used her cell phone and called in her suspicions to the police. With Blossom already being in the amber alert system, the local police were able to trace back the original missing child alerts. They thought that this might be Blossom.

"Within a half hour, they pulled the lady over just as she pulled into a motel at the end of town.

"She had changed the child's name to Heather, but Blossom said, 'No, my name is Blossom Blue.'

"The lady who had kidnapped her from school turned out to be wearing a black wig. Her name is Jean Allen and she lives in Westwood."

Deni screamed. "What? Jean is my best friend. She's been to my home!"

"Well, she's been arrested for child kidnapping and endangerment."

After Robert Franklin drove to San Luis Obispo to assist bringing Blossom home from the S.L.O. police station, the social worker and he drove the child down to Los Angeles's Children's Hospital. Deni, Coleman, Miss Johntrice, and Britton met them at the hospital. Coleman made sure he took Blossom's blankie.

Everyone was relieved that Blossom's physical examination revealed no molestation or physical abuse.

Later Deni found out the story as to how Jean had kidnapped Blossom. Jean disguised herself by wearing a dark wig and sunglasses. She had confessed after she was apprehended by law enforcement.

Jean had pretended that Coleman had sent her to pick Blossom up from school early that day. The staff had gotten busy and forgot to make the woman sign Blossom out and since she wore a school board badge, they hadn't paid her much attention.

After she drove off with Blossom, Jean had told the child they were going on a little trip. It turned out her husband Abe knew nothing about this plan and Jean had concocted this all herself, so he was not arrested as an accomplice. No one knew how sick Jean had become over wanting a child. She had fallen in love with Blossom at first sight, especially since she loved Black children in general, and even more so, because she saw how precocious Blossom was. Her wanting a child had become such an obsession for Jean, it had just pushed her over the edge.

That evening the rejoicing over Blossom's return morphed into a large dinner, which included the Blue family,

Deni's newfound father, and even her relatives, whom she invited and was truly glad to have come meet Robert, Coleman, and his family. Before the evening was over, Shana and Lionel and their crew of seven children in tow arrived like gangbusters. Shana had already lost her pregnancy weight since giving birth to baby Deni. Shana proudly held up Deni's namesake, and was pleased how Deni made a fuss over the baby. When Deni wasn't entertaining and serving guests, she held little Deni.

Even Mother Ticey had come out with Aunt Martha and Uncle George.

Mother Ticey, Aunt Martha, and Uncle George all remembered Robert Franklin. They were very friendly toward him and they spoke highly of him.

"He asked to marry your mother," Mother Ticey told Deni, "but she wanted to go to college and so she wanted to wait until Robert got out the service before they got married."

Deni didn't have to ask what happened to her mother's college plans. She knew her birth was what had sabotaged that. But one thing about it. Her mother had never complained or blamed Deni for the failed dreams because she had given life to her. She'd always made Deni feel special; wanted. Now Deni had found that she'd truly been a child born of love.

"Robert, man, we heard you got captured," Uncle George said. "That had to be hard."

A sad look flitted across Robert's face, but he didn't comment. Deni remembered all the terrible things she'd read had happened to the prisoners of war in Vietnam and she shivered.

Miss Johntrice went into the kitchen and cooked up a pot of gumbo. Robert and Uncle George barbecued and tried to see who could out-barbecue the next man.

All the adults kissed, hugged, and made a fuss over

Blossom and all the other children as well. It seemed like children seemed more important, more valuable since Blossom's return. Eventually, Blossom was so excited to have "play cousins" to run and jump with, she'd forgotten about being the center of attention.

To burn up their energy, Deni allowed the children to go swimming in the community pool as long as there was an adult present, which it turned out to be Coleman. He didn't want Blossom out of his sight again.

All evening long, the adults played bid whist, dominoes, and chess.

And everyone ate as much as they wanted, returning for plate after plate.

Near the end of the night, everyone got up and danced to the Electric Slide. Deni looked around and she felt a sense of contentment she hadn't experienced in a long time. For the first time, she was happy to have her relatives to share her happiness with. For the first time, she felt like she belonged.

"That Coleman is fine," Shana whispered to her. "You better scoop him up."

Deni didn't answer, but the glow in her face said it all. She and Coleman calypsoed together and they also danced the Charlie Brown.

At one point in the evening, Deni caught her father, Robert, studying her. When he caught her eye, he smiled across the room at her.

"Deni, thank you for letting me into your life again," he said. "I'm your father and if there is anything I can do for you, I will. I know it's going to take time to build a relationship, but I want to be a part of your life. I think you can never have enough people who love you."

Deni slowly smiled back and nodded her head.

Chapter 20

Garden of the Gods

Three months later . . .

Coleman had arrived at the Elegance Hotel in Beverly Hills early. He was so excited he could hardly contain himself. He thought of Deni's kindness in sharing her home with his family. That could not have been easy for her. Her home was immaculate when they moved in. It still was neat and clean, but it looked more lived in with a few Kool-Aid stains on the carpet. Yet, she had been so gracious with his rambunctious brood.

He thought over the intimacy they had shared outside of the bedroom. The walks on the beach. The boardwalk at Santa Monica. The opera. The jazz club. Even the ordeal of Blossom's kidnapping.

He ordered a huge bowl of strawberries, grapes, and berries. He also ordered a bouquet of red roses.

He'd never been this excited about the possibility of being with a woman, he mused. The feeling of wanting to impress, as well as please her was something new for him.

He pulled out his bag and took out his aromatherapy oils. Sandalwood to promote calmness, which Deni usually needed at the end of a workweek. He pulled out the bomb—ylang-ylang, which opened and enhanced one's sensuality and sexuality. Last, he pulled out jasmine, an aphrodisiac that eased emotional constriction. He lit a stick of lavender incense that gave the room a healing feel, to activate the crown chakra, allowing the light of intuition and inner guidance to clear the negative energy out of the room. He even set up his rock garden with its gentle, tinkling waterfall.

Coleman surveyed the room to make sure everything was perfect. The terry cloth robes were neatly packaged and the triple-thick towels were hung neatly in the bathroom. He had vanilla-scented candles lit in the bedroom and around the bathtub. He had slippers waiting for her.

Just the thought of Deni had his manhood calling for her body. He hadn't felt like this since Mellon, but this time, he was stimulated just as much by Deni's mind as he was with her body.

When her cell phone rang earlier that afternoon, she was pleasantly surprised to hear Coleman's voice at the other end. "Your highness, I'm your servant at your command for the evening. We will have a night of gentle caresses and thoughtful kisses. When you arrive at the Elegance Hotel in Beverly Hills, your bubble bath will be waiting for you. I'll have other pleasant surprises. Your wish is my command. I've made arrangements for our dinner too, so have a light lunch."

Deni closed her eyes and reflected on the message. She had come to know this man who worried about his children, took care of his widowed mother, lost everything and still could find some joy in life.

After she got out of court, Deni came straight to the hotel room. She had looked forward to seeing Coleman all day. The past three months had heightened her sexual attraction to him. They had developed a special bond—especially after what they went through with Blossom. Her only sadness was knowing that Jean had been placed in a mental hospital. Abe still went to visit Jean, but it was unknown if she would ever recover.

The soft knock at the hotel door alerted Coleman to Deni's arrival. When he opened the door, he stood drinking in her appearance, from head to toe.

"You look lovely," he said, approvingly. She was wearing a designer pant suit with a demure V-shaped neckline.

Deni stepped inside the room, where a sensual melodic jazz tune drifted out the room's speaker.

Coleman took her by the hand and escorted her into the living-room section of the suite.

He gazed into her eyes and they had their first kiss as he gently pulled her close into his arms.

"I've always thought a kiss was more intimate than sex," he said, kissing Deni on her nose.

Deni stared at him curiously, but she looked eager to follow his lead in this rhapsody of love. He helped her sit down on the sofa, and then he pulled out his saxophone and her violin.

"What are you doing with my old violin?"

"Is it like riding a bike—where you never forget?"

"I don't know. I haven't practiced in years."

"Give it a try."

At first Deni was awkward, as she held the bow and the violin, but after a while, she found that old rhythm and the notes that she and Coleman played somehow harmonized. Deni had forgotten how beautiful an instrument a violin could be when played against a backdrop of jazz.

The music led to them slow dancing to some of the old rock 'n' roll tunes like Smokey Robinson's "Oooh, Baby, Baby" and Marvin Gaye's "Sexual Healing."

Before Deni knew it, Coleman was slowly undressing her. He began feeding her the strawberries and berries.

When they undressed, they eased into the deep sunken tub of bubble bath. The exquisite alchemy of soap, water, and body slithering against body began a friction, which heated up the water all over again.

Coleman sat behind Deni and massaged and washed her back, her buttocks, and her pelvis area. He nibbled on the back of her neck and she began to moan.

Afterwards, Coleman patted Deni's skin dry and she in turn patted his skin dry. They began to whisper back and forth about the pleasures that each was giving one another.

Deni had never had a lover so considerate. Coleman seemed to anticipate her needs before she voiced them. Now she felt like a woman had never been made love to until they'd been molded in the hands of an artist—a jazz musician at that.

They never ordered their meal service until the next morning, as they became each other's treat.

Epilogue

Family

August 2006

"Coleman Blue's music is cutting edge, accessible to the public, and highly individual and embodies all the best of jazz, according to the *LA Times*," Deni read out loud. "This is great, baby."

Coleman cast a proud glance across the family room at his wife who was suffering through the early stages of morning sickness in her first trimester of pregnancy. His work was getting so well known, he'd been featured in the *Los Angeles Times*—no mean feat.

Recently Deni had turned her family room into an office for her new business. Deni wanted to be able to service her own community more effectively than she could as a court-appointed county counsel. She'd left her job at the Los Angeles County children's court in June and started her own nonprofit legal aid foundation.

This took place right after she and Coleman married in May in a private ceremony attended only by family members and close friends.